PRAISE FOR THE
BEAUTIFUL CREATURES
NOVELS

BEAUTIFUL CREATURES ✦ *BEAUTIFUL DARKNESS*
BEAUTIFUL CHAOS ✦ *BEAUTIFUL REDEMPTION*

"In the **Gothic** tradition of Anne Rice.... Give this to fans of Stephenie Meyer's *Twilight* or HBO's *True Blood* series."
—*SLJ*

★"The authors ground their Caster world in the concrete, skillfully juxtaposing the arcane, **magical** world with Gatlin's normal southern lifestyle.... [Fans will] plead for more."
—*VOYA* (starred review)

"A **lush** Southern gothic."
—**HOLLY BLACK,** *New York Times* bestselling author of *Tithe: A Modern Faerie Tale* and *The Coldest Girl in Coldtown*

"Smart, textured and **romantic.**"
—*Kirkus Reviews*

"**Magical, breathless.**"
—*Just Jared Jr.*

DANGEROUS CREATURES

DANGEROUS CREATURES

BY

KAMI GARCIA &
MARGARET STOHL

LITTLE, BROWN AND COMPANY
Boston • New York

Little, Brown and Company

Hachette Book Group
237 Park Avenue, New York, NY 10017
Visit our website at lb-teens.com

Little, Brown and Company is a division of Hachette Book Group, Inc.
The Little, Brown name and logo are trademarks of Hachette Book Group, Inc.

First Edition: May 2014
First International Edition: May 2014

Library of Congress Cataloging-in-Publication Data

Garcia, Kami, author.
Dangerous creatures / by Kami Garcia & Margaret Stohl.
pages cm
Summary: "Siren Ridley and her rocker boyfriend Link move to New York City to make it big with their supernatural band mates in Sirensong, but Caster trouble follows them"— Provided by publisher.
ISBN 978-0-316-37031-8 (hardback) — ISBN 978-0-316-37626-6 (special edition hardcover) — ISBN 978-0-316-40545-4 (international paperback edition) [1. Supernatural—Fiction. 2. Sirens (Mythology)—Fiction. 3. Rock groups—Fiction. 4. Love—Fiction.] I. Stohl, Margaret, author. II. Title.
PZ7.G155627Dan 2014   [Fic]—dc23   2013048080

10 9 8 7 6 5 4 3 2 1
RRD-C
Printed in the United States of America

For Link and Ridley,
because we knew there
was more to their story—
and for our readers,
because they asked to read it.

Odi et amo. Quare id faciam, fortasse requiris?
Nescio, sed fieri sentio et excrucior.

I hate and I love. You ask why I do this?
I do not know, but I feel and I am tormented.

— CATULLUS

DANGEROUS CREATURES

Ridley

There are only two kinds of Mortals in the backwater town of Gatlin, South Carolina—the stupid and the stuck. At least, that's what they say.

As if there are other kinds of Mortals anywhere else.

Please.

Luckily, there's only one kind of Siren, no matter where you go in this world or the Otherworld.

Stuck, no.

Stuck-*up*? Maybe.

Stupid?

It's all a matter of perspective. Here's mine: I've been called a lot of things, but what I really am is a survivor—and while there are more than a few stupid Sirens, there are zero stupid survivors.

Consider my record. I outlasted some of the Darkest Casters

1

and creatures alive. I withstood whole *months* of Stonewall Jackson High School. Beyond that, I survived a thousand terrible love songs written by one Wesley Lincoln, a clueless Mortal boy who became an equally clueless quarter Incubus. And who, by the way, is not the most gifted musician.

For a while, I survived wanting to write him a love song of my own.

That was harder.

This Siren gig is meant to be a one-way street. Ask Odysseus and two thousand years' worth of dead sailors if you don't believe me.

We didn't choose for it to be that way. It's the hand we were dealt, and you won't hear me whining about it. I'm not my cousin Lena.

Let's get something straight: I'm *supposed* to be the bad guy. I will always disappoint you. Your parents will hate me. You should not root for me. I am not your role model.

I don't know why everyone seems to forget that. I never do.

No matter what she says, Lena was meant to be Light. I was meant to be Dark. Respect the teams, people. At least learn the rules.

My own parents disowned me after the Dark Claimed me as a Siren on my Sixteenth Moon. Since then, nothing rattles me— nothing and no one.

I always knew my incarceration in the sanitarium that my Uncle Macon called Ravenwood Manor was a temporary pit stop on the way to *bigger* and *better*, my two favorite words. Actually, that's a lie.

My two favorite words are my name, *Ridley Duchannes.*

Why wouldn't they be?

Sure, Lena gets the credit for being the most powerful Caster of all time.

Whatever. It doesn't make *me* any less excellent. Neither does her too-good-to-be-true Mortal boyfriend, Ethan "the Wayward" Wate, who defeats Darkness in the name of true love every day of the week.

So what?

I was never going for perfect. I think that should be clear by now.

I've done my part, played my hand, even thrown in my cards when I had to. I've bet what I didn't have and bluffed until I had it. Link once said: *Ridley Duchannes is always playing a game.* I never told him, but he was right.

What's so bad about that? I always knew I'd rather play than watch from the sidelines.

Except once.

There was one game I regretted. At least, one that I regretted losing. And one Dark Caster I regretted losing to.

Lennox Gates.

Two markers. That's all I owed him, and it was enough to change everything. But I'm getting ahead of myself.

It all started long before that. There were blood debts to be paid—though this time it wasn't up to my cousin and her boyfriend to pay them.

Ethan and Lena? Liv and John? Macon and Marian? This wasn't about them anymore.

This was about Link and me.

I should've known we wouldn't get off easy. No Caster goes

down without a fight, even when you think the fight is over. No Caster lets you ride off into the sunset on some lame white unicorn or in your boyfriend's beat-up excuse for a car.

What's a Caster fairy-tale ending?

I don't know, because Casters don't get to have fairy tales— especially not Dark Casters. Forget the sunset—the whole castle burns to the ground, taking Prince Charming down with it. Then the seven dwarves go all ninja and drop-kick your butt straight out of the kingdom.

That's what a Dark Caster fairy tale looks like.

What can I say? Payback's a bitch.

But here's the thing:

So am I.

⊰ CHAPTER 1 ⊱

Home Sweet Home

It was their last night of summer, their last night of freedom, their last night of being frozen in time together in Gatlin, South Carolina—and technically speaking, Ridley Duchannes and Wesley Lincoln were in a fight.

When are we ever not? Ridley wondered. But this wasn't just any fight. It was the knockdown, drag-out, mother-of-all supernatural takedowns—*Siren Predator versus Hybrid Incubus Alien.* That was what Link had called it, behind her back. Which was about the same as saying it to her face, at least in Gatlin.

It had started right after graduation, and three months later, it was still going strong. Not that you'd know from looking at them.

If Link and Ridley openly admitted that they were still fighting, it would mean openly admitting that they still cared. If they openly admitted that they still cared, it would mean openly admitting to things like feelings. Feelings implied all sorts of gushy, messy, fuzzy complications.

Feelings were how they'd gotten into this fight in the first place.

Disgusting.

Ridley would rather have Link stab her through the heart with a pair of gardening shears than admit to any of those things. She'd rather fall on her face like Abraham Ravenwood did, in His Garden of Perpetual Peace, drawing his last breath unloved and alone—a far fall for the most powerful Blood Incubus in the Caster world.

At least Ridley understood Abraham Ravenwood. She was an expert on being unloved and alone.

Worshipped and obeyed? Great. Feared and hated? She'd take it.

But loved and together? That was harder.

That was Lena's territory.

So Ridley wasn't about to admit that she and Link were still fighting. Not tonight, or any other night. You couldn't hit one relationship domino without toppling all the others. And if they couldn't discuss whether they were in a fight, she didn't even want to *think* about what else might come toppling down.

It wasn't worth the risk.

Which was the reason Ridley didn't mention anything she was thinking as she trudged through Gatlin's stickiest marsh, heading for Lake Moultrie in her mile-high snakeskin platforms.

"I should have worn kitten heels," Rid lamented.

"Pretty sure kittens don't have heels." Link grinned.

Rid had caved and asked him for a ride to the stupid farewell party her cousin had organized. It was the first time the two of them had been alone together for longer than five minutes, ever since that night at the beginning of the summer when Link made the mistake of telling Rid he loved her at the Dar-ee Keen.

"Meow," Ridley said, annoyed.

Link looked amused. "I don't really think a you as a cat person, Rid."

"I love cats," she said, wrenching one foot out of a patch of drying mud. "Half my closet is leopard." Her shoe made a gross sucking sound that reminded Ridley of her little sister, Ryan, slurping on an ICEE.

"And the rest is leather, Greenpeace." Link's spiky hair stood straight up, as usual—more bed head than boy band. But you could see what he was going for. His faded T-shirt said GRANNY BROKE BOTH HIPSTERS, and the chain hanging from his wallet made him sound like a puppy on a leash. In other words, Link looked like he'd looked every day of his life, hybrid Incubus or not. Gaining supernatural powers had done nothing to improve his sense of style.

Just like the boy I fell for, Ridley thought. *Even if everything else between us is different.*

She yanked her foot up out of the muck again and went toppling over backward. Link caught her on her way to a full-body mud bath. Before Rid could say a word, he hoisted her over his shoulder and bounded across the marsh, all the way to the edge of the lake.

"Put me down." Rid squirmed, tugging her miniskirt back into place.

"Fine. You're a real brat sometimes." Link laughed. "Want me to put you down again? 'Cause I gotta whole lotta blond jokes…"

"Oh my god, stop it—" She hit his back, kneeing his chest in the process, but deep down, she didn't mind the ride. Or the jokes. Or the superstrength. There were some perks to having a quarter Incubus for an ex-boyfriend. Hanging upside down wasn't one of them, though, and Rid tried to push her way back upright in his arms.

Lena waved them over from her spot at the campsite, a makeshift fire pit at the water's edge. Macon's massive black dog, Boo Radley, was curled at her feet. Ethan and John were still working on the fire itself, the Mortal way, under Liv's direction—not that she'd ever made a fire before. Which was probably why it was still only smoking.

"Hey, Rid." Lena smiled. "Nice ride."

"I have a name," Link said, holding Ridley with one arm.

"Hey, Link." Lena's black curls were pulled up into a loose knot, and her familiar charm necklace hung from her neck. Even her old black Chucks never changed. Ridley noticed that the ornament from Lena's graduation had already joined her charm collection. *Meaningless Mortal ceremonies.* Rid smirked at the memory of Emily Asher's diploma turning into a live snake, right as Emily shook Principal Harper's hand. *Some of my better work*, Ridley thought. *Nothing like a few snakes to end a boring graduation, and fast.* But Lena looked a thousand times happier now that Ethan was back.

"Down. Now." Ridley gave Link one last kick for good measure.

Link dumped Ridley back on her feet, grinning. "Don't ever say I didn't do anything for you."

"Aw, Shrinky Dink. If it's the thought that counts, you didn't." She smiled sweetly back at him. She reached up and patted his head. "That thing's like an air mattress."

"My mom says balloon." Link was unfazed.

"Pound it, Pudding Head." Ethan dropped a last log on the smoking pile of sticks. He bumped fists with Link.

Liv sighed. "There's plenty of oxygen going to all the logs. I used a classic tepee structure. Unless the laws of physics have changed, I don't know why—"

"Do we have to do this the Mortal way?" Ethan looked at Lena.

She nodded. "More fun."

John struck another match. "For who?"

Ridley held up her hand. "Hold on. That sounds like camping. Is this camping? Am I *camping*?"

Link moved across the fire pit. "You may not know this, but Rid is not a happy camper."

"Sit." Lena gave her the Look. "Because I'm about to make you all very happy. Camping or not." She fluttered her fingers, and the fire ignited.

"Are you kidding me?" Liv looked from Lena to the crackling fire, insulted, while the boys laughed.

"You want me to put it out?" Lena raised an eyebrow. Liv sighed but reached for the marshmallows, chocolate, and graham crackers. Between her love of snack foods, her faded Grateful Dead T-shirts, and her messy braids, Liv seemed like she should be heading back to high school, not college. Once Liv opened her mouth, though, she seemed like she should be one of the professors.

"I'd pay serious money to see Rid campin' for real." Link flopped down next to Ethan.

"Your allowance isn't serious enough to get me to go camping, Shrinky Dink." Rid tried to figure out a way to sit down on a stone near the fire pit without ripping the thin black spandex skirt she was rocking.

"Havin' a little trouble with your nano-skirt, there?" Link patted the makeshift seat next to him.

"No." Ridley twirled the pink stripe in her hair. Lena speared a marshmallow on a stick, laughing as Ridley took another pass at sitting on the rock.

"Can't rest your dogs while you're strapped in that butt Band-Aid?" Link was enjoying himself.

Ridley was not. "It's a micro-mini. From Miu Miu. And what would you know? You can't even dress a salad."

"I've got my own kind of flair, Babe. And I don't need to buy mine at Meow Meow."

Ridley gave up on the rock, squatting instead at the edge of a log just down from Link. "Flair? You? You wash your face with shampoo and brush your teeth with a washcloth."

"What's your point?" Link raised an eyebrow.

Lena looked up. "Enough. Don't tell me you two are still going at it. This has to be some kind of record, even for you." She waved her stick and her marshmallow caught on fire.

"I mean, if you're referring to that one night—" Rid began.

"It was more of a conversation," Link said. "And she did blow me off—"

"I said I was sorry," Rid countered. "But you know what they say. Once a Mortal…"

Link snorted. "Mortal? I wouldn't believe a Siren if she—"

Lena held up her hand. "I said not to tell me." Ridley and Link looked away from each other, embarrassed.

"It's all good," Link said stiffly.

"Camping." Ridley changed the subject.

Lena shook her head. "No, this is not camping. This is…I don't actually know the verb for it. S'moring?" Lena caught a glop of brown and white goo between two graham crackers, shoving the whole thing into Ethan's mouth.

Ethan made a sound like he was trying to say something, but he couldn't open his mouth enough to make any actual words.

"I take it you like my s'moring?" Lena smiled at him.

Ethan nodded. Tonight, in his oldest Harley-Davidson T-shirt and ratty jeans, he looked the same as he had the day Ridley first met him, after basketball practice at the Stop & Steal. Which was crazy, if you thought about everything that had happened to him since then. *The things that boy has been through in the name of my cousin. And people think Sirens are hard on the opposite sex. He'd do anything for her.*

A little voice in Ridley's head pointed out the obvious: *Loved and together is the opposite of unloved and alone.* Ridley could barely stand to watch a relationship that functional.

She shuddered and shook her head, recovering. "S'moring? Don't you mean snoring? Because this is no way to spend our last night together. There are enemies to be made. Laws to be broken. Cheerleaders to—"

"Not tonight." Lena shook her head, spearing another marshmallow.

Rid gave up, grabbing a bag of chocolate bars to console herself. Sirens loved their sugar, especially this one.

"Speak for yourself. I think this is brilliant," said Liv, stuffing her face with a gooey chocolate–marshmallow–graham cracker mess. "Melted chocolate and warm marshmallow coming together as one—on the same graham cracker? That's democracy at its best. This is why I love America. S'mores."

"Is that the only reason?" John nudged her.

"The only reason? Yes. No," Liv teased, licking a finger. "S'mores, the Dar-ee Keen, and the CW." She shot him a playful look and he smiled, tossing a marshmallow into Boo Radley's open mouth. Boo thumped his tail appreciatively.

Twenty-five marshmallows later, Boo was a little less appreciative and the fire was burning down to embers, but the night was far from over.

"See? No tears. No good-byes," Lena said, breaking up the ash with her burnt-black stick. "And when we go, no one is allowed to say anything you'd read in a cheesy greeting card."

Ethan drew his arm around her. Lena was trying, but all the sugar in the world wasn't going to make this good-bye go down any easier.

Not for the six of them.

Ridley made a face. "If you want to boss people around, Cuz, start a sorority." She rummaged through a bag of empty chocolate wrappers. "It's our last night together. So what? Accept it and move on. Tough love, people." Ridley talked a good game, but deep down she knew her own tough love wasn't all that much tougher than her cousin's marshmallow meltdown.

They just had different ways of showing it.

Lena grew still, gazing into the dying fire. "I can't." She shook her head. "I've left too many people behind too many times. I won't do it again. Not to you guys. I don't want everything to change." She reached for Boo, burying her hands deep in his dark fur. His head dropped down to his paws.

12

The six friends fell silent, until only the crackling remnants of the campfire could be heard.

Ridley was uncomfortable with the silence, but more uncomfortable with all the feelings talk that had preceded it, so she kept her mouth shut.

It was finally Link who spoke up. "Yeah, well, change happens. I used to really love these things," he said, squeezing a marshmallow between his fingers. He shoved John, who was sitting on a rock between Link and Liv. "Dude. When you turned me into an Incubus, you shoulda warned me about the whole we-don't-need-to-eat-and-everything-tastes-like-crap thing. I would've eaten a bunch a stuff for my last meal."

John held up a fist. "You're only a quarter Incubus, you big stud, and I did you a favor. No one would've ever called you a big stud if you'd kept eating those things."

"No one calls him that now," Ethan said.

"What are you saying?" Link was indignant.

"I'm saying, you used to be kinda sorry, Stay Puft, and now the chicks are lining up. You're welcome." John sat back.

"Oh, please," Ridley said. "As if his head could get any bigger."

"That's not the only thing that's bigger." Link winked, and everyone groaned. Ridley rolled her eyes, but he didn't care. "Oh, come on. Like you didn't see that one comin'."

Lena sat up straight, looking over the fire at the faces of her five closest friends in the world.

"All right. Forget this. Forget good-bye. So what if we're going to college tomorrow?" Lena glanced at Ethan.

"And England." Liv sighed, taking John's hand.

"And Hell," Link added, "if you ask my mother."

"Which no one is," Rid said.

"What I mean is, we don't have to do this the Mortal way," Lena said. Ethan stared at her strangely, but Lena kept going. "Let's make a pact instead."

"Just no blood oaths," John said. "Which would be the Blood Incubus way."

Link perked up at the thought. "Is that another camp thing? 'Cause we definitely didn't get to do that at church camp."

Lena shook her head. "Not blood."

"Maybe like a spit promise?" Link looked hopeful.

"Eww," Rid said, shoving him off his log.

"Not a spit promise." Lena leaned in, holding her hand over the fire. The flames reflected against her palm, turning orange and red and even blue.

Rid shivered. Her cousin was up to something, and with powers as unpredictable as Lena's, that wasn't always a good idea.

The embers glowed under Lena's fingertips. "We need to mark this occasion with something a little stronger than s'mores. We don't need to say good-bye. We just need a Cast."

⊰ CHAPTER 2 ⊱

Symptom of the Universe

The six friends had talked circles around the idea, until the moon had risen and the fire had all but died, and even then Link wasn't really sure what was going on.

They're just feeling low, he thought. *Don't think there's a Cast for that.* Still, he wasn't going to be the one to break the news. If Lena and Liv wanted to pretend there was something anyone could do to change the fact that they were all getting the hell out of Gatlin tomorrow, Link wasn't going to pop that bubble. He'd learned to stay out of the way when it came to Casters and their Casts.

"Here's what we want: something that says that no matter where we go, no matter what we do, we will always, always be there for each other." Lena nudged Ethan in the moonlight. "Right?"

"Do you really have to ask?" Ethan mumbled, sleepily nuzzling her neck. "We don't need a Cast for that."

"Anywhere? Even across an ocean?" Liv asked, squeezing John's hand.

Link looked away. It was a long-established fact that John was basically following Liv halfway across the world like a whipped dog so Liv could finish studying at Oxford while completing her Keeper training. It was nothing like what Link had ever had with Rid, even back when they did have something.

But tonight John and Liv were happy as clams because they were staying together, while you couldn't chisel Ethan and Lena apart with a spatula the size of Link's Beater. They were headed to schools in the same state but different cities; that was the compromise they had reached with their families. Link couldn't even remember the names, though he'd pretended to listen to a thousand conversations about them—the schools, their dorms, their reading lists. *Blah, blah, blah.* All he knew was they'd be at rival schools in sleepy old towns up in Massachusetts (or Michigan, or maybe Minnesota—heck, what was the difference?) ninety minutes apart. *You would think it was nine hundred miles, the way they're acting.*

Whipped as Thanksgiving potatoes.

Still, Link smiled at the sweet stupidity of it all. Who was he to judge? If anybody had a shot, it was Ethan and Lena. Even John and Liv had managed to keep it together. It was only Link and Ridley who were Gatlin's biggest basket case of a relationship.

Ex-relationship, he reminded himself.

"Nothing's going to change." Lena's tone turned serious.

"We won't let it. We've been through enough together to know that the people you care about are the only thing that matters."

Link caught Ridley's eye in the flickering firelight, in spite of everything. Ridley looked away, pretending to listen to what Lena was saying, as if she cared. *Anything to ignore me*, Link thought. *That's her trick, same as always, and she still thinks I don't know what she's up to.*

Just like the old days.

"So, you think a Cast will keep us together?" Ridley asked, pretending to listen. "Can't we just, I don't know, send postcards?"

Lena ignored her. "Maybe Marian would have an idea."

"Or maybe she wouldn't. Because it's a bad idea," Ridley said.

"No, wait. I think I've got it." Liv's braids were coming undone, and she sounded exhausted. But the sparks in her eyes burned as bright as the remnants of the campfire. "A Binding Cast. It's how Ravenwood protects itself and keeps those who would do harm out, right? Binds a person to a place? Couldn't it also Bind six people together? Theoretically."

Lena shrugged. "A Binding Cast for people? It could work. I can't think of a reason why it wouldn't."

Link scratched his head. "Work how? Like, our hands are permanently stuck together in a group hug? Or like, we can read each other's minds? Can you get a little more specific?" *Not that I'd mind being Bound to Rid*, he thought. *At least, it wouldn't suck.*

Lena stared into the glowing embers. "Who knows? We're kind of winging it here. There aren't a whole lot of Casts about Binding people."

"Or, you know. Any." Ridley sighed. "So why am I the only person who thinks we should get out the peach schnapps and go bowling instead?" No takers. "How about breakfast, then?"

Link kicked a clod of dirt toward the fire. When had Rid gotten so worried about using her powers? She'd been like that ever since the summer. Skittish as a new pup, and about as nervous.

"This isn't black magic, Rid," Lena said. "If we do something wrong, we'll undo it."

"When have those words ever *not* come back to haunt you?" Ridley shook her head at her cousin.

"Nothing big," Lena said. "Just a little something so we don't forget about each other. Like a Forget-Me-Not. A memento. I could do it in my sleep."

Rid raised an eyebrow. "Someone's gotten a little cocky since she brought Boyfriend back from the dead."

Lena ignored the dig and held out her hand to Ridley. "Everyone join hands."

Ridley sighed and took Lena's hand, also taking Link's warm and sweaty one.

He grinned and gave her a squeeze. "Is this gonna be kinky? Please let this be kinky."

"Please let you shut up," said Rid. But it was hard not to smile, and she had to make an effort to keep her bratty expression in place.

John took Liv's hand, and Liv took Link's. Ethan grabbed hands with John and Lena to complete the circle.

Lena closed her eyes and began to speak in a low tone. *"There is a time beyond mountains and men—"*

"Is that it?" Link asked. "The Cast? Or are you just makin' it up? Because I thought all your Casts were in Lat—"

18

Lena opened her eyes and glared, one green eye and one gold flashing in the remaining firelight. Link's mouth shut and his voice was silenced for him, Caster-style. Link swallowed, hard. Lena might as well have slapped duct tape across his face.

He got the message.

Then she closed her eyes again. As she spoke, Link could almost see the words on the page, as if a scroll had opened itself for them.

> *"There is a time beyond mountains and men*
> *When our six-faced moon must rise.*
> *If you call for me, I will come to you then,*
> *And our six-headed horse will ride.*
> *Though Sixteen Moons began our thread,*
> *And Nineteen Moons must end us,*
> *Let us always be Bound by the Southern Star,*
> *And when in grave danger—*
> *Send us."*

Lightning flashed in the sky, ripping across the dark clouds and reflecting in the still surface of the lake. Boo growled.

A shiver rolled through all six of them—like a cold current coming from the lake itself—and they dropped hands, as if some invisible force had ripped them apart.

The circle was broken.

Link tried his voice and found to his relief that he could use it. Which was good, since he had something to say.

"Sweet buckets of crap! What was that?" Link opened his eyes. "'Grave danger'? And 'send us'? Send us where? What are you talkin' about?" His voice was raspy, as if he'd just been yelling.

Lena looked uncomfortable. "Those are just the words that came to me."

John sat up on his rock. "Wait, what?"

Lena squirmed. "I wasn't expecting the danger part. But it's all good, right?" She frowned as soon as she said it. "I guess it doesn't sound that great, does it?"

"You think?" Ridley tried another position on her hard log seat. She didn't look happy.

"Could it be an omen?" Liv's face clouded. "A warning or a threat about something that's going to end us?"

Lena shrugged. "I don't know. It's meant to be whatever it is. I mean, it's just what came out when I tried to focus on the Binding."

That was when Link lost it. "What do you mean, that's what came out? How could you work a Cast without knowin' what you're Castin'? What if it's somethin' really bad? Because Lord knows that's never happened to us before!"

Ethan punched Link's arm. "Chill out, Mrs. Lincoln."

Link shot him a dirty look, which Ethan deserved. It was basically the meanest thing you could say to Link.

Still.

Get control of yourself, dude.

"Lena knows what she's doing." Ridley tried to sound confident.

If she says it enough times, maybe it will be true, Link thought.

"Ridley's right. It's fine. Everything's okay. No one panic." But Liv didn't look like she believed a word she was saying.

Lena didn't look all that relieved, either. "Well, we should be Bound now. See? Something's happening." She motioned to the fire.

There, beneath the rising mound of gray ash and log, was a strange pulsing light. Lena leaned forward, blowing away the ash.

What remained were six glowing blue lumps of burning ember.

"Beautiful," Liv said.

As everyone watched, the lumps—more like orbs—rose into the air, spinning and hovering above the flames. Boo whined at Lena's feet.

"Whoa," Link said.

Lena reached forward with a finger, closer and still closer, until the blue orbs burst into a shower of sparks and vanished.

"Is that it? The finale?" Ethan studied the dying embers.

"I don't know." Lena grabbed a stick and poked tentatively at the ash.

"Look. It's still sparking." Liv leaned closer.

Lena dug in the hot ash with her fingers. "There." She held something up. "Six of them. One for each of us."

"What is that thing?" Ethan was staring. Everyone was. It wasn't an everyday sight, not in Gatlin County or the whole Mortal world. There was a tiny ring in Lena's hand, delicate and translucent. If you looked at it from a distance, it resembled some sort of delicately blown glass.

Lena slipped the ring on her finger. It fit perfectly, and the light inside it flared brightly and then died out.

"Go on. It won't hurt you." She stared at her finger as she spoke.

Ethan reached for a ring, then paused. "You think."

"I *know*," Lena said. "The whole point of a Binding Cast is protection." She didn't sound sure.

Ethan took a breath and slipped a ring on his finger. John followed suit, then Liv.

Rid slowly did the same.

Five rings were on five fingers. The sixth just sat there, glowing in the embers. Waiting.

"Hey, man." Ethan elbowed Link. "Take it."

"Give me a minute, Frodo. I gotta think about this." Link ran his hand through his hair.

"Really? We're going to start that now?" John shook his head.

But one look from Rid and the sixth ring went on before Link could say another word.

Personally, Ridley thought the whole ring thing was kind of stupid. She didn't make Link wear his to please her cousin. To be honest, she didn't remotely understand the concept of peer pressure that Mortals talked about all the time. *Who would ever do something because someone else wanted them to do it?* When someone wanted Ridley to do something, she almost automatically wanted to do the exact opposite.

Binding Rings included.

But given the brief history of her friends in Gatlin County, Ridley didn't feel like taking any chances. Nobody could argue that lightning wouldn't strike twice. Not for the Casters and Mortals of Gatlin County.

Not even Ridley.

If a stupid ring from a Natural would keep bad things from

happening, she'd wear it. She'd wear one on every finger if it helped her get out of the trouble she had gotten herself into this summer.

Everyone else was going off to start their future tomorrow. Ridley was going to try to undo her past.

⊰ CHAPTER 3 ⊱

Master of Puppets

In the shadows of the Underground, anything can look evil.

That was what the guy standing on the edge of an ancient New York City subway platform thought. He was eighteen years old, and he still dreaded coming down here. He shook the unruly lengths of caramel-colored hair away from his gold-flecked eyes.

It's impossible to know the difference between darkness and Darkness down here, even for a Dark Caster like me.

And Lennox Gates was plenty Dark.

The pale girl sitting on the edge of the platform across the tracks from him was not plagued by the same philosophical questions. Slumping inside a fitted black leather jacket quilted in diagonal stripes, she looked like a futuristic criminal. Her hair was buzzed down to an inch, except for a stripe of spiky blue that ran down the center of her head. Only her baby face looked innocent.

Dangerous, but innocent.

Lennox thought about her future. He wished he hadn't seen it, but he couldn't stop himself from picking up on the things he did, every time he accidentally looked into a fireplace, a lit candle, or even a flickering lighter. Her future, like so many others, had come to him in bursts, like the flash on a camera, streaming a high-speed flood of information he couldn't control. He had seen anguish and guilt, blood and betrayal.

Love.

The Dark Caster Necromancer was in for a wild ride.

Leaning against one of the support beams, her eyes milky white and opaque instead of their normal Dark Caster gold, she didn't look conscious. He felt bad about their arrangement, though she'd agreed to the contract. It had been her idea to wipe it from her mind, for security reasons. Like so many Necromancers, she didn't want to know what she was saying or who was saying it. Though the girl wouldn't remember any of this, he would—every dull, wasted moment.

Why did I have to inherit this mess, along with everything else they left me?

The ring of candles surrounding her on three sides had burned down to waxy puddles. Spirals of smoke drifted up toward her blank face. Her legs dangled over the edge of the tracks, kicking involuntarily to an unknown rhythm.

It's a good thing these tracks are abandoned. If a train came by, those legs would be cut from her body, Necromancer or not, Lennox thought. As good as she was, she couldn't protect herself in this state. She relied on him, and he could never forget it.

Occupational hazard of her job.

He slid a cigar from the inside pocket of his black trench and considered it. He hated the smell of cigars—and the smell of this one in particular.

Occupational hazard of mine.

He stared at the cigar as if he wanted it to disappear—as if he wanted to disappear right along with it. But he couldn't. He was the last of his family line, and there was still work to be done, even if he didn't want any part of it.

Do any of us really have control over our destinies? Maybe we're all just as helpless as little Mortals in the end.

He heard a sound from across the tracks. The girl would wake up soon. No more time for self-pity.

Time for an offering.

So he held the cigar up in the air in front of him, raising his voice. "Barbadian. Your favorite. I'd give one to your *obeah* there, but I don't think she'd appreciate it." He lit the cigar, letting the match burn out and drop onto the tracks. Nox didn't look directly at the flame, not even the burning cigar. Fire made him see things he didn't like to see. "I understand you want to talk. Here I am. What do you want from me?"

He looked over at the girl across the tracks.

She was still comatose, but she raised her head when the cigar smoke reached her, and her mouth opened like a puppet's. The voice that came out belonged to an old man—low and gravelly, with a distinct Southern accent. "What I want is to avenge my family's honor. For my blood debt to be paid."

His blood debt? After all the blood he's shed?

Lennox tried to keep the rage out of his voice. "Some people say the ones who are to blame have paid over and over again.

Even their friends have paid. Your family got what was coming to them. At least, you did."

"Accordin' to who?" The girl's face twisted into a sneer.

"Me," Lennox said coldly.

"Think again, boy."

Careful, Lennox thought. *He might be dead, but he's still dangerous.*

Lennox shook his head at the possessed girl. "I did what you asked. I set certain events in motion. I'm knee-deep in a pile of bones and moldering bodies, as Homer would say." He knocked the ash from the cigar without ever touching it to his lips. "I'm glad my mother isn't here to see it."

"I wouldn't worry yourself. Your mamma never gave a thought to what you did."

Lennox snapped. "She didn't have a chance. You made sure of that." *When you tortured her.*

"I make sure of everythin'." The girl took a moment to savor the smoke, and smiled cruelly. "Your job isn't close to done."

Lennox wanted to hurl the cigar at her.

At him.

"The Wheel of Fate crushes us all. Isn't that what they say, old man?" Lennox shook his head. "That's a dangerous business. Messing with so many people's fates at once. Are you sure it's worth it?"

"Don't be a coward, like your father," the girl muttered. "I will have my vengeance."

Lennox only smiled. "So you've said." *My father should've killed you when he had the chance.*

"What you grinnin' at, boy?" The girl snarled at him from

across the darkness. "Until I find my rest, you won't have any peace, either."

Lennox waved the cigar in the air between them. "I'm glad we're moving on to the threats. I was starting to feel slighted."

"Not just a threat. A promise. I'll see to it myself. That, and a whole lot more."

The Dark Caster cocked an eyebrow. "No wonder I turned out to be a model citizen. Considering I was raised in such a loving community."

"You are not my blood." The animated girl spat.

"Thank god for that." Lennox was tired of the old man. Even death hadn't lifted the burden of his presence. "Why don't you move on already? Cross over? You spent a lifetime exacting revenge on everyone you ever met. Aren't you bored yet?"

"I'm not goin' anywhere, boy." She growled. "I want them all gone. Not just the hand that drove the blade. Not just the traitor who led me there. Everyone who got them to that point, to that hour of that day."

"All of them?"

"Every last one. You hearin' straight? Because I want to be perfectly clear. You. Kill them. For me."

Lennox stared down the tracks. There was nothing but darkness.

What choice did he have, really?

When it came right down to it, there was only one answer. There was always only one answer. He sighed. "I'll do what I can."

The words sounded strange in his mouth, as if someone else was saying them.

"I take it that's a yes?"

"If only in the name of family honor."

The Necromancer smiled, raising her hands. "My family thanks you."

Lennox looked repulsed. "I meant mine, not yours. Don't flatter yourself."

"But our families were so *close*, Lennox." The voice echoed through the Tunnel. "Almost hard to tell where the one ended and the other began."

Not for me, thought Lennox.

He tossed the empty matchbook down to the tracks. Six letters were printed on the crimson cover. One word.

SIRENE.

Above the tracks, the girl slumped to the ground like a rag doll. The old man was gone. As many times as he'd seen it, Lennox was still unsettled. He waited just long enough to make sure his Necromancer was coming out of it.

She would be sick in the morning. Sick, and stinking of cigars. He'd have to work harder to make her forget this one. Maybe put a little something extra in her paycheck. It wasn't her fault she was particularly good at communicating with dead psychopaths, but it was one of the reasons she was so valuable.

Another occupational hazard.

Lennox walked away, disappearing into the deeper dark. There was always more darkness waiting for him. He'd lived his whole life in the shadow.

He couldn't help but spread it around.

⊰ CHAPTER 4 ⊱

Learning to Fly

By the time the last burnt marshmallow dropped into the fire, no Mortal or Caster was still awake to see it. The two hybrid Incubuses watched in protective silence as their four friends slept around the campsite.

Ridley could hear them murmuring as she drifted off to sleep. Her last waking thought was of Link, just to know he was there.

Like the old days.

After that, Ridley's dreams were filled with old memories. She wasn't thinking of good-byes or boys or rings coming from the embers. She couldn't know that plans much more dangerous than any fire—and infinitely stickier than any marshmallow— had already been set in motion.

How could she?

Instead, she slept on, dreaming of things that were far eerier than a ring. Even eerier than an unknown Cast—forever Binding a Siren, a Natural, a Keeper, a Wayward, and two Incubuses—under a full summer moon in a Caster county.

A full moon was for making magic.

Magic and memories.

A little fair-haired girl sat tucked between the twisting branches of the oldest oak on the grounds of the infamous Ravenwood Plantation, reading a book that was even older than that. She hooked her scrawny legs around a bark-covered branch thicker than her waist, but all the same, it wasn't really the safest spot for either a little girl or a big book.

"You know you're not supposed to be reading that, Rid," a girlish voice called up from below.

"Baby," teased Ridley, without looking up from the book. "You know you're not supposed to change your own diaper."

"Auntie Del's going to skin you when she finds out you've been stealing things out of her closet again," Lena, with a dark mess of curls and bright green eyes, shouted up from the safety of the grass beneath the tree.

"Tattler," said Ridley, flipping another page. "Where's your tail?"

The pages were so enormous, they brushed against her faded blue jeans when she tried to turn them, nearly ripping. The book's spine was almost as long as hers.

"Your funeral." As she spoke, Lena flung herself down on the grass, sliding a notebook and a pen out of her pocket. She pulled the cap off the pen, flipping to a clean page in her book with a sigh. "Well, go on. What's happening now, Rid?"

"There's a ship, Leanie-Beanie." Ridley twisted a blond ringlet around one finger absentmindedly.

"Don't call me that. And?"

"And three mermaids. Only they're not mermaids, because they have wings. And they're singing—at least, one is. And another one is playing a kind of strange flute. And the last one is playing a little gold harp."

As Ridley watched, the figures on the page moved through the story, exactly as she had described.

"Go on, Rid," breathed Lena, bright-eyed. "Tell the rest."

A ship came into view. A ship with sails. Surrounded by waves and rocks.

"There are sailors. And they come to visit the mermaids. They think the mermaids are the most beautiful creatures they've ever seen. I think they want to marry them. I think they're in love."

"Eww." Beneath the tree, Lena giggled. "And now?"

"Now the mermaids are singing more loudly. Can you hear them? Close your eyes." Ridley closed her eyes. Beneath the tree, her cousin Lena did the same.

"Can you?"

Lyrical music blew up from the pages of the book and into Ridley's face. It grew louder and louder, filling the whole tree with harmonies, until the branches began to shake and the leaves fluttered to the ground beneath it.

Ridley didn't care. She felt like she was a million miles away.

Lena covered her head with her hands, but the leaves and branches pelted her all the same. "Rid! Are you okay?"

But Ridley was transfixed. She sat clutching the book with both hands, a golden light radiating from its depths onto her face.

The music was beautiful, even hypnotic. Until hypnotic became horrific.

The sopranos turned to screeching, and the operatic melodies might as well have been nails scratching against stone. The noise was deafening, growing louder by the second, until it hurt to hear.

Ridley still didn't move. She couldn't. It didn't even look like she was breathing.

Beneath the tree, Lena pressed her hands over her ears, as hard as she could. "Stop it. Make it go away, Rid. Stop it now!"

Ridley froze.

She opened her mouth and closed it again, without a word.

It was as if everything she'd ever wanted was trapped right there, in those pages—but the longer she listened to them, the more certain she became that she'd never have any of it.

The sorrow was more than she could bear. Her eyes brimmed with tears as her fingers curled even more tightly around the page.

The song intensified into a howl. The breeze became a fierce wind, blowing in circles around the golden-haired little girl.

"Hold on, Rid!"

Lena crawled slowly up the tree trunk, a finger in one ear, the other tucked down against her shoulder.

She pulled her finger from her ear, yelling like what their Gramma would call a banshee. "I can't hear you I can't hear you I can't hear anything and I especially can't hear you!"

She reached up and up until her fingers were scrabbling against the gold-edged paper. With one last burst of energy, she yanked on the book as hard as she could, knocking it out of

Ridley's arms and sending it flying down and out of the tree in an explosion of bright blue sparks.

It landed, facedown in the dirt, with a thud.

Then silence.

Ridley opened her eyes to see Lena pulling herself up next to her. The girls clung to each other, trying to catch their breath, trying to slow their hammering hearts.

"What were those things?" Lena's face was pale. "And don't say mermaids."

"Sirens," breathed Ridley. Her voice was quiet, almost a whisper. "They're called Sirens. Dark. With wings and claws and fangs. They ripped the sailors' hearts right out of their chests." Her eyes were stricken. "I saw them."

Lena shook her head. "I would never, ever want to be one of those."

"Me neither," Ridley said. Her eyes were beginning to pool and prickle with tears.

"We won't be." Lena reached over, patting her cousin's cheek. "Don't worry, Rid. Gramma says if our hearts are good, we'll grow up that way, too. Light as sunshine."

"Yeah? How do you know if your heart's any good?" The tiniest wet streak wobbled past the corner of Ridley's eye.

"Yours is," Lena said solemnly. "I just know it." She drew a linty red lollipop out of her pocket and handed it to Ridley. "Promise."

For a minute, the younger cousin almost seemed like the older one.

They traded the lollipop back and forth, up in the branches of that old oak tree, until Ridley didn't remember the gnashing teeth or the jagged claws or the heartless sailors anymore.

Not one bit.
Promise.

When Ridley woke up, she was crying and she didn't know why. She remembered that she'd been dreaming, but the details had already begun to fade.

"What's wrong, Rid?" Lena was next to her, hugging her close in the morning light.

"Nothing." She tried to think, but it felt like she was pressing on a raw nerve.

"You hate good-byes, you big ball of mush. You barely said a word last night." Lena frowned, pulling her faded blue quilt tightly around the two of them. "Is that the only thing bothering you?"

"I told you. It's nothing." Rid looked around, taking in the dead campfire and the abandoned blankets. Only Ethan was still there, his face half buried in Boo's fur. "Where is everyone?"

"Link still had packing to do. John and Liv, too. I told them not to wake you up." Lena smiled. "Knowing you."

Ridley was relieved.

Lena brushed a long pink strand behind Ridley's ear. "You know, it's not too late. Just because you didn't finish high school with us doesn't mean you can't finish it at all. You could get your GED, go to night school—"

Mother of all that is holy in the world—

Rid grabbed Lena's wrist with five dagger-like glitter nails. "Wait a minute. Are you suggesting that you think it bothers me that I haven't graduated from Stonewall Jackson High? Have you lost what little is left of your mind?"

Lena gently detached Ridley from her arm. "You just don't seem like yourself."

Rid was furious. "You mean I don't seem like a cold witch? Or I do? Because last time I checked, that's what I was."

"Ridley."

"I don't know why everyone in Gat-dung has such a hard time remembering I'm not like them. I'm not even like you. I'm a heartless Siren."

"You are not heartless." Lena was matter-of-fact. They could replay this conversation all Ridley wanted, but she was never going to change her position on this particular matter.

"How do you know?" Ridley sounded as miserable as she felt.

"I just know." Lena kissed her cousin's cheek. "Trust me."

Truthfully, Ridley didn't trust anybody. But if she had, her cousin would've been first on her list.

They sat like that, arm in arm in the silence, for a long moment.

"Promise," Ridley whispered. She hated herself for saying the word—for cracking like that, the moment she did it—like always.

"Promise," Lena whispered back, reaching in the pocket of her sweatshirt and pulling out a bright green lollipop.

"Green?"

"Change is good. Live a little."

Ridley took the lollipop, waving it in her cousin's face. "You rebel." She stood up, awkwardly stretching her long, bare legs. "So, yeah. I gotta jet." It was as close as Rid could come to saying good-bye to her only real friend.

"I know," Lena said. She knew everything. What Rid was

saying—and what she couldn't. She held out a set of car keys. "I just Cast a *Manifesto*. It's on the corner."

Ridley shook her head. "You're good."

"I know," shrugged Lena, her eyes twinkling.

"Say good-bye to Ethan for me. And you behave, Cuz." Ridley smiled, in spite of everything.

"I always do. I'm the good one, remember?"

Ridley never forgot.

CHAPTER 5

Sweet Child o' Mine

A shower and a change of clothes fixed everything.

Well, a shower, a vintage pink silk kimono, a shot of hot chocolate, a final layer of Chanel Rouge Allure Incandescente—in other words, Siren Red—lipstick, and Rid's favorite Hervé Léger bandage dress.

Siren battle clothes.

Time to do your thing, Rid thought.

As soon as the red MINI Cooper made it down the hill and across Route 9 into town, Ridley was in better spirits. The moment she saw Link, she could tell he was halfway out of his mind. For all the usual reasons, she guessed. Not to mention the Pepto-Bismol–pink housecoat that one of those reasons happened to be wearing this morning.

"Wesley Lincoln! You won't be needin' that *garbage* at Georgia College a the Redeemer." Mrs. Lincoln stood in the driveway, trying to tear the *Star Wars* poster out of Link's hand. "In fact, at Georgia Redeemer you won't be needin' any a that mess from your room."

Link yanked harder on the poster, frustrated. The Beater was mostly packed, but he was supposed to have been on the road an hour ago. Ridley knew better than anyone that standing in the driveway arguing over his action figures one by one with his mother was Link's idea of Hell. "Aww, come on, Mom. That's my stuff. And I gotta get outta here. You want to make me late for all that good college orientin'?"

Mrs. Lincoln responded by yanking the poster up and out of Link's reach until it tore.

"Ma!"

Ridley chose that moment for her entrance. "Mrs. Lincoln. How *lovely* you look! I mean, the way your *housecoat* matches your *curlers*." Try as she might, Ridley could never manage not to irritate Link's mom. It was pretty much her specialty. That, and getting Mrs. Lincoln to turn a particular shade of red previously reserved only for old beets and sunburned pigs.

Link looked so relieved to see her that Rid thought he was going to break down and kiss her right then and there.

But then she looked at his mother and thought again.

Mrs. Lincoln seethed: "Is that sass? Do you think I want advice on how to cover my own God-given body from a shameless half-dressed harlot like you?"

Rid momentarily considered her thigh-high boots and her halter dress—more than a few bandages shy of a true bandage dress—and waggled one long red nail. "Now, now. No harlot shaming. Haven't you heard? There's a Democrat in the White House, ma'am."

Mrs. Lincoln gasped.

Ridley smiled. Her mood was improving. It felt good to mix it up with the Mortals. Flex the old chainsaw mouth.

Being good Ridley was so dull that sometimes she was tempted to make new friends just so she could lose them later.

"Lay off, Rid." Link turned to his mom, taking the poster out of her hand. "Rid's here to say good-bye. You might cut her some slack, seein' as she's not comin' to Georgia Redeemer with me. Especially seein' as you wrote all those letters to the Board to make sure."

Mrs. Lincoln forced a smile onto her face. "No, she certainly is not. She would burst into flames if she set one foot on a good Christian campus, and don't you forget it."

"Jesus loves everyone, Mom."

Mrs. Lincoln scowled at Ridley. "That right there is the one child Jesus forgot."

Link tried to keep a straight face. Nothing made his mom madder than a smile or a sass during a beatdown. "I don't know about that. They gotta call it Redeemer for a reason."

"I promise you, she's not it. Do not so much as dial her number." Mrs. Lincoln was almost turning purple.

"That's not really your business," Link said sulkily.

"Oh, you can bet your sweet corncakes it is. As far as I'm concerned, I'm the CEO a your business, Wesley Lincoln."

"I'm just here to see you off," Ridley said, sweet as pie.

First things first.

Ridley was here to get her boyfriend back, and she intended to get the job done.

Link held out his hand to her. She looked at it. "A hand-shake? What do you want me to do with that?"

"Sayin' good-bye, I guess. Like you said." He reached for her hand with a smile and a wink. "See ya around, Rid. Been nice knowin' you."

Ridley took his hand. Mrs. Lincoln's eyes narrowed. Ridley yanked Link toward her, grabbing his face with both hands. She tilted his head and kissed him so hard that his toes curled and his face turned bright red.

Almost as red as his mother's.

It was the kind of kiss that had made Sirens famous, the kind of kiss that stung worse than a whole army of wasps—the kind that made you forget your own name and your destiny. The kind that could make a sailor steer his ship straight into the rocks.

Until he would be the one wearing the bandages, Rid thought, with more than a little satisfaction. Or at least, pride in workmanship. She didn't have a tongue long trained by years of cherry lollipops for nothing.

Then, as quickly as Ridley had caught him, she threw him back, breathless and stammering. When she pulled away, Link looked like he was going to pass out.

"Bye, then," Rid said sweetly.

Link stumbled toward his car. His mother came after him with two open arms, then let them drop, disgusted.

"Well, Wesley Lincoln, are you happy now? What kind a mother could kiss her own son after a sordid display like that?" Mrs. Lincoln snapped. "You'd better go in the house and wash your mouth out or I'll never be able to kiss you again."

"Aww now, wouldn't that be a shame," Ridley purred.

Five minutes later, Rid stood on the sidewalk and watched as the Beater drove away. The Who—she thought it was "Teenage

41

Wasteland"—drifted through the air in its wake, almost like the sound track to the end of the movie that had been Link's crappy life in Gatlin.

Mrs. Lincoln sniffed, blotting her eyes with her handkerchief.

Ridley clapped her on the back. "Well, Mamma. I guess I should be off, too." She ducked to Mrs. Lincoln's cheek and kissed it loudly, leaving behind a red smear. "You don't mind if I call you that, do you, Mrs. L? Seein' as we're bound to be family, any day now." She leaned toward the woman who hated her more than all the banned books in the Gatlin County Library combined. "You know he's saving for a ring, don't you?"

Mrs. Lincoln could barely speak. "Get off my property, you little hussy."

Ridley wiggled her fingers, the Binding Ring still on her hand. *How about this one?* She couldn't resist flexing a little Siren power on Link's repulsive mother.

Mrs. Lincoln's face turned purple, but she couldn't get out whatever hideous thing it was that she wanted to say.

Ridley smiled. "Love you, too, Mamma. Can't wait to inherit your good china!" She blew Mrs. Lincoln a kiss and walked straight through her best flower bed, kicking up dirt as she went.

Ridley climbed back into her MINI and laughed to herself all the way down Route 9, her pink scarf flapping happily in the wind behind her.

By the time Ridley caught up to the Beater, Link was parked at the BP gas station on the edge of town and leaning on the hood.

Rid honked and rolled down her window, reaching into her

ashtray to hold up the torn corner of his old *Star Wars* poster. "You forgot something."

Link grinned, taking the scrap of poster from her. "I think you gave my mother a heart attack."

"Just wanted to give her a little something to remember me by. She's really starting to warm up to me." Ridley smiled, pulling down her sun visor to gloss her red lips in its mirror.

"Think you overshot a little? My mom will probably be having nightmares for the next three months."

"Only three? You sure know how to hurt a girl, Hot Rod." She pursed her lips. Link just stared.

Bandage dress, two. Wesley Lincoln, zero.

"Speaking of good-bye, you think your mom bought it?" She looked at Link.

"Yeah, she bought it." Link grinned. "Hook, line, and Redeemer. I'm a free man." He had been planning his escape for months. Everything, even the fake acceptance letter from the fake church college, had been gone over a thousand times. Link's practice at forging notes in high school had finally paid off.

Enough. It's time. Rid snapped her mirror shut. "And what was that handshake about? Did you really think your mom would believe we were just friends?"

"Why not? Aren't we?" Link leaned back over the edge of the car.

Ridley turned off the motor. "That all depends." She pushed open her car door, shoving Link backward as it swung away from her. Then she sauntered around the car and untied her scarf, slowly dropping it on the backseat.

It's like dancing sometimes. Even if only one of you can hear the music.

"Where are you goin'?" Link watched her, suspicious.

Ridley didn't answer. She just bent over to pop open the trunk of the car, pausing to make sure Link caught the view. Tight dress. Thigh-high boots. Just the way Heaven intended her to look.

One.

Two.

Three.

Now.

Ridley pulled out three identical Louis Vuitton bags and handed them to Link, one after another. From the look on his face, she could tell he'd caught the view, all right.

She'd closed the deal. Now all that was left was to break the news to the boy.

Rid walked up to the gas station attendant and handed him her keys. "My car goes back in the carriage house at Ravenwood Manor. Park it as far away from my Uncle Macon's hearse as possible. My cousin drives that thing like a maniac." She grabbed his hand. "And I was never here."

Rid didn't even need a lollipop anymore, not for most folks in Gatlin. She had a reputation, which was even more powerful. The attendant swallowed and nodded. He took the keys and disappeared back into the garage.

"Does this mean what I think it means?" Link stared at Rid. "You're comin' to New York with me?"

"Well, I'm sure as hell not going to Georgia Redeemer with you."

Link tried not to smile. "You're serious?"

Surprisingly, Ridley found she had to try just as hard. "As the grave."

44

He took a deep breath. "You and me?"

"You see another Siren standing here?" She took a steadying breath herself. "Or you got a problem with that?"

Ridley knew there were a lot of things Link could have said at that moment. He could've asked Rid about her change of heart. He could've pointed out how she had given John hell for following Liv to England. He could've cited their endless non-fight, their big breakup.

Breakups.

But Link didn't do any of those things. Instead, he gave her a smile as wide as the Mississippi River.

"Well," Link said.

"Yep," Rid said.

"I guess we should—"

"Right."

It only took about ten seconds for Link to awkwardly help Rid cram her three monogrammed bags into the back of the Beater.

"That's all you brought?" Link seemed shocked.

"That's just my underwear. One thing I know about the big city, Shrinky Dink, is where to shop."

Well, I'll be shopping. You'll be doing what I need you to do.

That was the plan, anyway. Even if she couldn't tell Link about it. Ridley felt a pang of guilt, but she pushed it away as quickly as it came.

Whatever. I'll think about that later.

By the time they were back in the Beater, the awkwardness had passed, and all they were left with was the scandalous thrill of having pulled it off.

Ridley settled into the seat next to Link.

He turned up the music, pulling her close. "I've been waitin' to do this since last night." He leaned in for a kiss, and she felt an unexpected burst of happiness.

God. I really did miss him, after all. Him, and this.

"Your wait is over, darlin'." She kissed him back, climbing halfway onto his lap in the process. It was going to be a long drive, and she figured she might as well get comfortable.

Link couldn't stop smiling, kissing aside. "You just couldn't stay away, could you?"

"Couldn't do it to you." She kissed him again.

He pulled away for a second, grinning at her. "Church college my ass."

She fluttered her eyelashes. "I've been a bad, bad girl, Wesley Lincoln. Think you can redeem me?"

His answer was lost on his tongue.

Or maybe hers.

CHAPTER 6

Welcome to the Jungle

The good-byes were over. By the time John and Liv had boarded their plane for Heathrow and Ethan and Lena were headed for the Massachusetts Turnpike, Link and Ridley were on the way to New York City—the one-and-only setting of Link's one-and-only dream. It had been a long time coming.

"Remember last time we were in New York City?" Link stole a sideways glance at her.

"You mean the time you pretended to be at church camp?"

"Best band camp ever. Sneakin' into clubs in the East Village. Crashin' at youth hostels and YMCAs. Sleepin' in the Beater." He patted the dashboard.

"How could I forget." Ridley smiled. It had been an entirely magical hallucination, laced with powerful Siren mojo.

"Makin' it in New York, Rid. That's right up there with signin' a record label or performin' at the VMAs."

"Slow down, Hot Rod. Maybe first you can just try to find a new band." *And I know just where to start looking*, Ridley thought.

Link was thinking bigger. "Who knows? This could be the first chapter in my autobiography. *Rock On: The Making of a Carolina Icon*." He said it like he hadn't already told her a thousand times.

Ridley smiled. "And with any luck, maybe you can get your mother to ban your own book from the Stonewall Jackson High School Library."

Link laughed, settling in behind the wheel. "A guy can dream." He turned up the music.

Ridley shook her head. At least it wasn't going to be called Meatstik, the name of his last band. And she had thought the Holy Rollers were bad. The Holy Rollers were the Rolling Stones compared to Meatstik, which was probably the reason that Link hadn't been able to convince any of the members of his band to come with him to New York. Grable Honeycutt was going full-time at the Summerville Suds-It-Up, and Daryl Homer was just Daryl Homer. He'd probably still be sitting on his mother's couch this time next year, unless his mother sold it out from under him the way she'd threatened.

"My money's on Daryl," Link had said when the band first announced they were breaking up, right before graduation. "Plus, who wants a gold velvet sofa smellin' like a Homer's butt?"

It wasn't like any of them were leaving a great career behind. "(You're My) Mystery Meat" and "(Feels Like I'm Chewin' On) Indigestible Gristle," Meatstik's two most requested songs at the Summerville Community Center dances, showcased some of the worst lyrics Link had ever written, in Ridley's opinion. (*"Butcher my heart, fillet my soul, and when I bleed, sop it up with your roll."*) Actually, the very worst. And that was saying something, considering that Rid had sat through more Holy Rollers concerts than anyone.

"Now that the band's broken up, maybe you should try writing about something other than meat," she'd said.

"But meat's what I miss the most," Link had sighed. "Now that I'm not eating. And now that we're together again." Then he'd winked at her. "Our love is rare, medium rare."

"Don't you dare quote Meatstik to me."

Ridley didn't push it. Now wasn't the time to be hurting Link's feelings, especially not when she knew what was coming. Sooner or later, she'd have to tell him that this trip wasn't about dreams. Not anymore. It was about TFPs—talents, favors, and powers. In particular, the favors she'd lost in a card game called Liar's Trade at the club called Suffer. She was still too humiliated to admit the truth to anyone—and too afraid.

She owed a debt to Lennox Gates, who was more than just a powerful Dark Caster club owner. If Link didn't go to New York, he would be giving up more than his dream. He would be getting Ridley into a mess of trouble even she couldn't escape. Or, depending on how you looked at it, delivering her into the hot mess of trouble she'd just gotten herself into.

Maybe I should tell him to turn around now. I already gambled Link's future away, she thought, with a pang of guilt. *It's too late to worry about mine.* But she shook it off, as quickly as it came. She couldn't do what she needed to do if she let stupid feelings get in the way.

I'm doing him a favor. I need to deliver a drummer to

Lennox to settle this first marker, and Link is going to New York to be a drummer. Is there anything so wrong with doing us both a favor? And that band, what were they called? Devil's Horsemen? Hangmen? They weren't really all that bad, were they?

There have to be worse things in the world than spending a year with a few Caster rockers with a solid in to good gigs.

In fact, Ridley knew there were. It was the other thing she'd lost that night—the one she couldn't even begin to let herself think about. The part where she owed not just a drummer but a second marker, a house marker, which meant it was up to the house to decide when to cash it in, and for what.

In other words, Lennox Gates owned the house and the club, so he owned her marker. In other words, he owned her until a year from the day she lost the game.

She owed him one favor. Or worse—a talent, maybe even a power.

No limits.

Anything he asked.

He could make her step off the top of the world's tallest building if he decided to. Drown herself in Lake Moultrie. Shut herself in an Arclight.

In fact, Lennox Gates could make Ridley do anything she'd ever made anyone else do, using her own Power of Persuasion. He could collect whenever he wanted, and there was nothing she could do about it.

Ridley could still see him gloating, that night at Suffer.

More like insufferable. That's what he was.

She put it all out of her mind.

First things first.

She had to settle her gambling debt, and to do that, she had to get Link to New York. One drummer, coming right up.

In Philadelphia, Rid only let Link out of the Beater long enough at the local truck stop to buy a Coke, not that he could drink it.

In East Brunswick, New Jersey, she was relieved to see signs posted everywhere that only an attendant could pump the gas, so getting out of the car wasn't even an option. "Sorry, Hot Rod. It's the law."

Ridley couldn't help but feel an irrational panic that he might turn around and drive right back home. She could sense his nerves all the way from the other side of the car. Link couldn't keep his hands on the wheel. He was too busy tapping on every other surface of the Beater.

"I just gotta pull over and breathe for a second." He exhaled loudly, like a smoker without a cigarette.

"You're fine." Ridley reached out her hand. *I should pat something, right? Maybe his arm?*

She let her hand fall on his leg, awkwardly.

"You don't know that. What if I suck? What if I never get a new band? What if this was all just a stupid idea?" He said the words like they were new thoughts, and Ridley tried not to smile.

"When has that ever stopped you before?" She gave up on the patting.

After that, Ridley was on standby, ready to implement emergency measures. Link was freaking out at the wheel, and Ridley was stuck in his passenger seat. If she didn't do something, she was going down with this ship.

Like it or not, they were in this together.

Link shrugged. "I could get a job at the Suds-It-Up, I guess."

It was the saddest thing she had ever heard. It gave her a thought so un-Ridley it felt like heartburn in her brain.

This must be what it's really like to be Bound to a person. You can't just wave it away, turn it magically on or off. Really connecting yourself to another person is infinitely more complicated than that.

She looked at the fire-forged Binding Ring on her finger. Ridley had to do something, for both of them.

Rid wriggled her fingers, watching as the colors of the ring shifted from a bright blue to a milky green. *Caster green*, she thought. *Like some big old Caster mood ring.*

She closed her eyes.

No. It wasn't a Cast. It wasn't even a Charm. It wasn't the same as a cherry lollipop or a piece of gum or anything she could chew on or suck on or sweeten up her Siren powers with.

It was a wish.

But as she wished, she felt a strange pull—as if something was giving way in the deepest part of her own mind, the way it did when she was Kelting with a Caster or Charming her way past some unsuspecting Boy Scout.

I wish this Beater could Travel. If John were here, he'd be able to figure out a way to do it. We'd Rip from here to New York City in a heartbeat.

Ridley's heart pounded and she opened her eyes just in time to see the Beater crossing the Brooklyn Bridge, over the water from Manhattan into Brooklyn.

"Wait," she said, turning to Link. "Did you see that?"

"It's kinda hard to miss the Brooklyn Bridge, Rid. Even for

a boy from Gatlin." Link grinned. He was back to his old self. Something about the city always charmed Link as completely as anything Rid could do to him.

"You didn't notice anything weird just now? Between New Jersey and here?"

"You mean, aside from the license plates bein' the wrong color and the radio stations bein' all jacked up? And how you gotta pay money just to drive on the highway? Everything's weird, Babe. This is the North." Then "Stairway to Heaven" came on and all conversation came to a mandatory stop. It was one of the only rules in the Beater. You had to respect the Stairway.

Rid held up her hand in the moonlight, staring at the ring. *What were the words of that Binding Cast? Something send us? Did the ring do it?*

It had faded back to blue again, and now it didn't look any more powerful than the other pieces of jewelry she was wearing.

Link didn't make the Beater Travel. He didn't even notice it. And I didn't imagine it. I couldn't have.

Because they were in New York.

She didn't know how or why, or even who was responsible— but at least nothing bad had happened. She had gotten her wish. There was no turning back from New York now.

Ridley couldn't tell if it was because of the ring, but as they crossed through the darkness from one stretch of sparkling lights to the next, the Brooklyn Bridge seemed like the most magical place in the world, or the second most magical. It reminded Ridley of the Caster bridge that led to the seam, the great boundary between the Mortal world and the Otherworld. Except where that bridge had been a splintery old dock, this one was almost a monument to Mortals. She wondered why she'd never noticed it before. The immense scale of everything—the cables rising high into the night sky overhead, the support beams striping them with shadow and light as the Beater sped by—it wasn't like anything either of them was used to seeing around Gatlin.

It was Mortal and breathtaking, and Ridley couldn't imagine ever getting used to the idea that the pathetic, broken-down human race could pull off something this beautiful.

Just when you think they can't surprise you, she thought. *Then you have to start worrying that they can.*

⊰ CHAPTER 7 ⊱

Another Brick in the Wall

We're not lost. How big can Brooklyn be? And I got a nose like a houndog, remember?"

"*Hound dog* is two words," Ridley said. "And you mean bloodhound."

"Whatever." He took a swig from the Coke can wedged between his seat and the door. Cars as old as the Beater didn't have luxury amenities like cup holders or windshield wiper fluid, let alone both headlights.

"You sure you even know where you're going? Where your apartment is?" Ridley looked at him suspiciously.

He spat the Coke back into the can with a sigh. It was as close as he could come to drinking one; like any Incubus, Link didn't need food, or even want it. But that didn't mean he didn't miss it.

Link sighed, rattling the can. "It's not an apartment. Not exactly."

"What is it, exactly?"

"A parking lot." He stole a sideways look at her.

"Excellent." She tried to look annoyed, but really, she wasn't that surprised.

"I figured I'd sleep in the Beater. Seems to me we had some pretty good times in this old girl." He patted the dashboard affectionately.

"Your plan was to move to New York until you made it big and you were going to sleep in your car the whole time?"

Link shrugged. "How long could it take? I'm a talented guy."

Ridley pulled a slip of paper out of her bag and grabbed Link's ancient and not-at-all-smart phone off the dashboard. She found the keypad and slowly typed in letters with the tips of her long red nails. "Never mind. I've got this."

It was time for the next phase of her plan—time to meet the band, and Link couldn't have made things any easier. The roadie at Suffer had given her the lead guitarist's number and told her to call when they got to town. *Here we are.*

on our way address pls—Rid frm Suffer

"You have? Got what?" Link frowned.

"I know some people." She patted his arm. "I always do."

"Since when?" Now it was Link's turn to be suspicious.

The next text was almost instantaneous, and incomprehensible.

puking clown myrtle duane

Ridley tried to decipher the message. "It seems like we're staying with this guy named Duane," she said. "And maybe a girl named Myrtle."

"How come I never heard a these people?"

Ridley scrambled. "They're friends of John's. I texted him, and he hooked us up."

"John's supposed to be on a plane all night, remember?" Link said. "Who is this Duane guy for real?"

"They have Wi-Fi now on planes," Ridley said smoothly. *The lies are starting to come so easily. Even more quickly than usual.* "Which you'd know, if you'd ever been on one."

"Hey, I've been places."

"The Greyhound bus to Myrtle Beach doesn't count." Rid didn't even look up. "Speaking of Myrtle." She kept typing.

what puking clown

The response came just as quickly.

puke on myrtle

What?

Link scoffed, and Rid forced herself to stop looking at the phone. He glanced away from the street signs long enough to raise an eyebrow at her. "Why do I need a plane? John's stupid for not Traveling."

"That's funny, because last time I checked we were sitting in a car for ten thousand hours driving all the way from South Carolina to New York City. Instead of Traveling." *Except for the part when we were*, Ridley thought.

"That's different. I couldn't leave this sweet old girl home. She'd kill me." Link patted the dashboard. "Isn't that right, Sugarpie?"

"We have a place to crash with Duane and Myrtle. That's the important thing. I'm sure everything will be fine."

Ridley almost believed herself as she said it. She tried the phone once more.

puking clown what the hell who is myrtle

This time, there was no response at all.

"She's a street, not a person." Ridley stood under the sign that said MYRTLE AVE. It was a miracle they'd found it, considering that it was the middle of the night and pitch-dark and every conceivable surrounding sign, wall, and surface was covered in layers of graffiti.

"I kinda picked up on that about Myrtle." Link sighed. "Let's get back in the car. That dude's place has to be around here somewhere."

Ridley shook her head. "Isn't it obvious? Duane's screwing with us."

"Actually, he's not." Link pointed, with a laugh. "But Duane really wants you to come in for your flu shot. Because he's also not a person." There it was, the sign announcing two-for-one vaccination day at Duane Reade.

Duane Reade, the drugstore.

Damn, she thought. *They are screwing with me. Of course. Devil's Hairspray. This band already sucks worse than Meatstik.*

Link looked down at Ridley. "There's no Duane, Babe. And no Myrtle. Do you have any idea where we're goin', or who we're goin' to see?"

"A puking clown." She sat down on the curb. It was true, and all she had left to go on. Ridley was so frustrated she felt like crying. It didn't help that the people they were looking for still wouldn't answer her texts.

"Of course. Why didn't you say so?" Link exhaled, trying not to lose it.

"That's all the guy said. I'm so stupid for listening to some idiotic Caster I don't even know and thinking he would help." She caught herself. "Even if he is John's friend." *Right.* It wasn't that far off. There were lots of idiotic Casters she never should have listened to in her life.

Damn Casters.

And damn that one Mortal roadie. If she'd never met him, she would never have gotten into the game of Liar's Trade that landed her in this mess in the first place.

Damn Mortals.

"So who is this Not Duane guy? Dark Caster?" Link sat down on the curb next to her.

"Probably." She shrugged, improvising. "If he's one of John's friends. He didn't have the Lightest childhood."

"Come on. John never had any friends, Rid. We both know that. Who is this guy, really?"

"Well..." Ridley took a breath and looked up at Link. "He's in a band."

"What?" Link stiffened. There was no way Ridley could work the word *band* into any conversation without Link knowing she'd been up to something.

The band was his thing, not hers.

She had pretty much avoided all other music since she and Link had gotten together. Considering the kind of music Link's bands played, it was better if she didn't have anything else to compare it to.

Now everything came tumbling out. *Everything, up to a*

point. "I don't even remember his name. He's in a band and I saw him play at Suffer." *After we broke up. After I ran out on you. After I went on a bender through half of Europe. After I lost everything at one bad game of Liar's Trade.*

"Go on." Link looked even more suspicious. Another band was annoying enough. Another band from a Dark Caster club was worse.

The rest of Ridley's defense came out in one long—and surprisingly partially true—monologue. "I didn't want to tell you because I didn't want to fight about it, and because I knew you'd hate him if you associated him with our breakup." (Sort of true.) "But that's where we met and his band needs a drummer and otherwise they seemed pretty good." (Also sort of true.) "And I told him I knew someone who would be perfect and now here we are." She took another deep breath. "See? It's all fine. Now let's go find a puking clown."

She tried to sound upbeat, but saying the words *puking clown* made her give up again.

"I can't believe you." Link stared at her, and not in a good way. Not in an I-love-this-Siren way. The bandage dress wasn't even a factor in this conversation, which proved how badly it was going.

I'm off my game, Ridley thought. *I should be able to swing this, but I'm not. What's wrong with me?*

"Which part can't you believe?" She tried to remember which part was true, but it had gotten so convoluted that she was having trouble sorting it out for herself.

"Any of it. You knew I was comin' here to break into the music scene. Then you sat in the car the whole way up here and never said one word about me auditionin' for a band."

60

"It's not an audition. You've already got the job." *Which is the whole problem*, she thought. *Irony sucks.*

"What are you talkin' about?"

"They need a drummer. You're a drummer. It's math. You plus them equals band. Done. Can we go find the clown now?"

"Rid. Stop. This is a big deal to me. You don't get to decide my whole future for me. That's not how this is going to go down."

"Why not?"

"It's my dream. You have to stay out of it. I'm supposed to get there myself."

"You are."

"Yeah? How many lollipops did you have to suck to swing this one, Rid?" he asked.

The words stung. She looked away.

"Regular girlfriends don't do things like that, Rid."

"Then why don't you go ahead and get yourself one of those?" *Don't snap, Rid. Back it down.* "Because I was only trying to help." *Myself*, she added, as badly as she felt about it.

He looked skeptical.

"Really, Link. I'm just trying to be honest with you." *Nice touch.*

"Whatever." He looked away, back in the direction of the graffiti-covered Duane Reade.

"Why don't you ever believe me when I say I'm sorry?" Ridley attempted to appear sorry, but she was having trouble remembering how that particular expression looked. She went with sick instead, because she'd faked that one enough times growing up that it was almost second nature.

"Because you're never sorry," Link said, as if the thought had only just now come to him. "Because you never really believe there's anything to be sorry for. This is all just a game to you. It's never goin' to be anythin' more real than that. Not for Ridley Duchannes."

Ridley knew what he was talking about. Earlier in the summer, when Link had confessed that he loved her, she had freaked out and bailed on him. Neither one of them had said a word about it since.

Sometimes real was too real, especially for Ridley.

"No. That's not true," she said, suddenly feeling sort of awful.

Link stood up. "I need to walk."

"No, please don't," she said. "Link."

He took off down the street—away from Ridley and the Beater and the Duane Reade and the whole conversation.

She'd been tricking Mortals her entire life. At least, manipulating them. She'd always gotten by before. Why did she feel so bad about it now? And who was Link to make her feel so rotten for doing what she'd always done?

Most Dark Casters didn't give Mortals a second thought. They were there to be taken advantage of—it was why they existed.

Like for target practice, or Casting lessons.

They're just, you know, Mortals.

Ridley sat alone on the curb in the circle of a sad yellow streetlight. The night was dark, even in the city, and once again she was alone.

This is who I am. A girl sitting alone on a curb. This is all I know how to be.

She knew she needed to tell Link the truth, but which truth?

And what did it matter? In the end, she'd still find herself alone on the curb.

Maybe that's where I belong.

She shivered, feeling conspicuous, like the world was watching.

Literally watching.

She looked up.

Because someone is *watching me*, Rid thought. She could feel it, the eyes on her. She glanced up and down the street. The night grew darker in the cracks and crannies beneath cars and stoops, inside doorways and behind bushes. There were so many places to hide.

But as she watched, everything remained still.

Maybe I'm imagining things.

There were no footsteps, no sounds.

I don't have that great of an imagination.

Ridley was still trying to hammer it out when Link shouted back to her.

"Rid!"

"Go away," Ridley said. "I don't want to hear it." It was what he expected her to say, the Siren alone on the curb. So she said it.

"Well, that's too bad, because I found us a puking clown."

CHAPTER 8

Stairway to Heaven

"Where are you taking me?"

"Have a little faith, Rid," Link said.

"Right." *As if.*

Link stopped and pulled her in front of him, putting a hand on each of her shoulders. "Look. I'm tryin' to help, here. I'm not sayin' it's a slam dunk. I gotta make sure it's a good fit, I mean. The band."

Ridley held her breath.

"Yeah?"

"If it's important to you, I'll give it a shot. I mean, I'm your guy. But you gotta be straight with me."

"I am." She reached up to push a spike of hair out of his eyes.

"You sure there's nothin' else goin' on here?"

She shook her head. *Nothing I can tell you, anyway.* But she was still spooked by the feeling that she was being watched. And more than a little guilty about having to lie to her own boyfriend.

She had a bad feeling about this whole night.

"I'm fine," Ridley said, as much to herself as to him.

Link looked relieved and grabbed her hand. "Then let's go."

She followed him across the street from the Duane Reade— the very real drugstore, not the infinitely less real person—where there was a small, run-down, otherwise nondescript one-story diner. Though the street itself was dark, the front window of the building was lit by a blinking neon light that said one word: DINER. It looked like it hadn't changed much, or been cleaned much, in half a century.

"Does that mean it's a diner? Or that the name of the place is Diner?" Ridley stared up at it. "I don't get it."

"Marilyn's Diner. Can't you see where the rest of the neon's blown out?"

She examined it more closely, but she could barely make out anything in the window. Now that he had transformed, the hybrid Incubus Link could see and hear things well beyond the abilities of a Mortal, or even a Caster.

"Anyway, I'm not talking about that. Look at this." Link pointed to a wall on the side of the diner, the one that faced the corner of the intersection. It was a relatively average wall of brick covered with graffiti. Tagged words became abstract spray-painted shapes, swirling one into the next. A row of monsters. A sea of faces. Hands lining the ground like flowers.

And one word, arching over it all.

NECRO

The lettering reminded Ridley of something, but she couldn't recall exactly what. The name was familiar, or maybe just the artwork. "It's like those paintings by that one guy. You know, in the museums in Paris, or Spain."

"Oh, that guy. I see what you're saying." But Link didn't see, since he had never set foot inside a museum in his entire life. Not even the gift shop.

"Dalí," she said, snapping her fingers. "Salvador Dalí, the guy with the droopy clocks and bizarre faces and skulls that have skulls for eyes. Monster heads walking around on chicken legs and whatever."

"Last time I checked, you paid about as much attention to museums as I did." Link grinned. "You're so full of it."

"See right there? Where the monster coming out of the creepy egg thing with legs is eating those little guys? That's what I'm talking about." Ridley gestured to the wall.

"I think you're missing the point." Link looked smug.

"Yeah? What is it, then, Picasso?"

Link reached toward the white monster. "It's that."

He touched the wall right behind the white monster, where another creature, one that looked like a cross between a squid and a giraffe—with a strangely round, red nose—was spewing what looked like a bunch of eyeballs out of his enormous mouth.

"He's throwing up," Rid said. "Clown Nose is throwing up." Suddenly, she saw it. Clown Nose. Throwing up. *Puking clown!*

"Pukin' like Savannah Snow at Senior Night." Link seemed

66

more chipper than he'd been since they left Gatlin. "Or Emily Asher at prom. Or that really drunk Summerville kid with food poisoning at Meatstik's last gig. Or—"

"Yeah, yeah. I've got it." Rid reached for the mouth. Her hand slid inside, until it disappeared all the way up to her wrist.

"Doorknob?" Link looked hopeful.

In answer, she grabbed his sleeve and yanked, until they both disappeared into the swirls of paint that were the graffiti mural...

...and reappeared on the other side of a door, in what seemed to be the mail room of an average-looking apartment building.

Link doubled over, his hands on his knees. Then he stood upright, shaking his head like a big dog that had just come out of the water. "Whoa. I don't think I'll ever get used to that."

"A basic *Occultus Vox* Cast? Oh, please, whatever. Illusionist kid stuff. Larkin did the same thing to his clubhouse when he was five." Ridley wasn't so impressed with the doorway; anyone could do that. But through the glass of another doorway, she saw stairs zigzagging up into the darkness—apartments above Marilyn's, hidden from the outside by a Cast. Illusioning away a whole apartment building was pretty cool. Only the diner on the bottom floor was visible, and Ridley realized there was a second way in.

"The diner's the threshold," Ridley said. "I think we came in the back door. They were probably trying to throw us off."

"Why would they want to do that?"

Ridley shrugged. "They're Dark Casters, not the Stonewall Jackson PTA. They're not here to meet the neighbors."

She stared at the mailboxes, where a row of names appeared in pencil next to their corresponding—and very Mortal, very battered-looking—metal boxes. She ran her fingers down the list.

FLOYD: #2D

She tapped her finger on the name. "I met that girl. She's the Illusionist."

"Floyd?"

"I guess so." Ridley shrugged. To be honest, she hadn't paid much attention to anything that night at Suffer beyond her own predicament. "She was good at Liar's Trade. But I was better."

"What else?" Link looked at her like she was forgetting the important stuff.

"Oh, right. Bass guitar, I think." She tried to remember, then gave up. "Whatever. She's just some rocker chick."

"I like rocker chicks." Link grinned.

Ridley ignored him. She just pointed at a different name on the wall. "She didn't do it all by herself. Look."

There it was.

NECRO: #2D

"So they're friends," Link said.

Ridley nodded. "One did the tagging and the other hid the door. I met them both, but I don't think I said two words to them all night." *Another poser rock loser.*

"Necro? Probably a Necromancer." Link looked anxious. He wasn't interested in talking to the dead any more than he already had in the last few years. Having your best friend go to the Otherworld and back will do that to a guy.

"You think? What gave that away?"

Link raised his hands in surrender.

One name was scratched out. Ridley looked more closely but she couldn't read it. "That one must have been their blowhole of a drummer. The one you're replacing."

"I'm not—"

Careful. Pull back. "The one *they think* you're replacing. I know, I know. It's not up to me. You don't have to do anything you don't want to do. I'm not the boss of you. So we'll just go inside and clear the whole thing up."

"What about this one?" Link stooped over to read the name. "It looks like Sam. Sam something."

SAMPSON: #2D

Ridley felt seriously ill seeing the name of the strange Dark-born who had beaten her in the final hand of Liar's Trade. The one who was playing for the house. "Sampson, he's...something different."

"Dark? Light? Incubus?"

If only she knew.

"Just different." Her tone said *leave it*, and he did.

Ridley took a breath.

Now or never. I got us into this mess. This is how I'll get us out.

So she did the opposite of every single thing she felt like doing. She found apartment 2D—up one flight of stairs, with nothing obviously Caster about them—and pushed the buzzer.

The door opened.

It was the pretty-boyish girl with the blue faux-hawk.

69

Ridley recognized the close-cropped blue hair from the club. She couldn't remember her name. They were all a blur now.

"Hey, *Duane*." She attempted a smile. "Knock, knock. It's us." Ridley had taken a step closer toward the door when the blue faux-hawk tried to slam it shut, in her face. "Not expecting us, were you? Thanks for the great directions. You really made things easy."

Link pushed the door open, and they stared at two very different girls. Ridley remembered them both from Suffer.

One was tall and gangly, sporting ratty jeans, a ripped Pink Floyd T-shirt, and more stringy blond hair than she seemed to know what to do with. Right now it was spilling out of two knots on the top of her head. "Hi, Floyd," Ridley said.

Next to her, the one with the faux-hawk was short and slight. Where there wasn't blue hair or black leather there were so many piercings it looked like she had a stapler fetish. "Necro." Ridley nodded. It occurred to her that she had never realized Necro was actually a girl before, when they'd met at Suffer.

Neither girl answered.

"Hey, Floyd." Link pointed at her shirt. "I get it. Awesome." He made a small, worshipful bow. Floyd swallowed a smile.

He looked at Necro. "What's up, Gaga?"

Ridley snorted. "Link. Don't be rude. It's not Gaga. I'm not even sure it's a Lady."

"It? Are you talking about me?" Necro examined her fist like she was considering her options. "Ouch, Barbie. Where'd you learn your manners?"

"On the streets of Brooklyn," Ridley shot back. "Thanks to your excellent directions." She looked at Link. "This is my boyfriend, Link." She nodded at the girls. "This is Devil's Hairspray."

"Hangmen," Floyd corrected.

"As if that's any better." Ridley rolled her eyes.

Necro looked annoyed. "Aren't Sirens supposed to keep their killer talons hidden under soft, sweet exteriors?"

Ridley waved a hand of talon-like nails.

Necro smiled. "Oh, I see the talons. I'm just having a hard time finding the sweet exterior."

"Bite me," Ridley said. "See how sweet I taste then."

Necro raised an eyebrow. "Funny, I'm going to pass."

Ridley smiled back. "Funny, I'm not going anywhere."

They stood eye to eye, talon to talon. Necromancer to Siren, at an unspoken impasse.

In the end, the Necromancer blinked.

Don't they always?

Necro shoved the door open with a sweeping gesture. "Fine. Lennox warned us you were coming. You can hang at the Devil's Hangout until you find a place of your own." Ridley took a step toward the door, but Necro stopped her. "I hope your boyfriend's better at the drums than you are at cards, Siren."

Ridley pushed past her. She didn't laugh.

There was nothing funny about Lennox Gates.

CHAPTER 9

Use Your Illusion

Apartment 2D was even stranger on the inside than the outside. The moment the door shut behind Link and Ridley, Rid realized she was standing in an inch of clear water.

"What the—"

Beneath her feet she could see golden sand.

Rid looked up to see a beach, and not just the depressing kind you found on a poster in a travel agency.

It was real. The sun was hot. The water was wet. She could tell by the way it was seeping between her toes.

"Is that an illusion?"

Necro shrugged. "Floyd missed the waves."

Floyd nodded. "I'm a California girl. Totally."

Link kicked at the water with his Doc Martens. "Killer surf."

Whatever.

"Can you tone down the water? I can barely hear myself think." Rid glared at Floyd, and instantly a wave the size of the Beater crashed over Rid's head. Floyd even made Rid's hair and clothes look—and feel, to Ridley's horror—sopping wet.

"Funny." She tried not to sound impressed.

When Ridley turned her back on the beach, she was dry again—irritated, but dry.

And on the other three sides of the beach, the loft was practically empty. The space was constructed with high, whitewashed ceilings and plaster walls—at least where you could see them behind the hundreds of Pink Floyd and heavy metal posters.

Like Link's bedroom in Gatlin, Rid thought. *Maybe that's a good sign.*

"What's that?" She pointed. At one end of the massive room was a sort of stage, with microphone stands and amps stacked to one side, and speakers mounted on the ceiling. A drum kit and three guitars sat on the stage.

"Practice room," said Floyd, banging the cymbal on the drum kit as she walked by. Necro moved next to her. These were going to be Ridley's new roommates. At least two of them. She sighed. Thankfully, Sampson, the Darkborn, was nowhere in sight.

"Unbelievable." Link's face lit up when he saw the stage, and he stood staring at it as if he could imagine himself hanging out there already. He took a step toward the stage, and a stadium-sized crowd appeared behind it, as if they were looking out from backstage.

Link took a step back, and the crowd disappeared.

Forward, back. Forward, back.

Crowd, no crowd. Crowd, no crowd.

He laughed. "I am so down with this." He took another step forward. Then another. The crowd started to scream, until their chanting drowned out the noise of the water.

"*Dev-il's H. Dev-il's H. Dev-il's H.*"

Link grinned over his shoulder. "Could we get them to chant my name?"

Rid yanked him back and the stage fell silent. "Can we not?"

"Aw, come on. Look at this." Link gestured to the posters on the walls, nodding his approval. "Metallica. Guns N' Roses. Black Sabbath. Iron Maiden. AC/DC." As he looked at them, each one played a riff of their most famous songs. You had to love Caster fandoms. "Someone's got good taste." Link nodded.

"That would be me." The blond girl smiled, mostly at Link.

"Figured it was you, Floyd." He grinned. "Your name says it all."

Wonderful, thought Ridley. *A She-Link.*

Floyd held up both hands. "No, no. I'm not named for the band. It's a family name. Frances Floyd the Third."

Link looked disappointed. "Aw, man. Well, your loss. It's all good."

Floyd broke into a grin and pointed at his face, laughing at him. "I'm messing with you. Pink Floyd is the greatest band of all time." Her arm morphed into an electric guitar, and she played a few bars of "The Wall" with one hand.

"*We don't need no ed-u-ca-tion,*" she sang.

Ridley had to admit Floyd sounded pretty good, which made her even more annoying. Especially when Link started playing bad drums against the coffee table with his hands. Her last hope that they'd get along evaporated as Floyd zeroed in on her boyfriend.

"*We don't need no thought con-trol*," he sang back. She wondered if he knew how bad he sounded. If Floyd thought so, she didn't let on.

Ridley raised her voice. "Okay, okay. You're a two-man band. Link Floyd. I feel we've established that."

"Link Floyd," Floyd said. "Look at that name. It was meant to be."

Meant to be?

"You know it." Link held out his fist to Floyd. "Pound it."

"Did I say Link Floyd?" Ridley shook her head. "I meant *Supertramp*." She glared meaningfully at the blond chick staring at her boyfriend.

Back off.

Floyd bumped fists with Link and added, "Or superhot."

Excuse me?

Ridley frowned. This wasn't what she was expecting. "Did I say Supertramp? I meant *Bitch*."

Link's eyes flickered over to her, surprised. Even Floyd looked at her like she was psycho.

Rid shrugged. "What? It's a band. Look it up." She stifled the urge to kick the coffee table to pieces. It would be bad for her boots.

"Da-ang," said Link and Floyd, accidentally and in unison. They looked at each other and laughed.

It was the final straw.

"You two want to get a room?" Ridley rolled her eyes. "Or maybe you can just show me mine. I'm exhausted."

"Yeah. Sorry. Sampson needs his own room, and Floyd and I share the other one." Necro glanced at Floyd, like there was a story there and she was warning her not to tell it.

Which was fine, since if there was, Ridley definitely didn't want to hear it. "Nice. I see who the boss is around here."

A shadow flickered across Necro's face. "You know any Darkborns? They're unpredictable. Not exactly roommate material."

"Darkborn?" Link was confused.

"Long story," Rid said. She looked at Necro and Floyd. "Some kind of mutant Caster. But he's nothing I can't handle."

"What are you gonna do? Charm him?" Necro laughed. "I'd love to see you try, Siren."

Apparently, Darkborn immunity had advantages beyond Underground card games. Ridley had lost everything back at Suffer, when Sampson had beaten her in spite of her Power of Persuasion. She wasn't interested in going head to head with him anytime soon.

Not like I'd admit that to these two fashion victims.

"So my mojo doesn't work on him. That doesn't mean he's invincible." Ridley was irritated. She just wanted this day to be over.

That and my own bedroom.

"Watching you try to Cast something on Sam? That would be like watching a fly try to high-five an elephant. You barely exist to him." Necro was happy to remind her of what she already knew.

"We'll see about that," Rid said. "Just show me my bed, Nympho."

Floyd looked at Necro, who stood there with a hand on her

hip. "Find it yourself. You can't miss it. It's the only mattress on the kitchen floor. The dirty one."

Then Necro smiled—her first smile of the night. "By the way. A friend of yours wanted me to tell you something."

"I don't have any friends," Ridley said.

"Sure you do. I don't know his name, but I think he gave me some kind of sick message for you. You seem to bring that out in people. It's been stuck in my head, like a bad dream. Happens sometimes." Necro extended an arm around Ridley, pulling her close.

"Keep your sick dreams to yourself," Ridley hissed.

"*Vindicabo*," Necro said. "One word. Four syllables. Noun. Vengeance Cast." Her lip rings clicked against her teeth as she spoke. "I think you have friends in low places, Siren."

Vindicabo.

The word hung in the air between them like a threat. Ridley stepped back, stumbling against the wall, pulling away from Necro. "What kind of message is that? *I will avenge* what? What are you talking about?" She'd seen enough *Vindicabo* Casts to know they were bad news for everyone involved. A *Vindicabo* was the Casting equivalent of a Vex: It showed no mercy, took no prisoners, and left a vast trail of destruction in its wake.

Ridley swallowed.

"That's all I got." Necro shrugged. "This stuff comes to me at night. I don't control it. And I'm not your secretary."

"Nice try, Nutbag." Ridley rolled her eyes. Her heart was pounding, but she could see Link watching her curiously from the doorway, and now she had no choice but to try to play off the whole conversation.

No big deal. Whatever.

"Don't say I didn't warn you. My kind, we hear these things. Watch your back. Something's coming for you. Or someone." Necro's eyes flickered to Link.

"Both of you."

⊰ CHAPTER 10 ⊱

Dream of Mirrors

Ridley thought it had to be a joke. But Nympho or Nightmare or whoever wasn't kidding. According to Miss Piercing Pagoda, not only was Ridley's life in danger, but her bedroom was the kitchen.

The kitchen floor.

The second of the two was the bigger problem, as far as Rid was concerned. She was familiar with death threats, but sleeping on a bare mattress on a dirty linoleum floor was something new. Ridley suspected her new roommates were trying to punish her, and if they were, they were a couple of sadistic geniuses. She had never slept on the floor of anything, anywhere, in her life.

Even when Abraham Ravenwood himself had kept her in a literal gilded cage, she'd had a divan for a bed.

For the record, she wasn't certain she'd ever been in a kitchen.

It wasn't entirely her own doing. Back at Ravenwood, Kitchen wouldn't stand for that sort of thing.

By the time Link returned from the Beater with her three bags, a big gray box, and his old Stonewall Jackson basketball team duffel, Rid was lying on the mattress, fully dressed.

"There is no way I can sleep on this thing," she said.

Link laughed. "A mattress in the kitchen. Sure you don't wanna sleep in the Beater?"

"How about in a cab on the way to a hotel in Manhattan?" Ridley wasn't kidding. Necro's warning had shaken her up.

Who is Casting a Vindicabo *on me? Maybe the same person who was watching me outside the apartment? If I wasn't imagining the whole thing?*

Ridley flung her arm over her eyes, blacking out the world around her, as if she could make it all go away.

Is any of this real, or is the Necromancer just messing with me?

Link slid his arm around her. "Come on. Where's your spirit of adventure, Babe?"

"Don't call me Babe." Ridley shrugged him off. "And that's easy for you to say. You don't even sleep."

"I wish I could. This day has been too freakin' long." Link dropped the bags and box from the car in front of her. The kitchen was so small there wasn't much room for anything but the mattress.

He sighed, falling next to her onto the mattress. Then he shoved the gray box in her direction.

"What is it, a present?" Ridley hated surprises. She always imagined the worst.

A head in a box. A bomb. Link's mother, miniaturized.

"I guess I shoulda told you," Link said sheepishly. "But I didn't know you were comin', remember?"

Rid reached for the lid and knocked it to one side, tentatively, as if she were afraid whatever was in the box would bite her.

Turned out, she wasn't that far off.

Lucille Ball stared back at her, curled up inside an old pink bath rug, looking as if she'd just woken up from a twenty-four-hour catnap.

"Are you kidding me? You brought the cat?"

Lucille howled, equally offended.

"Aunt Mercy said she'd never been up North. Aunt Grace said Lucille Ball would be better off crossin' the Mason-Dixon Line in the sky. Then Ethan promised he'd ask, and I promised I'd think about it, and before I knew it—"

"Your big plan was to run off to New York City to become a rock star with your best friend's great-aunts' cat as your sidekick?" Ridley looked from Lucille Ball to Link.

"I thought it might be nice, you know, to have a familiar face from back home."

"A cat's face?"

Lucille Ball howled again. Link tried to muzzle her, and Lucille bit his hand.

"Bite her, not me! I'm not the one who hates you." Link tried to slam the lid back on the box, but Lucille leaped out and onto the mattress.

He grabbed for her, but she slipped out of his hands and disappeared through the crack in the door.

"Hope the windows are closed. Otherwise I gotta tell the Sisters that I lost Lucille before she even got to see the Statue a Liberty."

"Don't worry." Ridley sighed. "Nobody is lucky enough to get rid of that cat."

"Yeah?" He sounded hopeful.

"Believe me, I've tried." Rid wanted to look angry, but she started giggling, and then Link cracked up, and soon they were both laughing so hard they could barely breathe.

Ridley flopped back on the mattress, and Link lowered himself down next to her. They lay there, staring at the ceiling.

"You want to snuggle up and keep warm? You know, body heat?" Link rubbed her arm.

"I'm hot." Ridley pulled her arm away. Seeing Lucille had made her feel better. But the cat had disappeared, and so had Ridley's good mood.

"Third Degree Burns. Can't argue with that," Link said, grinning down at her.

"It's late. I want to get some sleep." She wiggled out of his arms.

"What did Necro say when we were comin' to check out our room that got you so rattled?" he asked.

"Nothing."

"You can tell me."

Yeah, right.

A few minutes later, Link gave up. He disappeared to the practice room and Ridley was left staring up at the ceiling, wondering if this was her real punishment for that night at Suffer.

She heard Link's voice, and then a girl's laugh.

Supertramp. At it again.

Moments later, the bass guitar began to thump, followed by the drums. Soon the crowd was chanting.

Ridley pulled the pillow over her head.

"*Li-ink Floyd. Li-ink Floyd. Li-ink Floyd.*" You couldn't ignore it. Rid turned on her side.

Could this night get any better?

She didn't bother to take off her shoes. She wanted to be ready to bolt at the first sign of trouble. (It was already difficult enough to bolt in four-inch heels.) Plus, the mattress smelled like an old swimming pool. It wasn't exactly the kind of place where you wanted to strip.

Ridley fell into a fitful sleep, alone on a hard mattress, in a city full of threats and lies, while her boyfriend hung out with another girl.

Only the dim green glow of her Binding Ring lit the way.

The salty wind on her face felt good, tickling her like kisses. "The breeze is blowing the sunshine away, Reece." When she looked up, she saw sunspots—and two small dark spots on the horizon. She rubbed her eyes.

They were still there, past the palms, all the way down on the sand.

"Look. What's that?" Ridley sat up, still sucking on two sugar cubes that she had stolen from Gramma's tea tray. In the fourteen summers she and her siblings and Lena had spent visiting their grandmother, she had never once been caught.

"You mean who?" Her big sister, Reece, asked as she tied the back of her bathing suit even more tightly than usual. Because now they could see that the dark spots were moving, or more precisely, walking.

They were two people—two dark figures following along the aquamarine shoreline of Bathsheba Beach.

"Fine. Who's that?" Rid's eyes narrowed. She kept sucking, but now the cubes were so small that she could barely taste the sweetness anymore.

"Lost Shorelings, probably. Why don't you ask them yourself?" Shoreling was Gramma's made-up word for all the curious folk who wandered up and down the sandy stretch in front of their house.

One of the black dots was headed right into the startling blue bay.

"We're too far east for swimming. They'll drown in the current. Someone should tell them."

"Mortals?" Reece shrugged. "Don't look at me." Though the Mortal and Caster populations of the island had mixed peaceably for centuries, the fundamental code seemed to be leave well enough alone.

If you drowned, you drowned.

Que sera, sera.

"Fine." Ridley hopped off the ancient wicker settee and started on the sandy path that snaked between beds of cliff grass down to Bathsheba Beach.

"Hat," yelled Reece from the veranda above, but Ridley just waved her off.

The balcony that wrapped around Ravenwood Abbey, Gramma's Barbados house, was carved of broad stone, a graceful contrast to the otherwise severe coastal cliffs beneath it. Their house had guarded the edge of the island—the bay, and Bathsheba Beach—ever since the sixteen hundreds. Ravenwood Abbey was even older than Ravenwood Plantation; like so many others, Ridley's ancestors had stopped in Barbados on the way to the Carolinas, long ago.

Hundreds of years of nothing ever happening, *thought Ridley.*

That was a long, long time.

Unless you loved spending hours memorizing family ancestral charts, maps of constellations, herb and garden journals, Caster histories. And the history of the Abbey, of course, which was why Ridley knew an encyclopedia's worth of information about Gramma's summerhouse. Reece and Ridley and Lena had studied everything but the actual Casts themselves, which they weren't allowed to see. Even little Ryan wasn't spared hours in the Abbey library. "It's like she wants us to learn about power just to make sure we'll never have any," *Rid had complained when they first arrived this summer.*

"Don't say those things. Gramma loves us." *Reece frowned, looking worried.*

But she looks that way most of the time, *Ridley thought.*

"How do I know that? She's never nice to me. Sometimes I think she hates me." *It sounded strange to finally say the words out loud.*

"She doesn't hate you," *Reece said, pulling Ridley into her arms for a sisterly hug. These moments didn't happen very often, and Rid savored it while it lasted.* "I think, sometimes, Gramma is a tiny bit afraid of you."

"Me? Why me?"

Reece just put her hand on Ridley's cheek and looked into her eyes, as if she could see the answers to all her sister's questions there. "I wish I knew."

But Gramma wasn't even here today. She had gone with

Mamma to the easternmost tip of the islands to look at some ancient caves that Gramma was convinced had something to do with their family's future.

Why would anyone spend a whole day looking at a cave? *Ridley had no idea. But as she ran down the path, she tried not to think about anything but the sun and the sky and the tadpoles she had found in the pond by her room last night.*

Summer was meant to be fun.

Everything else could be ignored for now.

She was going to save the Shorelings and then tell Gramma all about it at dinner. Uncle Macon, too. They'd think she was brave and kind. They'd tell Reece and Ryan to be more like her, and then give Ridley an extra piece of dessert. Ridley had it all worked out.

"You! Shorelings! Get out of the water!"

A towheaded boy pulled himself to his feet. He walked up out of the foaming surf, right toward her. A girl, younger looking, with darker hair, sat at the edge of the water, on the sand.

"What did you call me?" The boy's eyes flashed.

Ridley sniffed. "The water's dangerous. If you drown, my Gramma will have to call the police. And she hates the police."

"I'm not going to drown." The light-haired, dark-eyed boy smiled. He couldn't have been that much older than she was. He was tan and tall, but not too tall. Not old.

Just a boy.

"You shouldn't be out here. It's private property," she said.

"Nobody owns the beach or the ocean." He crossed his arms.

"What are you doing here?"

"I'm here with my sister," he said. "We're bored."

"I know the feeling."

"We're stuck here while my grandfather is away for the day."

Ridley nodded. "Mine, too. I mean, Gramma."

"He's at some stupid caves."

"Mine, too," Ridley said, with an odd feeling in her stomach.

She wanted to run away. She wanted to run as fast as she could, all the way back up to the path and up the stairs and down the hall and into her room. She wanted to hide under the bed—only she didn't know why.

Kiss me, *she thought.* That's what I want.

I want him to kiss me.

My first kiss.

And I want it to be here, on the beach, with this dark-eyed boy.

Her eyes were wide. The boy smiled, his teeth as sharp and white as his eyes were round and dark. He leaned his face closer to hers.

Her wish was about to be granted.

Then he whispered, so quietly that she almost couldn't hear him over the ocean wind.

"You want me to kiss you, don't you?"

"No," she said. But it was a lie.

"You know why you want me to kiss you?" he asked.

She said nothing.

"Because I wanted you to."

Then he pulled his head back and started laughing. Ridley started crying.

"Don't mistake me for a Mortal again," he said. "I'm not your Shoreling, or whatever you called it. I'm one of the most powerful Casters alive."

"You wish," Ridley said, suddenly bold. "You're just a

dumb Caster boy. And my Gramma is a thousand times more powerful than you."

He took a sandy step closer to her. "Yeah? Prove it."

This fight was as exhilarating as the kiss.

As the kiss might have been, *she reminded herself.*

She closed her eyes.

Kiss me.

I want you to want to kiss me.

And as if he was listening, he brought his face toward hers, his eyes wide open, as if he couldn't believe it himself.

She felt her powers relaxing over him, enveloping them. She'd never used them before, not like this. Not so knowingly on another person, especially not another Caster.

She liked how they made her feel—strong, independent, invincible.

He brought his lips to hers...closer and closer.

Now his eyes were shut.

"This is for you," she whispered, her voice as low and husky as his had been moments before. "So you never forget. My name is Ridley Duchannes, and nobody tells me what to do. If I want you to kiss me, believe me, you'll want to kiss me."

The boy was speechless.

"Is that what you want?"

He nodded.

"More than anything?"

He nodded again.

"Good."

Then she slapped his face as hard as she could and turned and ran all the way back up the path.

Ridley sat up on the mattress, feeling like she'd just remembered something important. It was only when she heard Link playing "Burger Boy" from the practice room that she realized where she was—and why.

The crowd was gone, and so was Floyd. All Rid could hear was Link.

"Patty, oh, Patty, you're not real Fatty / and you're only kinda Bratty / my ham-burger Patty."

Ridley lay back down on the mattress, staring at the cracks in the ceiling until the set ended and the sun was high. By either measure, it was one of the longest nights of her life.

She would get Link in this Caster band and then get him right out again. *Devil's Hangnail. Whatever.* She wasn't going to let him ruin his life for her or for anyone else. And she sure as hell wasn't going to let her life be ruined by some stupid gambling debt.

Or by the crazy feeling she was being watched. Or by the even crazier thought that she was being threatened by a Necromancer with a *Vindicabo* Cast from the unseen world.

Or, craziest of all, by the idea that some rocker girl named Floyd thought she could steal her boyfriend.

Link Floyd? Never going to happen.

Because her name was Ridley Duchannes, and nobody told her what to do.

Nobody.

⊰ CHAPTER 11 ⊱

Read Between the Lies

In the morning, Ridley left apartment 2D and came downstairs to see Link sitting alone in a booth in Marilyn's Diner, talking into his cell phone.

Interesting.

A cold cup of untouched coffee sat in front of him. He was wearing Mario and Luigi on his T-shirt, which meant only one thing: Link was feeling nostalgic and sentimental. That usually meant trouble for Ridley, who never admitted to feeling much of either.

She moved toward Link, wary. She was wearing her favorite fishnets, her peep-toe suede booties, her buckled mini-kilt, and her oldest black T-shirt. All of her most trusted comfort clothes—yet somehow, this morning they weren't doing the trick.

Ridley didn't know why she felt so off her game. Nothing

around her looked that out of the ordinary. Spinning fans turned above a long counter in the center of the room. A faded New York City Department of Health certificate hung on the wall next to an out-of-date calendar* featuring Marilyn Monroe, the namesake of the diner. Not a Siren, as far as Ridley knew, but she should've been. Rising behind the counter, dusty glass shelves offered sticky doughnuts with frosting stained by old colored sprinkles. Stale slices of cake in plastic wrap leaned against oversize chocolate muffins or mini boxes of sugar cereal or small pitchers dripping with maple syrup—in other words, Siren bait. She could smell it in the air.

But Rid was the only Siren in the diner, of that she was pretty certain. The counter and vinyl-covered stools were crowded with nose-ringed students, tattooed arty types, even stressed-looking office folks in jackets and running shoes—mostly Mortals, it seemed. When she walked past them, they avoided her eyes, as if they knew something she didn't. As if there was something about her they didn't want to know.

Or were afraid to know.

Strange.

She felt the same familiar coldness—the one from the curb, the one from the *Vindicabo* Cast. From her dreams. She tried to shake it off. New York City was complicated enough—second-guessing herself wasn't a luxury she could afford.

Nothing here I can't handle, is there?

She tried not to consider the answer to her own question.

Besides, there were a few familiar faces. Upon closer inspection, Ridley picked out a Blood Incubus chopping up raw meat in the kitchen, a Dark Caster hunched over the *Marilyn's Sweetheart Specials* menu, and what appeared to be an aging Siren bartender nursing a coffee at the counter. A mixed crowd was relatively rare in the Caster world, and Ridley didn't know what to make of it.

She didn't know what to make of a lot of things since they'd arrived.

"What do you know? The joint is jumping," Ridley said, sliding into the booth across the table from Link.

He kept talking into his phone, holding up one hand. "Hang on. My roommate just walked into the dining hall."

Rid raised an eyebrow.

Link's mom.

He looked at her, pleading. She got the message.

Don't blow this for me.

"Gotta go, or I'll be late for the Righteous Freshman breakfast." He nodded. "I know." He nodded again. "Sure thing." And again. "Yes, ma'am." Again. "Yep. Yep. Yep. Flossed, too."

Ridley held up a canister of cutlery and shook it by Link's face, making a loud clattering noise. He started to laugh in spite of himself.

"Whoops—I'm losin' you. I think the band's practicin' or somethin'. Call you next week—I can't hear—" He clicked off with a sigh.

She smiled. "How's my favorite Mamma?"

He tossed the phone down to the tabletop. "Who cares, as long as she doesn't get in her car and haul all the way to Georgia Redeemer to make sure I change my underwear?"

"Did you?"

"Why? You wanna see for yourself?" He smiled at her, Rid's favorite smile. The one that said: *Third Degree Burns, Babe. That's how hot you are.* After last night, she hoped that was what it still meant. Instead of: *I'm feeling guilty because I crushed on some rocker girl.*

Either way, she smiled back, Link's favorite smile. The one that said: *I know, Hot Rod. I'm the one holding the match.*

Come play with fire.

My fire.

The moment she reached for his hand, Link pushed his coffee cup away from him. "I've been thinkin'."

Uh-oh.

She pulled back her hand. He kept going. "The thing is, Rid, you're right. You were right all along. I thought about it last night while I was working on some new lyrics in the practice room."

"So I heard. Seems you're getting along with the girls in the band. At least half of them." Ridley forced a smile.

"Whatever," Link said. He wasn't falling for that one.

Ridley made a mental note to change the stripe in her hair from pink to some other color. *Any other color, so long as it doesn't remind me of Pink Floyd.*

Link jiggled his leg beneath the table. "Why was I so mad at you yesterday? I came to New York to play my music, and you gave me that opportunity, right here and now."

"I did? I did." She tried not to sound surprised. *Right? You did. See? You're not such a terrible person.*

"You just did it in your own messed-up way."

"Messed up?" She tried to look confused.

Link ignored her. "Which used to be all right. But now we need to set a few ground rules," he said.

Um. O-kay. "You know I don't do well with rules."

"I do. That's why we're goin' to get it all out in the open."

93

Link looked unusually serious. "This is the way it's going to work with us. This is the only way I can handle it. If we can't do it the right way, I don't want to do it. Not anymore."

Not anymore? He'd better do it. Just like I promised he would.

In all their many breakups, Ridley couldn't remember Link ever being so reasonable. It was almost horrifying.

This wasn't how they talked. They threw things at each other. Insults, jokes, sometimes even remotes. They made war and made peace and made up and made out. They didn't do things like set ground rules. They didn't do feelings talk. They didn't get it *out in the open.*

Ridley looked down at the red, bowling-ball-speckled diner table. "It all sounds so grown-up when you say it like that."

A sad expression crossed Link's face. "So maybe we gotta grow up, Rid."

"But *ground rules?*"

"Yep." Link tapped on the tabletop. "First, no magic. No Siren stuff."

She looked liked he'd slapped her. "What are you talking about?" No one had ever dared say anything like that to her before. *No Siren stuff? Why didn't he just say no Ridley stuff?*

They were one and the same.

Ridley drew a deep breath.

"Wait," Link said, grabbing her hand before she could launch her attack. "It's just that I don't want you charmin' anyone or gettin' out your little Blow Pops to make sure everyone loves me. That's not everyone lovin' me, or my music. That's everyone lovin' you."

"I don't see the difference," Ridley lied, her voice still cold. It was one of those chicken-and-egg, tree-falling-in-the-forest problems. Siren School 101: *If a Siren charmed a Mortal to shoot someone, who was the real shooter?* Just because Ridley didn't want to debate the Power of Persuasion in a coffee shop with a Caster wearing gauges and a soul patch didn't mean she didn't get it.

Link wasn't finished. "Second, no more lies. Just tell me the truth. You want me to meet up with a band, just say it. You want to come with me to New York, same thing. There's nothin' you can't tell me, Rid. Nothin'."

Ridley raised an eyebrow.

She had been working as a Siren long enough to know that those words were the single biggest fantasy in any relationship. It wasn't even up for debate.

There was always, always something you couldn't tell the other person.

Look at Link, who could have kept three little words to himself and saved them both a breakup. Hadn't he learned anything?

When it came to relationships, the truth never set anyone free. The truth only set things on fire.

If you thought otherwise, you were deluding yourself, or you were seriously stupid. Ridley was neither, and as much as she wanted to believe those words, it was all she could do to nod, because she knew Link believed them.

Even the nod was a lie.

"Truce?" He held out his hand with a smile. "No Siren stuff? No more secrets and no more lies? Just you and me, and maybe or maybe not Lucille Ball? Trying to make it in the big city like a couple a regular people."

Regular people? Us? Did he really just say that?

95

She looked at him with a smile of her own. "Right. A couple of regular people. That's us."

What does he think? I'll just join the DAR and learn to make biscuits? He'll get a job pumping gas at the BP?

He has no idea.

"Rid? You shootin' straight with me? Tell me the truth." Link didn't seem convinced.

She squirmed on her vinyl seat cushion. "Honest."

For the thousandth time, Ridley wondered how the two of them had ever gotten together. But she couldn't ignore what he was saying. Link wanted something more out of their relationship—and somehow *more* translated to real and regular.

Like he was looking for a Lena, not a Ridley. Someone honest and kind, not deceptive and selfish. A girl who wrote poetry on her bedroom walls. Not a Siren sitting alone on the curb.

I hate my life, Ridley thought. *I hate myself. I just wish I hated him.*

It would make everything so much easier.

Ridley grabbed the menu off the table, suddenly desperate for a sweet fix. "Now it's time for some sugar, Sugar. And I'm not talking about *Marilyn's Megga Monty Christo*."

"That's my girl." Link grinned.

As Ridley started to order, she wondered if Link noticed that she never shook his hand.

Regular people? That's what he wants us to be?

Breakfast had come and gone, and Ridley still couldn't let

the idea drop. Now she had retreated to the curb in front of the diner.

Here I am again.

Link had gone upstairs to practice, and she needed to figure a few things out for herself.

I should give up now.

When Wesley Lincoln was the guy giving you relationship advice, it was a low point. The odds of that happening were about the same as Mrs. Lincoln telling Ridley to show a little skin. By Siren standards, Ridley was hitting rock bottom.

Regular people.

Regular people aren't Sirens.

Regular people don't use magic.

She had to face it. Her relationship was doomed.

She hadn't known hearing the words come out of Link's mouth would bother her the way it did. How could she? Not many intelligent words came out of his mouth in general.

Ridley traced the cracked edge of the curb with her finger. It reminded her of the cracked stone walkway that led up to her own front door—the one that her mamma had slammed in her face the morning after her Claiming.

She remembered stumbling up the stone steps, pounding on the chipping paint of the old wooden door. She could still feel the way her clothes constricted her, damp with sweat and fear, as she stood panting on the veranda.

You need to go, Ridley. You can't come back here. Not anymore.

She closed her eyes as she remembered the screaming and the

wailing, the way her voice seemed to belong to someone else. Someone small and fragile and alone.

Someone who still needed a mother and a family, no matter what the moon had told them.

You've been Claimed, child. The Dark is your family now.

Ridley pinched her red glitter nails into the soft flesh of her hand. The pain brought her back.

Wake up. That's not you. That's not now.

You're not that girl. Not only that girl.

Ridley looked out at the street in front of her. She could already see a pile of parking tickets on the Beater's windshield, a metal boot snapped around the tire.

This wasn't Gatlin. Things changed here.

Things could change.

Ridley couldn't promise she wouldn't use any magic. After all, she wasn't a miracle worker. You couldn't just go cold turkey.

The rest of it, she could at least try.

For Link.

It was the kind of thing a Lena would do for an Ethan, and if a Lena was what Link was looking for, Ridley could give it a shot.

Like a regular girlfriend would.

But there was a lot she didn't know, like what regular people did all day.

Work? It seemed like the obvious answer. Did he expect her to find a job? Earn Mortal money?

Learn all the rules? Stand in the lines? Wait for my turn, like everyone else, every day?

Play nice?

The last thought was too terrifying to imagine.

For the rest of the day, it was all she could think about.

But when Ridley fell asleep, her nightmares were anything but regular. They were filled with disasters, with fires and explosions, with gold-eyed Casters watching her in the shadows, figures of terror cloaked in darkness and fear.

Everywhere she looked was blood. Magic and blood.

Hers and Link's.

The longer she tossed and turned, desperately trying not to fall back asleep, the more regular life began to look like the lesser of two evils.

Finally, Ridley gave up, clutching her knees as she sat on the striped mattress, staring at the cracked wall. *Maybe it's a sign.*

The next day, Ridley Duchannes had made her decision. She was ready to face the regular world. At least, she thought she was.

She was ready to try.

"I need a job," Ridley said out loud, testing the words out. They might have sounded more legit if she hadn't been lying on the beach as she said them.

It's not my fault the living room floor is a beach, she thought, irritated. *Besides, it's only a fake one.*

Necro burst out laughing and sat down in the sand next to her, sloshing a cup of coffee that narrowly missed hitting Ridley's shiny red leather, heavily zippered jumpsuit—the one that made her look like a ninja-robot-assassin from the eighties. It was an outfit that signaled Getting Down to Business, which apparently Ridley intended to do. Even if the waves looked pretty nice, out on the horizon in front of her.

Necro put down her paper coffee cup, still smiling.

"Why is that so funny?" Ridley looked insulted, and this time, she didn't have to fake it. "Mortals have jobs. They work. They get up in the morning and get on their little train things and go places with telephones and plants and—"

"Elevators?" Necro asked innocently. She pulled out an apple and flipped open her switchblade. With an expert flick of her wrist, she began to carve, smiling to herself.

Ridley was a little unnerved. Yesterday she had met the homeless-punk-looking Necro, the one wearing the jacket made of old carpet samples and black high-top Docs, the one who liked to pass on threats from unnamed people or things from another world. Not the laughing, smiling Necro. Ridley was instantly suspicious. At least she knew where she stood when a girl was threatening her.

"Elevators. Sure. Whatever. Why couldn't I do that?" Ridley shrugged. "I could completely do that."

"Ride in an elevator?" Necro fingered the silver hoop in her nose, trying not to laugh. "You really are gifted."

"Is that a job?" Ridley wasn't sure. She kicked at the sand. It sprayed up and into the balmy breeze that wrapped itself around the living room.

"Not really. But, man—you're a Siren. That's not you."

"I'm also not a man." Ridley frowned. "Sirens have had jobs. Some are real pros."

Necro raised an eyebrow.

Ridley frowned. "Not *that* kind of job."

100

"There's probably an opening at the club somewhere. You could ask Nox."

"No," Ridley said quickly. "Not at the club." She didn't want to deal with his smug face any more than she had to.

"Hey, a job's a job. And you're the one who said you wanted one," Necro said. She snapped her knife all the way through half of her apple.

"Not that badly." Ridley shook her head. "Besides, I don't want a Caster job. I want a Mortal job."

At that, Necro began to really laugh, as if Ridley had told a joke. She tried to think what it could have been, but she couldn't come up with anything.

"Again, what's so funny?"

Necro tried to look serious. "What can you possibly do in the Mortal world? And why would you ever want to do it? Mortals are—"

"I know." At least they could agree on that. Rid sighed. "You never know. It might turn out to be useful someday. If things get old around here."

"Things like gambling debts?" Necro sliced through a section of apple.

Ridley ignored the implication. "Besides, I want to show Link that I can get by without the Power of Persuasion. Because he's part Mortal. And because he thinks that's all I know how to do. I'm more than just a Siren. I'm also—"

Necro leaned forward. Now she was interested. "Yeah?"

Unfortunately, Ridley couldn't finish that sentence. If she could, they wouldn't be having this conversation in the first place. Because she wasn't a regular person. She wasn't a regular anything. And aside from being a Siren, she wasn't sure what else she was.

Ridley gave up. "Enough with the interrogation."

Necro snapped her switchblade shut. "That's what I thought."

Ridley clenched her fists. She'd show Necro. Rid would make it in the Mortal world on her own. She could be regular. She could do more than any of these idiots thought she could.

Even if the idiot happened to be Ridley herself.

CHAPTER 12

Hell on High Heels

Hey there, Hot Rod."

Ridley used the term loosely, and for once, she wasn't talking about Link, who was busily rehearsing imaginary drum solos back at the apartment.

She was talking to Nerd Warrior Nick.

At least, according to his name tag.

It had taken her two hours to find the nearest Nerdworld in Brooklyn, which was where Necro had told her to go for a fast, free job search. This particular Nerd Warrior, which was apparently what you called the inhabitants of Nerdworld, looked more Nerd than Warrior.

"Are you talking to me?" Nerd Warrior Nick swallowed, taking in Ridley's red leather jumpsuit, head to toe. It was a serious eyeful. Rid smiled, satisfied. Score another point for robot-ninja-assassins.

Somewhere in Gatlin, the ladies of the DAR were turning over in their future plastic-flower-covered graves.

Ridley pointed at Nerd Warrior Nick's chest with one long, red fingernail. "I need you to show me how to work this thing."

"What thing?" He swallowed. Then he seemed to remember he was standing behind a long table full of the latest and greatest Nerdworld gadgets. "You mean, a tablet?"

Ridley nodded. "Yeah. The little square thing."

"To be honest, it's actually more of a rectangle." Nick pushed his glasses up against his eyes.

"Are you kidding me?" She blinked at him. "Honey, if I say it's a circle, it's a circle. You got that?"

"Wh—what can I help you with? Seven-inch? Nine-inch? Memory upgrades? Are you in the market for a—"

Ridley sighed. "I'm thinking I might need a job."

"Printing job?" He looked confused. "The tablet can wirelessly connect to almost any—"

"Nick." Ridley shook her head, edging her way up onto the table until she was sitting all the way atop it, swinging her legs. "I'm talking about a job job."

"Here?" He swallowed again.

"No, not here. Well, maybe. What is it you do here?"

"Fix computers and tablets and smartphones and—"

"And all the other little square things?"

"Rectangles." She glared at him the moment he said the word, and he looked down, ashamed. "Yes."

"No. This is a terrible job."

"Well, actually—"

"For me," Ridley said.

Nick looked relieved. "It's not for everyone."

104

Ridley thought about it. "I need something with a little glamour, a little style. Something exceptional. Something that only I could do. Something that would make everyone who ever met me—"

"Proud?"

Ridley looked at Nick like he was insane. "Hate me. In a fit of seething jealous rage."

Nick stared at her. "Are you still talking to me?"

She smiled, tugging playfully on his incredibly short and unevenly cut hair. *Nobody should pay for that haircut.* There really wasn't much to tug on. Still. She'd worked with less before. "Why don't you fire up that little squ—rectangle of yours and find me what I'm looking for, Smarty-Pants?"

He was searching *JOB EXCEPTIONAL GLAMOUR STYLE NEW YORK CITY* before Ridley had to unwrap a single lollipop.

There was persuasion, and then there was Persuasion. Sometimes it was even more satisfying for Ridley to remember she didn't need magic to be powerful.

She just needed red leather.

It felt good to be back in the game.

Nerd Warrior Nick had been a faithful soldier to the end, and now it was time for Ridley to cash in on his valiant Googling.

Even if that should be a made-up word.

"You don't have to do this," Necro said. She couldn't even imagine going into a place like the one they were standing in front of.

"Yes, I do." Ridley took a deep breath. "I can do this."

Necro had been kind enough to walk Ridley to work, saying, "This I gotta see with my own eyes." Now they both stared up at the sign over the door. Yesterday, it had seemed like the right thing to do. That was three phone interviews, one sleepless night, two pieces of pie—strawberry rhubarb and triple berry—and ten outfit changes ago.

Today, Rid wasn't so sure.

Apparently, to get a job you needed to have had other jobs. It had taken Ridley a few phone calls until she figured out how to say the things people most wanted to hear, which was usually her specialty. She didn't think of it as lying, not exactly. She thought of it more as charades. You had to pretend to be the kind of person who got jobs, to get a job. What was that jobbish-workery-going-on-elevators sort of person like?

Ridley learned everything the hard way. She learned that when people ask you to pick one word to describe yourself, you don't say *perfect*. You also don't say *hot*. After two misfires, Rid went with *persuasive*. While it didn't exactly seem to persuade anyone, it wasn't a conversation stopper, either.

Lesson learned.

She had also learned to apply for jobs Sirens could do in their sleep, for starters. She came close to getting a position as a *SKILLED COSMETIC TECHNICIAN*, but it turned out to be a gig applying makeup to corpses at a run-down funeral parlor in the Bronx, and Ridley had had enough close calls with the Otherworld as it was.

Rid had been excited about an opening billed as a *COUTURE RETAIL EXPERIENCE*—until it turned out to be at Connie's Cat Couture. Maybe Lucille Ball would be fine with it, but Ridley couldn't stand the thought of being a Cat Couturier. The owner had suggested that Ridley stop by to let Connie the Cat "sniff you and lick you and just love you until you get the hang of her." Ridley had said she'd rather lick Connie the Cat herself than do any of the above. The owner had told her where she could stick that mouthful of fur, and the conversation had ended pretty abruptly after that.

By the time Rid got the hang of it, there was really only one gig left, and now she was standing on the sidewalk right in front of it.

The Brooklyn Blowout

It was a hair salon, but they didn't call it that. This was supposed to be a party, or as the brochure said, a "Hair Experience."

Ridley wouldn't be a stylist. She'd be a Dry Girl, which as far as she could tell was like a Fly Girl, but with a hair dryer.

"You got this, right?" Necro looked through the stenciled glass, where a row of teased, painted, primped, polished Dry Girls were brandishing not only hair dryers and curling irons but straightening irons and hot rollers, as if they were weapons. "How hard could it be?"

Ridley would have preferred actual weapons.

Necro touched her blue spiky faux-hawk nervously. "I'd better get out of here before they drag me inside and make me look like Taylor Swift." She began to back away down the sidewalk.

"Necro," Ridley called after her, on an impulse.

"Yeah?" Necro didn't look back.

"I thought you hated me. Why are you being so nice?"

Necro turned. "For the record, I do hate you. If you say otherwise to anyone, I'll kick your butt. I'm only here to get out of

107

sound check, which I hate even more than I do you." Then she smiled in spite of herself.

"Right." Ridley smiled back. She turned to face the glass front door.

"Don't go soft on me, Siren," Necro called from safely down the street.

"Never," Ridley said as she went inside.

"Are you telling me I have to put my hands in *that*?" In the shampoo room, Ridley stood at a row of six sinks, pointing like she'd just seen a snake crawl up and out of the drain. Ten feet away from her, a woman with coarse peroxide curls and dark black roots lay with her head tilted back, into sink number six.

"Her hair?" Delia, the Blowout manager, looked amused. "Yes."

Ridley sighed. Being a regular person wasn't starting off well. She had taken the Mortal subway here, and the whole way she couldn't shake the feeling that someone was watching her.

Again.

Maybe that's what Mortals are like. Maybe they really are just always watching each other.

But Ridley had seen a man standing stock-still on the platform at Broadway Junction, grinning at her through the closing car doors.

Sirens didn't spook easily, but New York public transportation had proved to be up to the challenge.

Rid shook off the memory and glared back at the waiting customer.

"I'm sorry. Did you mean I had to *touch* it?" Ridley looked like she was going to be sick. "The skin parts?"

"Her head?" Delia started to laugh. The laughter didn't make her seem nice, though. She was completely tattooed and wearing a tank top, so the overall effect was more intimidating than even a manager probably needed to be.

"With my *bare hands*?" Ridley took a step back.

"Have you ever worked in a salon before, Riley?" Now Delia started to look irritated.

"Ridley," Ridley corrected her.

"Well?" Delia didn't really seem to care what Ridley's name was.

Mortals have no manners, Ridley thought. *They're all so rough around the edges.*

"Yes," Ridley lied. "All the time. I just never worked on heads."

"No heads?"

"That's right. I worked on—" Ridley tried to think of a less hairy place on the Mortal body. Hair was just so disgusting. She didn't know why she'd thought she could do this job. Her hair styled itself with the flick of her wrist, like it always had. Another Siren perk. "Feet. I worked on feet. And knees. And elbows. The occasional calf, but only the really smooth ones."

"Is this one of those shows where the movie star comes out and says it's a joke?" Delia looked around the shop tiredly.

"Does that happen?" Ridley felt interested for the first time that afternoon.

"You tell me," Delia said.

She stood there until Ridley walked back to the sink and put not one but two hands into the disgustingly hairy, greasy scalp of a complete stranger and scrubbed. It was horrific, but at least Delia left her alone after that.

When the woman in the chair leaned her head back, Ridley could see up her nose. She yanked harder on the woman's hair. *Let's just get this over with already.*

"Ow! Not so hard!"

"Beauty is pain," Ridley said.

"You're a pain," the woman said, sitting up.

"Well, you're no beauty."

"I need to see the manager," the woman said.

"Crybaby." Ridley threw her a towel. "Dry yourself off."

The stupid cow of a woman stared at her.

"What?" Ridley snapped. "Do you need an invitation? You're dripping water all over the floor."

The woman shook her head, muttering, and began to towel off her wet hair.

"Back to the chair," Ridley said. She tried to remember the lines she was supposed to recite as she took her client back to the Drying Chair, but she gave up. "Time for a hairy experience, lady."

The woman made it to the chair and kept on going right out the door. It was a real bummer, because Ridley had to pay the store back for the blowout, which was almost forty bucks. She was going to lose money on this job if she didn't figure something out, fast.

"Beauty is pain," Delia said as Ridley cleaned up her station.

"Am I fired?" Ridley asked. She hoped the answer was yes.

"I haven't decided." Now Delia was back to looking amused.

It's hard to keep up with her, Ridley thought.

"I really hated that lady. She's been stiffing me on my tip for years," Delia said. "And she does have one nasty scalp." She started laughing to herself. "Hairy experience," she said. Now she was spluttering so hard she was howling, even spitting a little around the edge of her mouth. At least Ridley couldn't see up her nose.

Mortals really were nauseating.

Ridley didn't know if she wanted to laugh or cry, but it didn't matter. By the time she got home on the very Mortal L train, she'd done both.

CHAPTER 13

Bleeding Me

I never thought you had it in you, Rid." Link sounded impressed. Shocked, even. There was that. But Ridley wasn't sure it was worth it.

Because regular people suck.

At breakfast, her feet hurt, her arms ached, and two of her nails were broken. *I can't believe I have to go back to that place, like a regular person.*

I'm a worker. I work. Six whole hours a day.

Even the thought was exhausting. It was all Rid could do to find the energy to finish her meal, a disappointing piece of *Marilyn's Coconut Dream Pie* with an even more disappointing piece of *Marilyn's Apple of My Pye*. Still, they were just sweet enough to do the trick. It was a Siren's version of morning coffee.

Rid pushed away the plate. "The only good thing about Gatdung was the pie."

"I don't know. Pecan fried chicken."

Ridley's eyes almost glassed over at the thought. "And Amma's Tunnel of Fudge cake. The one she only made Ethan. Warm."

"How about hot corn and a zombie flick at the Summerville Cineplex?" Link grinned.

"You mean making out in the back row," Ridley said with a smile.

"I mean, makin' out by the lake with a picnic basket full a biscuits." His eyes met hers.

She leaned toward him. "You and your biscuits."

He leaned toward her. "I used to wait outside Ethan's kitchen window on the days Amma was makin' hers."

Link's lips locked onto hers, and he slid his hand up around her neck. Ridley kissed away the memories, just like the old days and sweet as strawberry jam, until she felt an elbow in her side.

She opened her eyes as Necro slid into the booth.

"Adorable." Necro grinned. "Or should I say Adorkable?"

"Great timing," said Link, grouchy.

Ridley dotted at her lipstick with a paper napkin. Timing aside, she was relieved to see Necro, even if the faux-hawker looked like a hot mess of red leather (jacket), black vinyl (pants), and blue (hair) today. It was nice to see an almost friendly face. They had practically gotten along yesterday, the two of them.

"Pie?" Ridley slid the plate in Necro's direction. "Or is that not an approved Goth dessert?"

Necro flipped open her switchblade and slid it vertically through the quivering piece of deep-dish apple pie, as if that was some kind of answer. "We gotta get moving."

"Classy," Rid said.

"I take it that's a no?" Link ran his hand through his spiky hair with a sigh.

Sampson, the Darkborn, dropped into the seat beside Ridley. Every time she saw him, he seemed even better-looking than she remembered from the game at Suffer. He was hot, if you were into abnormally tall, leather-clad rock gods, with hands the size of dinner plates. Link had thought Sampson was full of himself, "and a whole lotta other things," he said after their first few encounters. "Besides, there's only room for one rock god in this apartment." Ridley had just rolled her eyes.

"You guys ready?" Sampson asked. Link didn't look too happy to see him, but then, Ridley didn't know why anyone would be happy to see a Darkborn.

She took the opportunity to inch away from Sampson on the pleather booth seat. His disturbing gray eyes matched the gray T-shirt he was wearing over his tight leather jeans. With tattooed arms and a bike chain around his neck, he looked like the kind of guy you didn't want to mess with. From what little Ridley had learned about him during the epic failure of a game at Suffer, it was true.

If he's immune to my powers, Ridley thought, *what else is he immune to?*

Rid had searched Uncle Macon's archives, and the *Lunae Libri*, trying to find out anything she could about Darkborns this summer after Liar's Trade went south. But these new Supernaturals were a result of the New Order, so there weren't any ancient scrolls detailing their history.

All she had learned since her game with Sampson was that a new race of Supernatural had evolved, radically and permanently, as a consequence of Lena more or less breaking the universe. They were born from the Dark Fire, from which all magic derived—complete and whole, as if they'd stepped out of cryogenically engineered pods. Magic had created them, and yet somehow they defied its laws.

Casters had no effect on a Darkborn. Beyond that, no one knew much of anything about them, except that they made Incubuses look like kittens.

Ridley had learned that firsthand. Sampson had caused her more than his share of trouble, that night at Suffer. He smiled at her now, and she resisted the impulse to claw his eyes out the old-fashioned way. *I'd like to see if he's immune to that.*

"You got enough eyeliner on, Maybelline?" Link said, looking at Sampson. "Because we can wait, if you have to, you know"—he gestured to his face—"freshen up." You put an Incubus and a Darkborn in the room together and they started to go at it within the first five minutes. That much everyone had learned this week.

"Jealous?" Sampson stretched his arms along the top of the booth. "Not everyone can pull it off."

"Or not anyone," said Link. "Just sayin'."

"I wouldn't say that if I were you." Necro shook her head at Link. "You know that whole Incubus superstrength thing?" She motioned to Sampson. "Yeah. You can't hurt him. He's immune."

Link swallowed. "How can you be immune to superstrength?"

Sampson smiled. "By being stronger."

Link held up a spoon. "Bend this fork with your mind."

"It's a spoon."

"Trick question."

Sampson grabbed it and crushed it in his hand.

Link swallowed. "So you think with your fists? Good to know."

"Let's get out of here. We're gonna be late." Floyd appeared behind Sampson, pounding on the diner table nervously with drumsticks that morphed into her fingers. Floyd looked like a long-lost member of a speed metal band. It wasn't clear which was more of a relic, her tattered black tour T-shirt—this one was from Judas Priest—or her battered black pants. Either way, Ridley was beginning to think Floyd shopped at some special thrift shop for retired rockers.

"Late for what? Where are you guys going?" If it meant she could avoid going back to her job for a few more hours, Rid was all in.

"The big audition." Floyd picked at the crust of Rid's pie. "Well, not yours. His. You don't even have to come."

"Wait. Audition?" Link turned to glare at Ridley. "How about that?"

"Nobody told me he had to audition," Ridley interrupted. "Just to be clear." She looked at them. "What are you going to do, not have a drummer? I mean, he has to be better than nothing, right?"

"Hey," Link said, trying to figure out if she was insulting him or not.

"Come on. What did you think would happen? We'd just show up with your boyfriend and start rocking the house, business as usual? Nox isn't like that," Necro said, shaking her head. "Anyway, it's not like a real audition—it's just one gig, in front of his house crowd. We haven't even played there yet, so in a way, he's auditioning all of us. They like us, he likes us, it's all good."

"And if he doesn't like us?" Link frowned.

"Let's just say the last guy Lennox Gates didn't like isn't around anymore." Floyd looked over at Necro.

"Where is he?" Link leaned forward in the booth.

"Some say it was a fire. Some say it was a *Mortem* Cast." Necro sounded ominous. "Either way, nobody ever saw him again."

"Lennox Gates sounds like a swell guy." Link shook his head. "This day is just gettin' better and better."

"Sirene's a cool club. I've checked it out. At least, it's a step up from Suffer," Floyd said.

"Sirene? That's the name of the club?" Ridley looked incredulous.

"Why, you know it?" Necro shrugged. "It just opened." She yanked a flyer out of her pocket. At first, it looked like a blank piece of black paper.

Slowly, shimmering burgundy letters began to appear, one at a time, as if they were ascending from a great depth.

SIRENE

There was nothing else—just the word.

But it was strangely evocative, especially to a Siren.

Is it a coincidence? Or is Lennox Gates messing with me? Why would he suddenly need my help at a club basically named after me?

Being a regular person suddenly seemed like the least of Ridley's problems. There was no way she was letting Link go anywhere near that club without her. Work would have to wait.

"Enough talk. Let's blow." Sampson stood up, and everyone followed.

Bandmate or not, you didn't mess with a Darkborn.

———∽

Out on the sidewalk, Rid caught up with Link, a few paces behind the others. "I didn't know you had to audition."

Link looked at her. "Nah, it's cool. It's one gig." He called up to Floyd. "Hey, Floyd. I was meanin' to ask. What happened to your last drummer?"

"I heard he sucked," Ridley said carefully.

The three Supernaturals stopped in their tracks. "Wait a minute. He doesn't know?" Necro looked amused, while Floyd looked amazed. Sampson seemed only mildly interested.

"Know what?" Link looked at Rid. She glared at the others. All three of them were there, the night she lost everything at Suffer. They knew what a mess she was in, and worse, how she'd gotten herself into it. She just had to keep them from telling Link all the gory details, until she fixed things. And until she figured out what the hell was going to happen with her second marker. She couldn't tell Link about that. It was too humiliating, she was too scared, and he might get too angry. At her, or at Nox, she didn't know, but she didn't want to find out.

But what are the odds of that?

Floyd clapped her hand on Link's back. "You realize this is all a scam. Your Siren's scamming you, bro."

"What are you sayin'?" Link looked even more confused than usual.

118

"Nothing," Ridley snapped. She looked at his bandmates, meaningfully. *Don't even think about it.*

Necro shook her head. "It's not nothing. You need to tell him—"

Floyd cut in. "Your girlfriend took down our drummer and crossed a badass dude in a big card game, and—"

"Won. I beat him." Ridley looked up at Link. "Believe me, Hot Rod. I was as surprised as you are."

"Yeah, right," said Floyd. "And then unicorns flew out of your ass." She twisted two fingers into a unicorn horn and held it up to her forehead.

"How did you know? It's my specialty." Ridley glared at Floyd, desperately wishing she would shut up. Then Rid turned back to Link. *Believe me*, she thought. *You have to believe me.*

"Come on, Ridley. That's not what happened," Necro began.

Link started to waver. "What went on that night? You never actually told me anything about it. One minute, you took off for Europe, the next thing I hear you're in that club in New York. Then suddenly you show up in Gatlin, actin' all kinds a sorry, and you just happen to know a band that needs a drummer? Since when do you even know bands?"

Ridley started to panic. *Think fast.* "What does it matter? I went out. I met the band. Their drummer sucked, and he left. They needed a new one. We made a deal at the club. End of story. That's it."

"Why didn't you just say that? Are you hiding something? Were you with someone? Is that what this is about?" Link looked like he might lose it, right there on the street.

"We were broken up!" She backpedaled when she saw the

119

pain in his eyes. "Why would you even think that?" Ridley gave up trying to explain. She didn't want to Charm Link, but the way she saw it, she didn't have a choice. Unfortunately for him, she did have a lollipop. Her fingers began to fumble for it in her pocket.

No magic. You promised. No Siren stuff.

She hesitated, but only for a second.

Who am I kidding?

Ridley smiled up at Link. "Of course not. I know you believe me. That's all that matters." As she spoke, she felt the candy wrapper come off in her fingers. *You know I'm right, Shrinky Dink.*

"Of course I believe you. It's just—"

"You're worried because you care about me and you want me to be happy." Her fingers curled around the lollipop. *You want me to be happy, Hot Rod.*

"That's all I want, darlin'."

"But I know that deep down, you trust me." *And you absolutely really truly believe me, Wesley Lincoln.*

She held her breath. She hadn't tried anything like this on Link in a long, long time. He didn't like it, and she didn't blame him. Truthfully, she didn't really like it, either.

Link smiled at her. "You know I do, Babe."

She smiled back. "I know." *Let's go to the gig, Link.*

He took her hand. "Now let's go get us a gig, Sugarplum."

As they walked away, Ridley tried not to think about what she had just done.

It worked, didn't it?

But if it was all for the best, why do I feel so bad?

She ducked her head and tried not to see their faces

120

everywhere she looked. If she let herself remember, they'd fall from the sky like so many autumn leaves. Hundreds. Thousands. The people she'd Charmed. The men she'd destroyed. The boys who had worshipped her. The women who had hated her.

Do I really want to add Wesley Lincoln to that pile of burning leaves?

Have I crossed a line?

Ridley wished Lena was here. She would know—and she'd tell Ridley, too. Lena was Ridley's barometer; she always had been.

What would Lena say now?

Ridley let her hand slip from Link's grasp. He and Sampson began talking about the set list and walked ahead of her. Rid fell back, trying not to think about it. She had bigger problems to think about than Charming one more hybrid Incubus.

"Hey, Siren."

Necro grabbed Ridley by the arm. She waited until the boys were out of earshot. "When this is over," she said, "we're going to have a little girl talk. Heart to Dark heart." Any goodwill between them was now long gone.

Floyd shot Ridley a nasty look. "She'd have to have a heart to do that."

"Why would I want one of those?" Ridley didn't smile.

Floyd leaned in. "I guess anyone desperate enough to Charm their own boyfriend really wouldn't understand, would they?"

"You know. Linky Charms." Necro shrugged. "I hear he's magically delicious. Oblivious, but delicious."

Ridley couldn't believe she'd thought this lame little fauxhawked dead detector was her friend.

I'm a Siren. What do they expect? Nobody gets in between a Siren and her sailor. They should know that by now.

Maybe it was time for Ridley to remind them.

"Patty," said Ridley, grabbing Floyd by the arm with her own long, red nails. "And Duane," she said, grabbing Necro, with the same fierceness. "Let's us girls get a little something straight. You ever try to turn my boyfriend against me again, and it will be a whole lot more than a girl talk. It'll be a catfight." Ridley leaned in. "Claws out."

"Meowch," Necro said, her gaze unwavering. Floyd said nothing. "No one messes with our bandmates, Rid. You don't get it, because you're not in the band. It's the line you don't cross."

Alone. On the curb. She got it.

Only, at this particular moment, Ridley Duchannes didn't care what anyone else had to say about it.

She didn't miss a beat. "I admit I can't control Sampson," she said. "But I can make the two of you fall in love with every stray pit bull from here to New Jersey, and don't think I won't do it. It's a Siren thing."

"And don't be surprised when every single one of them suddenly looks just like your cutie-pie boyfriend." Floyd pulled her arm away. "Illusionist thing." She smirked and took off after Sampson.

Cutie-pie boyfriend?

I will take you down.

Necro shook her head. "Now you've done it. Never screw with an Illusionist. They say you won't know what hit you. Literally."

"Bite me," whispered Ridley. "I'm not scared of you."

"Believe me," Necro whispered back, "you don't get it." The Necromancer stepped closer until she was almost breathing in Ridley's ear. "If my dreams mean anything, I'm not the one you should be afraid of."

Her last word raked the air between them.

"*Vindicabo.*"

⊰ CHAPTER 14 ⊱

Appetite for Destruction

Lennox Gates kicked and shouted. A stream of unintelligible gibberish came from his mouth, but it was loud and urgent.

So loud that he woke himself up.

He sat up on his couch, groggy, and then flopped back down.

Lennox was still wearing the clothes he'd had on when he came home from the club, early this morning. He'd been having nightmares again, courtesy of his friend on the other side, no doubt.

Vexes.

Vengeful manifestations from the Otherworld—black stretches of cold shadow had been everywhere. Swallowing up his friends, his family. Turning everything to fog and fear and doubt.

They had swarmed his club, his apartment, even his house on the island. He couldn't escape, and he couldn't hide. He would never be free of them, not until they dragged him back down to the world they came from.

Lennox Gates got the message. It didn't require any actual words to articulate the threat of this ticking clock.

He looked at his watch, cursing under his breath. He was late, and not just for his first appointment of the day, but for the other things he'd been asked to do. The sort of things he couldn't exactly put on his calendar.

Dark things. My specialty. How did that happen?

He was on a short timer, and his associates were impatient. At least it was only a nightmare.

For now.

Then Lennox felt the hair on his arms stand up. His room turned cold, so cold that he could feel a new sharpness to the air in his throat with every breath.

"What do you want?" His voice echoed through the empty room.

Silence.

"I know you're there. You can come out now."

The shadows in his room seemed to convulse, as if the walls themselves were trying to catch their breath.

The air churned around him.

Now. It's coming.

Slowly, a black figure rose from the floor, materializing up from the rug as if it were being pulled into the Mortal world against its will. In reality, Lennox knew it was the reverse. The spirit was willing itself into this world—a difficult feat, almost Herculean.

Vexes—real ones. Here. In my own apartment, for the very first time.

Then Lennox had another thought, colder than the air around him.

He's getting closer.

The apartment was the most Bound place Lennox knew of, with the exception of his club. The security in his building rivaled that of the UN building downtown. Stray Supernaturals were not welcome here, and neither were visitors from the Otherworld. Lennox would have thought it was impossible, if he hadn't been dealing with the angriest dead headcase in five hundred years.

He can get to me, anywhere I go.

I'll never be free of him.

Lennox raised his voice. "Which is your point, right? I understand, old man. You'll have your way, or I'm to join you down there?" He stood up, pacing across the room. "Your hybrid friend is going to show up at the club today, and your Siren is bound to follow. I've taken measures to incentivize them both. Have a little faith."

He knew he was asking the impossible, and he expected that his associate was laughing on the other side. Laughing, and making room for Lennox Gates in the Otherworld, right next to him.

"I'm not stupid or suicidal. This display really isn't necessary," he said.

But it is your style, he added silently. *Or your name wouldn't be Abraham Ravenwood. And I wouldn't be in this bind.*

CHAPTER 15

Rock of Ages

As Link walked down the Brooklyn street with Sampson, he couldn't remember what had been bothering him. Something had been, but it had slipped away. Ridley had that effect on him. A few words from her, and he almost always started feeling better. He'd almost have thought she was Charming him, except for the fact that she'd promised she wouldn't.

What kinda magic was that?

Link gave up.

To be honest, he didn't really pay attention to a word anyone said after *audition*. It was like listening to a bunch of chickens squawking over a spilled bag of feed. *Chickens or cheerleaders. The Jackson PTA, fightin' over which book to ban. My mom on the way home from choir practice, full up with a fresh load a gossip.* Link didn't have much to say. At least, not to the chickens. His mind was on the audition.

It was an awesome word, like *overtime* or *front row* or *state finals. Cheese-in-the-crust* or *double-stuffed* or *supersized.* Of all those words, *audition* was the granddaddy of them all. At least, Link was pretty sure it was.

He'd never actually had one.

Link didn't audition for bands. He always made sure it was his band, so they had to take him. That was the secret of his success. But it didn't help him now. He was terrified. Auditions were so good they were bad, so important they were paralyzing. Link's adrenaline was pushing and pounding so hard he felt sick, same as when he tried to eat his mom's red-eye gravy halfway through his transition from human to Incubus.

Like he could blow chunks.

Hope I don't puke onstage. Marilyn Manson puked onstage. Wait. It's cool, right? If Marilyn Manson did it?

Link was lost in thought until he and Sampson met up with the girls outside a stairwell that led to a subway station.

Don't think about the audition. Crap, you thought about it, you dumbucket.

"Earth to Link." Floyd looked at Link. "You sick?"

Link didn't say anything. *Not in front of her. Not in front of a girl.* He tried to focus on the yellow police tape that sealed off the entrance to the stairs.

"If you're gonna puke, do it now," Floyd said. "That's all I'm sayin'. Remember Marilyn Manson." She smiled. "That was a damn good hurl."

Link laughed, in spite of the bile in his throat. There weren't a lot of girls like Floyd. Even Ridley could see that, which was probably why her feathers had been so ruffled ever since they'd gotten here. He had to admit he kind of liked the attention.

That's just life in the henhouse, he thought. *Especially when the rooster's as smooth as this guy right here.*

Floyd looked both ways and ducked inside the stairwell. The second she passed the yellow tape, she disappeared. The air rippled in her wake.

Not something you'd see in any henhouse.

"Is she Rippin'? 'Cause I didn't hear anythin'." Link looked at Necro.

Necro shook her head. "Nope. Doorwell. You gotta look for the broken subway stops. They're not actually broken. They're ours."

"The regular old New York City subway? It's also a Caster subway?"

"The stops are. We rotate ours through the Mortal system, so it's a different stop every time, all over the five boroughs. Whole system. Someone got the idea when we saw all the New York City utility blockades during the last big storm. So long as we stick to the broken stops, nobody sees us come and go. And nobody bothers us."

Link looked at her. "Doesn't anyone ever wonder why there's so many broken stops?"

Necro smiled. "Who? Something's always broken. This is New York. Now come on." She disappeared as she said it, as if she'd explained something.

Link scratched his head. It was hard for him to imagine, seeing as every time a porch light burned out in Gatlin, it practically made the news. At least, it made his mom's personal broadcasting system.

"Try to keep up." Sampson looked at Ridley and Link like they were a couple of kindergartners, then disappeared after Necro.

"Fun guy," Link said.

"Or not," Rid said.

Link shrugged. "I guess Darkborns are stiffs."

"You think?" She sounded worried.

"You know what they say. With great power comes great nothing else." He laughed, but Rid wasn't having it. Not today.

She looks hotter than Myrtle Beach in July, but she's just as crabby, Link thought.

"Come on. You want to—" Link gestured at the yellow tape. "Or should I?"

"They're gone. We could bolt," Ridley said. She seemed more uneasy than she should have, considering this whole Devil's Hangmen thing was her idea.

"Yeah, right." Link laughed, but she didn't. *Rid's not jokin'. So that's weird.* "What are you talkin' about? We didn't come this far to hide like a scared cat now."

Rid sighed. "I'm not saying I'm worried. I'm just saying. We could, you know. Take off."

"You said that already." *So you're worried*, Link thought. "Why, Rid? I thought you said what happened at Suffer was no big deal."

Ridley shrugged. "This audition. Lennox Gates. Sirene. I don't know. I've got a bad feeling about this whole thing. Maybe I was wrong. Maybe I never should have gotten us into—"

"Whoa. Back it up. This is me." Link pulled his drumsticks out of his back pocket, where he liked to keep them. "These are mine. I got this. I'm good, and if I'm not, well, that's on me. You can't keep yankin' my chain, Rid. First you're pushin' me to do this whole Caster band thing, and now that I'm on board, you want out? No way."

She looked unconvinced, but at least she didn't take off. Link knew better than to push his luck more than that.

He grabbed her hand and pulled her across the yellow plastic tape before she could say another word. "Geronimo, Sugarplum."

The Doorwell to the subway must have used some powerful Illusionist mojo, because once Ridley and Link stepped through the yellow tape, they weren't in the same place at all. They were in something that looked like a tunnel. Then Link felt it—the energy and electricity, the power coursing through his veins and into the world that was beneath the world.

He didn't feel sick now. They weren't in just any tunnel. They were in the Caster Tunnels, the Underground that ran like an unseen labyrinth through the world, just beneath the Mortal Realm. Even when he expected it, it was still a surprise. Nothing else felt like this.

It never did, not even when I was full-on Mortal.

Link breathed deep and opened his eyes wide. He squeezed Rid's hand one more time. "You okay, Babe?"

She nodded. "I'm okay. I mean, better."

Of course she felt better. They were back in the Underground. It was hard to remember that there was ever a time these Tunnels scared the crap out of him, though they had. Him, and Ethan. For a while, even Liv had freaked out when she came down here. Back when John Breed was just a bad biker boy—and Vexes and Sheers roamed the Tunnels like rats and snakes.

But right now, the Caster Tunnels were the closest thing to home that Link and Rid had. The Tunnels had become the one place they were free from the eyes and opinions of Gatlin County Mortals—none of whom were too short on either. The Underground was practically a full-time home to Macon, seeing as the whole town thought he was dead. Just goes to show, you can get used to anything.

"Hurry up, man." Floyd was impatient. She was waiting with Necro and Sampson just ahead, and as Link and Rid followed them through the dimly lit carved stone cavern, it felt like old times. Flickering torches lit the way with uneven light, and Link could see as far as the straight stretch of tunnel before them reached, all the way to the unknown darkness.

Until a small something came weaving toward them through the shadows, and meowed.

Link looked ahead into the dark. "Lucille, what the hell are you doin' down here? I thought you were headin' out to see the Statue a Liberty? Maybe catch a show on Broadway? Too late for *Cats*." He grinned, turning to wink at Ridley.

She groaned.

"Anyway. No Mortal sights down here, Lucille. Just a bunch a dumb old rocks and Casters."

But Lucille didn't care. She sat in a pool of light, delicately licking her paw. When Link tried to pick her up, she hissed at him.

"Fine. Be that way. If you get mugged, I'm not going to be the one explainin' it to the Sisters. You're gonna have to grease that hog yourself."

"He's talking to that cat." Necro raised an eyebrow.

"I know," Ridley sighed. "Lucille Ball. She's sort of like the cousin of his best friend." Link ignored them, cooing at Lucille. It was the friendliest Link had heard Rid get with any of the band, and he didn't want to break up the moment.

"You're kidding." Necro looked from Link to Ridley. "She's kidding, right?"

Link kept walking, with Lucille following ten feet behind. He knew better than to mess with the Sisters' cat, even all the way up North. He should've known that cat could handle herself wherever she was.

She was tougher than any of them.

Now Link could see a light ahead of them in the Tunnels, where the passageway broadened into a crossroads. The words CASTER UNDERGROUND were laid into the tile mosaic in the walls where the pathways met. On the wall beneath the mosaic hung what looked like a hand-drawn map, held by an elaborately carved frame.

"Siren Hill." Floyd pointed at a spot on the map. "That's where we're headed." Then she pointed to a far tunnel. "That one."

Link peered over her shoulder. "That's how you get there? Not from the Mortal world?"

Floyd shrugged. "There are back doors, side doors, trapdoors. But yeah, more or less. The main entrance is from down here."

"Just try to keep up," Necro said, heading into the farthest tunnel. They followed her as she moved through the darkness, until she reached a stone staircase leading to a rusted metal door. By the time the others rejoined her, she was already pushing open the Doorwell—and the echoing stillness of the Underground gave way to something that could only be described as pure chaos.

Mardi Gras, Link thought. *Beale Street on a hot night.* Ever since he went to that creepy bokor's shop with Ethan, he'd used the Underground to retrace his steps to the City That Care Forgot on more than one occasion. *Doesn't smell much better here, either.*

The moment they stepped into the dim cavern, the noise overwhelmed them. Outside the Doorwell, the crowd was so thick that it was impossible to see past the first ten feet of people, even for a supersized quarter Incubus who was head and shoulders above almost everyone else.

"Can you see the door?" Floyd shouted up at him. She was a lot taller than Necro, but even she couldn't see a thing.

"I think it's that way. Hold on." He ducked through the crowd, the others following in his wake. "There." Link nodded and grabbed Floyd's arm with one hand, guiding Rid with the other. Necro held on to Floyd, while Sampson brought up the rear.

Ridley glared at Link until he dropped Floyd's arm.

"Look." Floyd pointed. "Sirenes."

Ridley scoffed. "Sirenes? That's not a real thing."

"It is now. Nox uses them to lure people into the club."

They weren't real Sirens, but they didn't have to be. They were women so hot they could've been on the covers of Link's car magazines. They wandered through the train station, selling tubes of bright red liquid to some folks and clear bubbling foam to others. Floyd was right—if you watched long enough, you could see they were pushing the crowd in the direction of the club.

Link was starstruck.

"Eyes forward, soldier," Ridley said. All he could do was nod. The Sirenes weren't wearing much; instead, they were wrapped in some kind of crazy lit-up fabric, like Chinese lanterns, or maybe human glow sticks.

As usual, when it came to Caster clubs, Link didn't get it. This time, he didn't mind. But he still didn't get it. *If my mamma could only see me now. She'd blow a gasket.* He shook his head. "Didn't we just come from breakfast?" he said loudly. "How is there so much nightlife with so little night?" It was the strangest thing he'd ever seen, and given the past few years, that was really saying something.

"Because," Floyd shouted back, "this is probably still last night."

"Or maybe tomorrow night," Necro said. "Give or take a few days. The Underground never sleeps around here. Especially not when Lennox Gates opens a new club in town."

"Big crowd for a new club," Ridley said.

"When you're hot you're on fire," Necro yelled.

"How would you know?" Ridley shouted back. Necro made a face and disappeared into the crowd, Floyd ducking after her.

"Come on, Rid. We gotta keep up." Now that they were actually at the club, Link started getting nervous again.

"I think they went in there." Rid nodded. "That way."

Above the crowd, the word SIRENE was spray-painted, graffiti-style, against the crumbling walls of the Tunnels.

The crowd parted, and all Link could see was the black velvet rope as Lucille Ball strutted right past it.

As far as Link could tell, Sirene was no place for Mortals. Sure, there were always a few strays who found their way to the Dark Caster clubs in the Tunnels—Link and Ethan had, not long ago. But as a general rule, Casters and Incubuses preferred to keep to their own. Dark to Dark, Light to Light. Especially when they were doing things like blowing off steam, drinking blood, and flexing their powers.

No, Casters didn't want Mortals here, and Mortals wouldn't make it for long. The Underground belonged to the Casters, and down here, the rules were different. Moderation was something only Mortals cared about, right along with respect for Mortal life. Rid used to tell Link that you didn't want to be a fly on the wall of any Underground club when some Supernatural decided to go Hershey's Special Dark and get out their swatter.

Not that many Mortals ever got to the point of risking it.

The idea of a place without Mortal judgments, not to mention a place where Darkness belonged as much as if not more than Light, was terrifying to most Mortals. Before he was bitten, Link's whole idea of good and bad—or as Mrs. Lincoln liked to call it, bad to worse—was based on sneaking out of Sunday school (bad) and into the girls' locker room (worse). Now it was based on making deals with Dark Casters (bad), drinking human blood (worse), or, say, stabbing your friend's great-great-uncle in the chest with gardening shears (the very worst).

Tonight, Link doubted Sirene would be an exception to the rule.

"Hey." Ridley nodded at the bouncer standing behind the black velvet rope at the entrance to the club itself. He was about the size of three Summerville football players, the kind who were never in good enough shape to play any other sport. "You have to let us in. We're with the band. They just came through this way, and—"

Before she could finish, the bouncer grunted and held up his hand. He rose to his feet, pulling back the black velvet rope, and a group of Incubuses instantly Ripped inside, materializing out of the air almost exactly where he stood. He nodded to them respectfully. "Your usual table is waiting, gentlemen."

Link swallowed, automatically stepping backward into the shadows.

Blood Incubuses. Here. A whole lot of them. Smelling like they just ate. This place is as bad as that other Caster club, Exile. Maybe worse.

Now the bouncer looked back at Ridley.

"Like I said, we're with the band," Ridley said.

"And that cat," Link added.

"They're expecting us." Ridley held up the flyer scrawled with the word *Sirene*.

"And what are they expecting, Blondie?" The bouncer leered at her. "Can I expect something, too?" His bald, sweating head was so heavily inked that you almost couldn't see his gold-lit snake eyes. When he smiled, he let his forked tongue slither in and out of his mouth. Each side was pierced.

Classy, Link thought.

The forks curled and uncurled almost to Ridley's cheek, getting closer, until Link realized they weren't tongues at all, but some kind of strange snakes that lived in the guy's mouth.

Link grabbed them and yanked, as hard as he could. "Yeah. They're expectin' you to show the lady some respect. Now step aside, Snake Eyes."

137

Three feet of hissing snakes fell out of their warm habitat and down to the ground in front of the bouncer. Six feet of Link joined them there, seconds later, knocked on his butt. *Hybrid Incubus. Right. Superstrength. Shoulda seen that one comin'. Seein' as he's the bouncer and all.*

"So, tough guy." The bouncer leaned over Link. "You think this is your big break? For you and your cat? Think again."

Link felt his cheeks getting hot, and he was pretty sure he'd snapped a drumstick beneath him. "That's not cool, Pool Cue."

The bald guy turned even redder beneath his tats. "No? How about this? Here's your big break. Only it's for your head. I know because I'll be the one doing the breaking."

"You talkin' about my melon, Rapunzel? Is that it?" Link sat up and the guy pushed him back down. "You feelin' a little jealous?"

If I can get back on my feet, I can take him.

The bouncer flexed his horse-sized muscles.

Maybe.

"Boys." Rid shook out her pink-striped hair. "This is getting boring."

Link tackled the bouncer and the two of them went flying into the crowd, beating the crap out of each other.

Ridley rolled her eyes. A second later, the cherry lollipop hit her tongue and the velvet rope hit the floor. She was that good. Just like always.

As he wiped the blood off the corner of his bruised mouth, Link wondered if she'd done it to him since they'd started going out—and if she had, how would he know?

"Your table is waiting," the bouncer said, helping Link up after him. Then he offered his arm to Ridley, as if he'd forgotten

138

about the whole beatdown thing. She let him guide her up the steps to the doorway.

"It sure is" was all Rid said to the bouncer. "Tomorrow, I want you to wave us straight through."

"You got it," the bouncer said. "Mr. Gates said we'd be seeing a lot of you from now on."

"He did?" Ridley faltered. "Of course he did."

Link didn't seem to hear him. Instead, he yanked his hair back up into its usual spikes and pushed his way up to the bouncer. "Hey, Baldy McThug. Next time I'm gonna kick your ass. Me, and my cat. What do you have to say to that?"

The bouncer ignored him. Link sighed.

It was humiliating, having your girlfriend run interference for you, but as Link brushed himself off from the dirty floor, he didn't know how to tell her that. This whole band thing might have been her idea, but it was still his audition. Link would never know his way around the Caster world the way Ridley did, but that didn't mean he was pathetic, and it didn't mean he couldn't take care of himself.

Couldn't he?

He was the one who belonged at an Incubus club more than any of them. He'd taken out Abraham Ravenwood with a pair of garden shears. There was no point in holding back now.

It was time for Wesley Lincoln to man up.

Tonight would be the beginning of all that. His supernatural rock career was coming, and it was about time.

I need a few cherry lollipops of my own.

Link followed Ridley and the bouncer up the steps.

Lucille waited for them at the top, like they were a couple of clueless idiots.

Link snorted. "Don't you look at me like that. I didn't see you helpin'."

Lucille stalked away in a silent huff.

"Women." Link shook his head at Rid.

"Don't." She took his hand as the massive warehouse doors slid open, and they were in the club.

Or at least, they were in some kind of long, dark hallway leading to the club. The crowd pushed them along like a river. Link held on to Ridley with one hand and felt for his broken drumsticks with the other.

The only light came from the outline of a mirrored bar running down the side of the chamber. Even though it was far too dark to see where you were going, Link could've sworn he saw something in the shadows. It felt like he was being watched, but he didn't see anyone.

Strange, he thought. *No stranger than anything else around here, though.*

It wasn't until the hall opened into a single room—maybe three or four stories high—that flashing lights hit his eyes and he could see again.

Barely.

It was what he saw that floored him.

More than that...who.

CHAPTER 16

For Those About to Rock

What is she doing here? Ridley thought. At least, that was her first thought. Her second was *I'm going to kill her.* The third was *My mother is going to kill me.*

"Link! Ridley!"

Link looked almost as shocked as Ridley. "Sweet Cheesus—" Ryan Duchannes was at Sirene.

Ridley froze. It was an animal instinct—fight, flight, or freeze. Her little sister was here, at the club. Ryan was thirteen years old and expected to go Light as the sun itself. A Dark Caster Underground club was the last place you'd think to find her.

True, she was wearing makeup and a mess of an outfit Ridley couldn't even begin to understand—plaid shorts, an argyle vest, knee-high duck boots, and a baseball cap. Ryan's attempt at a signature style.

She stood there in the crowd, holding the cat, sandwiched

between Dark Casters and looking about as out of place in the industrial warehouse as a Mortal Girl Scout would. Ridley's sister would never have found this place on her own. Someone else was involved.

Someone powerful.

Someone who wants me to know just how powerful he is.

Running wasn't an option. She couldn't leave Ryan alone here.

Fight was out, too. Ridley didn't know exactly what she was up against, but she had a pretty good idea.

This one move told her more than most. She could smell a predator a mile away, and more than anything, she knew when she was bested.

Checkmate, Lennox Gates.

She was in New York City, on his turf. She had dragged her boyfriend all the way here, and she'd put her future and his on the line. Now she was staring at her kid sister.

It was the first time Ridley understood that getting out of this whole mess was going to be trickier than she'd thought. She had underestimated her opponent. After Sarafine and Abraham, she thought she'd learned never to do that again.

Ridley's hand was around Ryan's wrist before Ryan could say another word. "Get out of here."

"Why?" Ryan looked shocked. "I thought you invited me? For Link's gig?"

"We didn't invite you." Ridley was already pulling Ryan toward the door, which wasn't easy, seeing as she nearly knocked over an Incubus carrying a pitcher of what she doubted was cherry soda. He glared as she pushed past.

"How did you get here, Ryan?" The sisterly inquisition was on.

"Tunnels."

"And Mom thinks?"

"Mamma thinks I'm sleeping at Jackie Eaton's." Ryan looked past Ridley. "Hey, Link."

"Hey yourself, Ryan. Lookin' sharp." Link leaned in for the same old awkward hug he usually gave Rid's little sister, the kind that avoided all unnecessary touching.

"Why are you here, Ryan?"

"That note you sent."

"I never sent you a note."

"Of course you did. I have it in my bag." Ryan slipped her suede backpack off her shoulders and unzipped it. She handed Ridley a slick black envelope sealed with red wax.

The wax had been stamped with the letter S, only the S was a serpent. " 'Ridley Duchannes and Wesley Lincoln request the pleasure of your company at a private concert benefiting the Sirensong Foundation. Come join us in celebrating the opening of the club Sirene. R.S.V.P. & H.T.V.T.' " Ridley looked up. "What the hell? Is this some kind of a joke?"

"H.T.V.T.?" Link looked blank.

"Hold to Virtually Teleport. It's a Rip letter. All Ryan had to do was go anywhere in the Tunnels with this thing in her hand and she Ripped right here."

Ryan's eyes were still glowing. "It was like riding in a Ferrari."

Ridley shook her head. "Not an easy Cast, more of a status thing. You know, big party, transportation provided. Check it out." Ridley held the letter out to Link.

He raised his hands. "No way. I'm not touchin' that thing. I have a bad enough time Rippin' as it is." Link looked as worried as she felt.

143

She knew they shouldn't have come here. *But then, if we hadn't, who would be taking care of Ryan right now?*

Ryan's face clouded over. "If you didn't invite me, Rid, then who did?"

"I did." The words sounded like they came from the sky, both above and behind her. But Ridley knew better.

Not the sky—the balcony. Ridley recognized the voice immediately, though she hadn't heard it in weeks now. It still made her shiver.

The one who looked as hot as he acted cold.

The one she owed not one but two markers.

One that could ruin her relationship, and one that could ruin her life.

He was the reason they were here tonight, and the reason she was in New York at all.

Ridley had finally met her match, and his name was Lennox Gates. Ryan was his move. It was a challenge, head to head. Siren versus whatever the hell kind of Dark Caster he was.

Forget Liar's Trade. The real game was only now beginning.

This might be Link's audition, but it was her game.

Her fist clenched in the sudden green light of her Binding Ring.

It's on.

The moment she turned to look at him, the club went quiet.

Not quiet—utterly and completely silent, because there was no one left inside. Every single person had disappeared, and now it was just the two of them. Ridley could hear her own heart pounding.

Lennox Gates was there, standing at the railing of a raised industrial platform. His eyes were as intense—and as gold-flecked—as she remembered. Something about them reminded her of what Dark Fire looked like.

Pure power.

Ridley couldn't see past what he wore under the leather jacket, but it was clear that whatever it was concealing included a compact, athletic build. His golden hair fell around his face and almost curled in places, especially near his neck. *He looks like ambition,* she thought.

He looks like danger.

Ridley didn't take her eyes off his face. She wouldn't give him the satisfaction of thinking he had impressed her with his little magic show.

Anyone could—what? Evaporate a room full of heavily Charmed and powerfully protected Supernaturals? Throw down a Temporal Distortion like that? Not really.

No one could, except maybe Lena. Even then, it wouldn't be easy.

Ridley had to admit that. Her heart was pounding, and she wondered if he could hear it, which only made it pound harder.

Get it together, Rid.

She spoke first. *Not broke first,* she thought. *Keep playing the long game. Focus on how you will destroy this person.* "You must be really proud of yourself for pulling that one off."

His eyes didn't waver from her face. "I'm almost never proud. They say it goes before a fall, and I'm not planning on falling."

"That's funny, since I'm not planning on caring. Now what did you do with the nice people in the club, Mr. Gates?"

He waved a hand dismissively. "They're still there. Having the night of their lives. Or so they think."

Condescending jerk. "You're talking about my sister and my boyfriend," Ridley said. "Put them back or you'll wish you never met me."

"How do you know I don't wish that already?" Now he was smiling.

"What's it to me, either way?" Ridley smiled back. "Whatever your problem is with me, I guarantee you it's about to get a thousand times worse. Ask around. I'm sort of famous for that."

"I'm looking forward to it." He snapped his fingers and the noise, the chaos, the wild adrenaline of the club instantly returned. He raised his voice over the noise. "Who said I had a problem with you? I've missed you since our little encounter at Suffer."

He snapped his fingers again, and the people disappeared for a second time.

"See? Everyone's happy as a soft-shell clam." He gestured toward her. "But this is me time. You and me time. What's that in your hand?"

Ridley looked down at the black envelope Ryan had given her. It only took a moment before the room around it went even blacker.

⊰ CHAPTER 17 ⊱

Runnin' with the Devil

Ridley's head was spinning. Then the darkness gave way to light. But it was no better, because the lights were too bright for her to see. Slowly, as the room began to solidify around her, she realized she was staring into a candle.

"Something sweet? You seem a little light-headed." Lennox's voice cut through the light.

Ridley looked up. She was sitting across from Lennox Gates, at what appeared to be a private table for two. *Transportation provided.* She had forgotten she was holding the damn invitation.

She winced. He'd gotten the better of her twice now. It was more than embarrassing. It was infuriating. "How did you manage to use a Rip letter inside the club, when a whole posse of Blood Incubuses had to Rip outside and walk in the door like everyone else?"

"I Bound the club myself. I can come and go as I like." He looked pleased with himself, which only made Rid more irritated.

"Just you?"

"Just me, and anyone I hand that invitation to." Lennox smiled. "Nectar of the Gods?" He lifted a decanter—a bottle so tall and thin that it looked like the neck of some poor dead goose. Golden bubbles rose to the surface of a thick, syrupy drink. Ridley sniffed and smelled sugarcane, the essence of sweetness in its purest form.

Siren catnip. He's good.

"Go to Hell, Lennox Gates." It was all she could manage to say.

He nodded pleasantly. "Please. Call me Nox. And I'm sure I will. You could say it's a family tradition. But until then, perhaps we should toast to our joint venture?"

Ridley dropped the black envelope like a hot coal. "No. And no more cheap party tricks. Please."

She was beginning to get her bearings. This room was nothing like the rest of the club. Quiet darkness was reflected everywhere—in the vintage-looking black velvet curtains, the black leather booths that curved like shells against the low, vaulted walls, and the massive black stone fireplace that dominated the far end of the chamber.

"Hungry, then? Even a Siren has to eat." A series of black leather triangles covered the polished metal disc of the tabletop. A silver goblet sat on a crystal plate in front of Ridley. When she looked at the goblet it was empty.

"Perhaps something from the Grand Bazaar? Do you like Istanbul?"

Ridley looked again, and the goblet was full of sweet honey-comb, dribbled with a golden syrup that smelled like wild honey-suckle. A fat bee buzzed lazily over the top wedge. Triangles of what looked like fresh pistachio baklava and Turkish Delight mounded up against the goblet, on the crystal plate.

So he can Manifest, too. Great. He's got some kind of Shifter blood in there.

Shifting. A Temporal Distortion. Ripping. His powers seemed to cross every conventional Supernatural distinction. Her debt to Lennox Gates was only getting more and more worrisome.

She tried not to panic. She willed her heart to beat more slowly.

There is nothing to be afraid of.

He's just another bully.

You've seen worse. You've beaten worse.

Ridley collected herself and looked up at Lennox Gates, shaking her head. "No, thanks. I'm not hungry. I'll pass."

On this. On you. On all of it.

"More of a Paris girl? A little *je ne sais quoi* from La Maison Angelina? For *la petite Sirène*?"

Now the plate was covered with dark chocolate truffles and a delicate teacup filled with rich, steaming hot chocolate.

Show-off.

Ridley stood up. "You've made your point. You grabbed my sister. You forced me to hand over my boyfriend. It's clear you're set on destroying my future."

"And?" Nox looked interested, as if he was actually enjoying himself. Which only made her hate him more.

"And on top of all that, I'm certainly not going to *flirt* with you."

"Flirt with me? Is that what you think this is about?" For the first time, Lennox started to laugh. It almost made him seem like a real person, which Ridley found more disturbing than she could explain.

"Don't flatter yourself, Little Siren." He poured some bubbling liquid into his own glass. "Sit down."

She did, against her better judgment—and what irritated her more was that she honestly couldn't tell if he was compelling her to or not. *He can't be*, she told herself; she hadn't seen a single Siren, and she'd know if there were one in the club.

Wouldn't I?

No one had ever turned the tables on her like this. Rid had no idea what it would feel like to be compelled, but the more she thought about it, the more she imagined it might feel remarkably like this.

"To Sirensong." He held up his glass. "Long may they rock."

She didn't hold up hers. "Siren what? Do you mean the Devil's Hangmen?"

"I've renamed the band for my new club. Catchy, isn't it?"

"Not really."

Nox clinked his glass against her untouched one and drank anyway. "Fine. Let me be perfectly clear. This is about business. You beat my drummer in that game and left him completely powerless. I had no way of knowing the drummer you offered up in return was your boyfriend. I admit, that's awkward for you."

"Why do I have the feeling you had every way of knowing that my boyfriend was a drummer?" She looked around. "And we both know I owe you more than that." She finally looked him in the eye.

"Ah, yes. You do owe me two markers, don't you? As you

150

know, your drummer boy only settles the first one. But don't worry. I'll tell you when I need to collect the second." Lennox smoothed the gold hair from his eyes. "House marker, paid on my call."

Ridley shivered. She didn't need to be reminded of it. She thought of it as she lay in bed every night. *How I've lost so much more than a game.*

"I'm not in a rush. You'll know what I want, when I want it. And I assure you I will." He looked at her. "Want it, that is."

She didn't respond.

"I have an exceptional memory." He smiled. "Especially when it comes to my markers."

Ridley faltered. For once, she had nothing in her arsenal. No clever comeback, no snappy insult—nothing was going to change the fact that she had lost the one thing she prized above all.

Power.

Power was her freedom.

Mine, and Link's.

Lennox raised an eyebrow, sipping again from the fluted glass. "Speaking of which, how does the hybrid boyfriend feel about your trading in his future for your own?"

"It's not like that." Ridley winced.

"What's it like, then, *Sugarplum*?"

The sound of Link's pet nickname for her was too much. "Leave Link out of this."

"Wesley Lincoln? The worst student in the entire fake freshman class of Georgia Redeemer? You know I can't do that." Lennox sighed. "But I have to say, I've enjoyed getting to know him."

"You don't." She felt a new cold, coiling in her gut. "Know

151

him, I mean." *Or me, for that matter. Otherwise, you wouldn't dare.*

"I keep an eye on all my investments. Your near-Mortal mistake will play in my band and work for my club and do whatever I want him to do, whenever I want it. Like all my employees."

"Over my dead body."

"Careful, now. You don't know how many people would line up for the chance to help you out with that." He held up his glass. "I, on the other hand, do. And congratulations. I honestly don't know how you managed to make so many people so angry in such a short time. So angry, and so impatient." He shook his head. "You're a gifted girl."

Ridley faltered no more. She grabbed her drink and splashed it at Lennox's face.

"What the—" He was spluttering now.

"Screw you, Lennox Gates. Screw your giant Caster ego and your poser Siren club and your loser band. I don't know what's really going on here, but I know that none of this is about what happened during that card game."

"You don't know what you're talking about, Little Siren."

"I'm talking about your rigged game and your creepy markers. I'm talking about you spying on my family and my boyfriend."

"Spying on you?" His dark eyes shone as he put down his glass. "You know what I see when I look at you, Little Siren? Flames. Smoke and fire. It's all over your future. I don't know what it all means, but I can translate some of it for you."

"Be my guest." *Great. He's a Seer, too?*

"How about, your future's going up in smoke?" He wasn't smiling.

152

"Screw with me and you're going to get burned." Ridley's eyes were deadly.

"You know, there are so many things I want to say to that." Nox winked.

"Here's one. You mess with my friends, and I will come for you." She stood up. "And if you ever speak to my sister again— any of my sisters—you better get yourself one hell of a bigger bouncer. Smoke that, *Lennox*."

Lennox held up both hands, including the black envelope—a sign of surrender.

"I think I'm happy to stay out of your future."

"Believe me. You were never in it."

"Duly noted. Here, give this back to your sister. She'll be home the second she touches it."

Ridley grabbed it out of his hand. She walked away in a huff without so much as a glance back at him, even though she had no idea where they were or where she was going.

"Stairs on your left. Can't miss them." She heard a chuckle from the table behind her. He really did seem to be enjoying this, and it only made her more furious.

She had almost made it to the door when she heard the unmistakable sound of music from the club below. The thumping bass. The screeching lead guitar. The drums. God, the drums.

She knew this melody. She'd been listening to him rehearse it last night, when he thought she was sleeping.

"Sweet Meatballs." That's "Sweet Meatballs."

Link is playing with the band.

What did Lennox Gates call them? Sirensong?

All of a sudden she could feel it. Lennox was standing right behind her. His voice was quiet and—if she had to pick a word

153

to describe it—dangerous. "Your boyfriend has bigger problems than just me, Little Siren. But I bet you know that, since we're both Dark Casters."

Ridley didn't answer for a long moment. When she did, she didn't look at Lennox. "Know what?"

Lennox pulled a matchbook from his pocket, fingering it idly. "That they'll come for him. That he's a walking dead man. That there's no happy ending, not when you're the idiot who took out Abraham Ravenwood." He took a step closer to her. "As I said, Casters have long memories. Incubuses, even longer. But I don't have to tell you that, do I?"

Ridley could feel his breath on her neck.

He continued. "Look around. Half of them are here. It's a Dark club. I'm a Dark guy. Who do you think my clients are?"

"Shut up." She couldn't look at him. "You don't know what you're talking about."

"Don't I? Why do you think we wanted him to play his little drums here? Right here?" Nox shrugged. "And why not? I'm in the business of giving the people what they want. It's what I do. If someone wants me to deliver a hybrid Incubus, why should I ask why?" Ridley's heart was pounding, but Nox didn't stop. "And if they wanted his friends? What then?"

What then?

Ridley didn't want to think about it. This was a risky conversation, for her and for Link. Risky, and potentially deadly. Lennox Gates could strip her of her powers, or he could exploit them. He could make her life a living hell, or end it.

But he could not—could not—mess with her Shrinky Dink.

Enough.

Ridley turned, slowly, and when she did her eyes were

blazing. "Two markers. That's between you and me. Leave Link out of this."

"How honorable of you."

"I'll pay my debts, and you'll keep your mouth shut."

Nox shrugged. "Tell him or not. They'll come either way." He tossed her the matchbook. "They always do."

⊰ CHAPTER 18 ⊱

Metal Gods

"She was so juicy, her name should be Lucy.
She was so tender, I loved her like my Fender.
Even when she had sauce, I knew she was my boss.
When she was in a toasted bun, I knew I'd get
*   my meatball fun."*

Sweet Meatballs" was Link's magnum opus as a songwriter—
a tragic ballad composed for a meatball sub he didn't get to eat
anymore. Which was no different than his singing about a broken heart, Ridley guessed. Or a hamburger Patty.

Love was love.

But it wasn't everything. The night was ruined for Ridley, and
as she made her way back to the main floor of the club, she felt

like all she could see were Incubuses moving toward her in the shadows, and Dark Casters staring at her from behind gold eyes.

Ridley and Link—and Ryan, oh god, Ryan—had to get themselves out of Sirene.

But Sirensong was still playing, and the crowd was still listening. The set was going well—better than it should have, in Rid's opinion. Which only made it take longer. When the chorus hit (*"Roll me in bread crumbs, I know you can't be all thumbs"*), the crowd even sang along.

That's a first.

As soon as Ridley spotted Ryan in the crowd—jumping up and down in front of the stage, yelling, *"Roll me! Bread crumbs!"*—Rid made a beeline in her direction.

But when she got there, Ryan was following Link with her eyes as if she'd never seen him before. As if he was someone from the cover of a teen magazine, rather than just another guy who refused to throw out his old car magazines.

Not you, too.

It was almost hard to watch.

Link was center stage, bending over the mic, dipping it backward on the stand as if they were slow dancing. It was his audition. They were letting him do whatever he wanted. That was clear by the way they were all watching him.

Link as lead singer? Were they setting him up to fail?

Either way, it didn't seem to matter much to Link. He looked like he was having the greatest night of his life.

"You know I love you, Saucy Bossy Girl," he crooned to his imaginary meatball. The mic crackled enthusiastically—and the crowd screamed.

That mic will probably make a better girlfriend than I ever will, Ridley thought, feeling guilty.

She sighed.

Downstage, Necro's blue faux-hawk was flying in every direction over the enormous keyboard, like it had a mind of its own. Sampson stood next to Link, singing into a mic—with the tattooed arms and hypnotic presence she remembered from the night she first met him at Suffer. His hands sped across the strings of an über-modern electric guitar. The body curved into a wide U shape, like a harp. Behind Sampson, Floyd jammed on a bass as big as she was. Ridley couldn't tell if the guitar was part of her body or not.

A red plaid hipster drum kit sat waiting for Link in the center of the stage. As the crowd screamed, Link threw down the mic and picked up the sticks, sliding back behind the drums. The drums had always been the one instrument you could safely hand him. At best, it was a loud banging. At worst, it was also a loud banging. There was something reassuring about that.

The crowd screamed louder. *"Roll me! Bread crumbs!"*

Sirensong was rocking the house.

She'd had enough.

"Ryan—"

Her little sister's eyes lit up the moment she saw Ridley back on the floor. "There you are, Saucy Bossy Girl."

"Don't ever say that." *No Sirensong. No Meatstik. No more lyrics.*

"You missed most of the set. Link has been so—"

"Uh-huh. Say hi to Mamma for me. Love you." Ridley shoved the envelope into Ryan's hand and she was gone. You couldn't even hear the Rip over the music.

Ridley breathed a sigh of relief. Her sister was safe. For the time being.

Your move, Gates.

She closed her eyes and stood there, in the middle of the crowd, listening to the music. Something wasn't right. She could smell it, almost taste it.

Her skin was crawling with it.

Come out. Show yourself.

I can feel you. I know what you're doing.

She opened her eyes. She didn't know what kind of answer she was expecting, but there was nothing.

She couldn't help but check inside her purse, where her last cherry lollipop remained firmly wrapped.

Yet, somehow, the Power of Persuasion was thick in the air around her. Ridley was sure of it, even if she wasn't the one responsible for it.

Which only left one question...

Who was?

Backstage, beneath the jungle of scaffolding and light stands and extra amps and extension cords, Sirensong was celebrating. Bottles were popping, and fountains of champagne—no, from the smell of it, make that shaken cans of cheap soda—sprayed in every direction.

Geez. You would have thought Sirensong had never played a hit song to a full house of screaming fans before.

Maybe because they hadn't.

"Dude. We smoked it." Floyd fist-bumped Link. "Like Roger Waters."

"Like bacon." Link fist-bumped her back.

"Like a cigar," Necro said. A shadow passed over her face, but Floyd sprayed both of them while Sampson ducked out of the way, and soon Necro was laughing as hard as everyone else. When Floyd's fist began to actually smoke, Ridley shook her head and pulled Link away.

Illusionists.

Link flung his arm over Rid's shoulder. "You just got me the greatest gig a my entire life, Babe." He kissed her, smack on the mouth, without even stopping smiling. "Did you see the crowd losin' it durin' our set? They loved us."

"Yeah. They did. And now we've got to get out of here."

Link pointed at Rid. "Roll me! Bread crumbs!"

"I got that," Rid said. "The whole recipe. I was there. Let's go."

Link took one look at her face and gave up. It was clear there wasn't going to be all that much celebrating tonight. "Aw, come on. Geez. What now? Why are you givin' me that stinkeye?"

"Link. Come on." Now she was frustrated. He just wasn't getting it. "Did you ever wonder why everyone was chanting that chorus?"

He shrugged. "Because meatballs are awesome. And so is Sirensong. And so am I." He couldn't stop smiling.

"Or?" Ridley looked at him. She could feel the anxiety tightening in her chest.

"Or what? What are you gettin' at? They loved us because we killed it. Because of Floyd bringin' it and Necro whalin' on it, and Sammy Boy tearin' it up out there. We made Meatstik look like beef jerky." Link was starting to look insulted.

160

Careful, Ridley told herself. But Ridley also never listened to anyone—including herself. And she had spent far too long with Lennox Gates tonight to not know how high the stakes were.

There was no time for careful.

"Really, Link?" Ridley crossed her arms. "Do you really want to do this now?"

"Yeah, really," Link said. He crossed his arms, too.

"Because I hate to break it to you, but everyone watching you was high." There. She'd said it.

"What?"

"Sirensong. The joy juice. The Power of Persuasion. Whatever you want to call it. They were Charmed. This whole place is. It's not you, it's them." She tossed her hair defiantly, just for emphasis.

"That's not what you're sayin'." Link stiffened. "You're sayin' it's not me, it's you." Link was madder than she could ever remember seeing him. Ridley hated to keep going, but she didn't have a choice.

She shook her head. "Just listen to me. I didn't Charm anyone tonight but the bouncer. I told you I wouldn't do it, and I didn't. But if someone else is messing with you like that, we need to get out of here."

Link looked at her in disbelief. "Do you hear how crazy that sounds? You're freakin' out because I did okay for once?"

Ridley grabbed his sweaty sleeve. "Nobody's going to be doing you any favors at Sirene. We can't trust Lennox Gates. This whole thing is a setup. Why can't you get it through your thick skull?"

"I don't know, Rid. Maybe on account a the hole where my brain is supposed to be?"

"Link—"

"Well, don't worry. Here's another hole for you, and I'll make sure it's an even bigger one. The one between you and me." Link took off before she could say a word.

Ridley was stunned.

She closed her eyes and held out her hands, using her powers to see what the club really felt like beneath the pounding beat of the bass, above the thick layer of conversation and clinking glasses, through the buzzing lights and the roar of the sound system.

What is going on in here?

She smelled the thick elixir of sugar in the air, the coppery scent of blood. A fire. A kitchen. Things cooking, like in any restaurant. Smoke from a cigar or two.

Her own sweet power.

Basically, it was the smell of Suffer, or Exile, or any Underground Caster club, so long as she was in it.

Ridley felt power, but it felt no different from her own. It spread thickly through the air around her, like the Power of Persuasion. But she didn't know who was behind it. She was the only Siren in the club, as far as she knew. And she wasn't using her powers on anyone.

Have I lost my mind? Or just my way?

But her boyfriend was disappearing through the crowd in front of her, and she didn't have time to wait for the answer.

⊰ CHAPTER 19 ⊱

Something to Believe In

L ink!" Ridley pushed her way through the crowd after him, trying to catch up. She followed him up the stairs, down the hall, and through the doors marked BROOKLYN. Moments later, she found herself standing on the empty street, in the miserable, rainy night, but it was too late.

He was gone, and she wasn't a hybrid Incubus. She couldn't keep up. She could barely walk in these shoes. And she didn't have a jacket.

Even Lucille Ball the cat looked sorry for her, dry as she was beneath the awning of the liquor store next door, beating her tail against a trash can lid.

Lucille let out a sympathetic howl.

What a mess.

This wasn't the way they'd come in, and Ridley was pretty sure it wasn't the way they should have come out. The doors that opened onto the street appeared to be the doors to a Chinese Laundromat. Signs in the windows in Mandarin advertised what looked like free detergent with every load. A neon sign in Kanji seemed to be the only marker for the club.

Ridley was a little rusty on her Kanji, but she knew this one. It was familiar to Sirens worldwide, and a popular tattoo—aside from the more magical Dark Caster variety. Plus, it was the same in Chinese characters, Japanese Kanji, or old Korean Hanja. In its most rudimentary form, the brushstrokes formed a square body with a tail.

A bird.

Sometimes the character was slightly different. Sometimes it was a person with wings; sometimes it was a bird rising from ashes, like a phoenix; and still other times it was the bird of long life and spirit, the crane.

But it was always the bird.

That was the mark of the Siren, even for a sophisticated, edgy club like Sirene. When it came right down to it, that was what Sirens were—pretty songbirds with nightmares for nests. Creatures with wings that still never managed to fly free. They sabotaged themselves too often for that. Talons for nails—so sharp they could draw blood, so fast you'd never know you were bleeding.

Even when, half the time, the blood was their own.

Sirens were messed-up Dark creations. There was no denying it.

Rid backed away from the door and the club, taking in the street. She was in Brooklyn. She knew that much.

Real Brooklyn. Mortal Brooklyn.

Home to a Siren club.

That was what this was. There was no doubt about it now. The sign, the name, the Sirenes—he wasn't trying to hide it. It was his little inside joke.

Lennox Gates has someone Charming his club. He has a Siren working for him. Ridley shivered. She'd heard of such a thing before. Abraham Ravenwood had once kept her locked in a cage until she agreed to do his bidding. It wasn't common, and it wasn't something she wanted to think about. *Sapping some poor Siren's powers. Making someone else do his dirty work.*

She shuddered.

But there was a Siren's hand in all of this—in Sirene, and Sirensong. Ridley was sure of it.

Why?

What does any of this have to do with me?

What does Lennox Gates really want from me? From us?

And where the hell is my boyfriend?

Ridley had to find him.

Ten blocks later, when it was raining ten times harder, Ridley found Link.

To be fair, it was Lucille who found him. Rid only saw the cat, standing in the street, complaining. Of course, Lucille had managed to stay completely dry. That cat had nine hundred lives, and she lived better than a Siren in every one of them.

Better than a part-Mortal, too. Especially this one.

Link was sitting on an abandoned couch tossed halfway on the sidewalk, halfway into the street. The sopping, puke green cushions were wetter than sponges in a fishbowl, as Link would normally say, but he didn't seem to care that sitting on them was only making him wetter. Not now.

She knew the mood. He was past caring about anything.

He was past furious.

She'd crossed a line, but in her mind, she had crossed it so long ago that she couldn't even remember when or why or how it had happened.

It was hard to keep track of the lines, there had been so many.

She sat down next to Link.

He didn't look at her. The rain hit his face as he stared out at the depressing park with the cracked pavement right across the intersection from them. "You don't believe anything good can happen to me. Ever."

"That's not true."

"You think I'm stupid." He sounded defeated.

"Don't be—" *Stupid.* She caught herself just in time. "I don't. And I don't care what anyone else thinks about you."

He shook his head. "See? There you go again. Why do you assume whatever someone thinks about me will be bad?"

"Because you act like a freaking idiot so much of the time." *There.* She'd said it. She couldn't help it.

"Thanks. Don't hold back, now." Link turned to her. "Answer me this, Rid. Did you use magic in there, at any time, when we were in Sirene?"

"No. I told you that. It wasn't me. But I have an idea—"

He cut her off. He was in no mood to listen. "Did you, for even one second, stick one of those stupid lollipops in your mouth and do your thing?"

"No. Not once we got inside." *I even double-checked,* she thought uncomfortably. *But I think someone did.*

166

Link looked relieved. "Then why are you freakin' me out about the best gig a my life? Maybe the greatest night a my life? Why can't you let me have that? Why can't I enjoy this for just a second before you come in and take it all away from me?"

Ridley didn't know.

She didn't know why she broke everything she played with. Why she hurt everyone she cared about. Lost everything she found. Pushed away everything she wanted.

"I don't want anything to happen to you. Anything else," she said carefully. "And if it wasn't me helping you tonight, then—"

Link held up a hand. "Face it, Rid. You're jealous."

"Jealous? What do you have that I could ever be jealous of? Except maybe me." She refused to bring up Floyd the Rockerette, because deep down, she knew that none of this was really about her. It was about something bigger.

"You're jealous of my dream," Link said.

"That's ridiculous," Ridley scoffed. "I'm looking out for you."

"No, you're not. You're jealous because you don't have a dream of your own." Link braced himself like he was afraid to say it. Like he was ready to duck from whatever she was going to throw at him.

What she wanted to throw was the couch. But she didn't. Instead, she used her words, and not even supernatural ones. *Lena would be proud.*

"That's really mean."

"But it's true." He shook his head sadly. "I just call it like I see it, Rid."

"Link." She took a breath.

"When something good happens to me, you act like it's an

accident, or magic, or some sorta joke. Like you can't believe I earned it."

"Link—" She tried again.

He held up his hand. "I want to be someone, make somethin' outta my life. You're afraid to let me have that, and I don't know why." He stared straight ahead as he said it, out into the cold, wet street. *Looking anywhere but at me*, Ridley thought. That was how she knew he was for real.

She was stunned. "What are you saying?"

"I'm saying, get your own dream."

The words sounded like rain to her. Gray and soggy and depressing.

"I have dreams. You'll see. And then you'll feel like the giant idiot that you actually are." Ridley stood in the rain. "I felt it. In the club, back there. Someone was using the Power of Persuasion. Someone was watching us, too."

"Yeah. It's called an audience."

Rid bristled. "What do you think that stunt with Ryan was?"

He shrugged. "Kids sneak out to see bands all the time."

She tried to control herself. She tried to stay calm. She had to make him understand, whether or not she felt like unleashing every Cast and hex in the Caster universe on him.

Which she did.

"Link. We're not safe here. This isn't me being jealous or crazy. This isn't about me wanting to be the center of attention. I know what the Power of Persuasion feels like, because I have it, too." She looked at him, daring him to even try to stop her.

He didn't.

"There are some things I still know better than a brand-new hybrid Incubus. This is one of them, whether or not you want to believe it. And I'm sorry if that means you suck as a band. I'm sorry if you're never going to be Sting. I'm sorry if nobody really wanted you for a drummer after all. But I'm not sorry that I'm telling you the truth."

There.

It had to be said, and now she'd said it. She only wished it didn't make her feel so awful. The way the words had sounded as they came out of her mouth was almost as bad as the look on Link's face.

"Why should I believe you now?" he asked.

She wanted to smack him.

"Why should you believe me ever?" She wiped the rain off her face. "Look. This is me doing the best I can. I'm not perfect, but I am trying to help you."

"Some help." He still wasn't buying it. She didn't know what more she could say to him.

"Someone's setting you up, and they're going to take you down. Maybe both of us. That's how it works. Trust me. I invented that game."

Tell him. Tell him what Lennox Gates said. Tell him that Abraham Ravenwood is going to come for him. That he will never be safe.

That you got him into this mess in the first place.

But she couldn't. She didn't want him to live in that world. It was no place for regular people. She had to take care of this.

She had to handle it for both of them.

Link didn't say a word.

Ridley felt herself swaying, on the inside. She felt little pieces of her breaking off, smashing into the street like that old couch Link was sitting on.

"I can't believe a word you say anymore, and that's the truth," Link said. "That's all the truth I'm ever going to get from you, isn't it, Rid?"

She knew she was going to burst into tears, and she couldn't let that happen. She was Ridley Duchannes. Nobody made her feel like this. Nobody but a dumb quarter Incubus from the middle of nowhere.

But deep down, she knew something else, too.

He's right.

She took a deep breath.

"I haven't been completely honest with you. Some things happened that night at Suffer. I didn't beat a Dark Caster in a game of Liar's Trade. I lost to Sampson. Because I didn't know he was a Darkborn, and I couldn't—" Rid shrugged.

"Cheat?"

"Pretty much."

"So you lost your shirt to Sammy Boy, huh?" Link smiled, in spite of his anger. "I guess he'd have a good poker face."

"I didn't lose my shirt to *him*. Not exactly. He was playing for the house."

"What house?" Link asked slowly.

"The club. Suffer."

"You mean Lennox Gates?" He didn't look at her.

Ridley nodded.

"What did you lose, Rid?" Link's tone was darker now.

She swallowed. "Two markers." She really didn't want to tell him the rest, but she knew she had to. It had all gotten too big for just one person.

"One was for a drummer. Because the drummer for Devil's

Hangmen lost his talent in the game. When I cheated it out of him." She didn't look at Link.

"A drummer?"

Rid nodded. She felt her eyes starting to water.

"So you had to hand me over in return? You lost me in a card game? Some sick Dark Caster game?"

"It wasn't like that."

"What was it like, Rid? You sold me out and then you lied to me about it ever since?"

"I feel awful, Shrinky Dink. You have to believe me. And I thought it would be good for you. I thought you'd get a chance to be in a real band, even if it was a Caster one."

"What else, Ridley?"

Rid didn't say anything.

"The other marker. You said there were two. What else do you owe him?" Link didn't even say his name. She had the feeling he was dreading the answer as much as she had been dreading the question.

"It was a house marker," she said.

"What does that even mean?"

"When you're playing for TFPs, it means the house calls it." She shrugged. "They can ask me for anything, and I'd have to do it." She took a breath. "I mean, I will have to do it."

"Anything." It wasn't a question, and she didn't answer it. He stared down the street into the rain. "For how long?"

"A year."

"What if you don't do it?"

"I don't have a choice. I'm Bound. Those were the terms of the game. I can't undo it. Believe me, if I could, I would've already."

"What if I don't want to be his drummer?" Link asked. *His. Nox's.* The unspoken name hanging over this whole conversation. "What if I say no?"

"I don't know what would happen to me. I guess I'd find out. One way or another." Ridley shivered.

They sat in silence while the rain fell.

"That's the truth, Link. Everything. No more lies. Not between us."

She reached out and put a hand on his arm. He shrugged it off.

The rain kept falling.

So this is what it feels like? To tell one truth? One time? To even just one person?

See what happens? See what it gets you?

When Link finally looked at her, Rid knew what he was going to say before he said it. "I can't, Rid. I can't do this anymore."

This wasn't a fight. It was something different.

Something worse.

"I know." She looked up into the rainy sky. "I don't blame you."

As she walked off down the Brooklyn street, Ridley realized she had absolutely no idea what she was going to do, or where she was going.

Only that she had to go.

Because telling the truth? It gets you nothing. The truth was too expensive. It wasn't worth it.

Because right now it felt just as sad, and just as heavy, as a lie. Ridley wondered if regular people knew that.

CHAPTER 20

The Divine Wings of Tragedy

Even through the double glass, the black-painted brick, and the exposed steel girders of Nox's suite, he could still hear the thump and whine of Sirene's house music.

The DJ was going wild, mashing up iconic Caster and Mortal music; listening to his remixes, you would think Madonna was a Siren herself.

She's not, but she could have been.

Nox stared out the floor-to-ceiling windows of his private office, looking down at the empty stage. It was his war room, his command central. Nox was more comfortable here than anywhere else in the world. The main floor of the club threatened too many perilous potential reunions.

Too many Ravenwoods to watch out for. Too many Incubuses in one place. That's not even counting the Darkborns.

He hardly even dared set foot in his apartment now, not since the Vexes had started showing up.

Nox loosened the skinny retro tie that hung around his neck.

As he watched, the roadies wheeled the drum kit offstage. It was done. One cog connected to the next, like he was an engineer instead of an entrepreneur. Nox should've considered the night a victory, which was a rare pleasure. Something he hadn't felt since the fateful game at Suffer. When the very first cog began to turn...

They never learn. Don't bet against the house.

His mind flickered to the image of a certain blond, with a certain pink stripe and a knack for trouble.

She was more than he'd imagined. He wondered if she remembered him. He didn't know if he wanted her to or not. It had been a long, long time.

Don't get attached. You're almost there. You could finally get Abraham Ravenwood off your back if you deliver the hybrid and the Siren.

The thought made him ill, so he thought about something else.

Anything.

The club. The crowd. The band.

So many powerful problems.

A troubled Necromancer. An Illusionist with a secret. An Incubus marked for death. A Darkborn in hiding. A Siren with a past.

His money was on the Siren.

She'd taken them all on—if by her attitude alone—and she'd

do it again. Nobody could rein her in. Except for the sister. The sister seemed to be an exception to the rule.

Just as his sister had been for him.

It was interesting, really. Family, as a concept. When it worked—which wasn't often, in the Caster world—the bond was like no other Binding in the universe.

And these two have the bond, he thought. The Siren and the Thaumaturge, if he'd read the younger girl's powers correctly. It was almost sad to watch. Nox was well aware of what some of his business associates would do with that kind of information. And with the leverage it afforded them.

Especially the Ravenwoods.

In terms of his associates and clients, the Ravenwoods were the worst. Some families were like that. You didn't reign for four hundred years as one of the most powerful families in the supernatural universe without developing a certain coldness, an indifference to suffering, Mortal and Caster alike.

The whole thing was really a shame. The little Siren was starting to grow on him. It would be a terrible waste to let anything happen to her.

What choice do I have?

The Incubus was another story. Nox disliked anything remotely Mortal, and this one was stinking of it. It wasn't his fault; it was how he was raised.

Still, that didn't stop Nox from wondering how it would all play out. He was trapped, just another one of Abraham Ravenwood's pawns.

Nox let his eyes flicker over to the cigar box on his desk.

No. I need to stay out of it.

There was no reason to get drawn into a battle that wasn't his to fight.

Nox pushed himself away from the window and went to sit at his desk. He leaned back in his chair, averting his eyes from the fireplace that lit the central part of his underground office.

The overstuffed chairs in front of the hearth sat empty, the way they always did. Nox never sat that close to the fire. He didn't like fire. He didn't like the things he saw when he looked into it: terrible things, wondrous things, images that tormented him in his sleep.

It was his gift, and his curse, like the old storybooks said. He could see the world, everything around him, and everyone. How it ended, and when, and why. How they ended, and when, and why.

Unless it involved him.

Lennox Gates was gifted with Sight and cursed with blindness—or vice versa, depending on how you looked at it.

Blindness could be a gift. His Sight had always felt more like the curse.

But when does power not feel like pain? His mother used to say it to him when he was a little boy. He'd always found it to be true.

She hadn't been wrong yet.

The fire beckoned.

Nox tried to pull himself away, but it was too late. The flames had taken hold of him. His eyes traveled down to the blue root of the fire itself.

The blue divided itself into strands of light that moved together and apart, again and again, until they formed shapes instead of lines, and pictures instead of light.

Nox was nearly overcome by the smell of burning flesh.

That, and the screaming. A girl.

The girl. The Siren.

The screaming was too much for Nox. It was a kind of ceaseless sobbing—a pure expression of death.

It gave him chills.

Nox could hear her but he couldn't see her.

He pushed and the billows of smoke parted, as if he'd walked through them.

In a way, he had.

There she was, surrounded by fire and pinned by a burning beam of wood. Probably the splintered support of a now-fallen ceiling.

Now the screaming became distinct words, familiar words.

Ancient words.

> *By the will of the Gods*
> *By the will of the Gods*
> *I see everything that happens*
> *On the known earth.*
> *I know you see this, Nox.*
> *I know you see me, right now.*
> *You told me you could,*
> *remember?*
> *Don't just sit there.*
> *Do something.*
> *Help me.*
> *Save me!*

The smoke stung his eyes, and he tried to keep looking at her, but he knew it wouldn't last. The room was caving in around her.

Soon she'd—

Soon the screaming would stop.

So would the vision.

The dead left no stories to tell.

At least, not the way Nox saw them.

Fire, he thought.

She dies by fire.

He saw a fleeting succession of images, one after another. A wooden staircase. Flames, reaching into the heavens. The sky.

Then the wood began to crash around him, and the sobbing was muffled, and with a sudden shock, Nox realized he knew exactly where she was.

Nox found himself standing next to the fireplace, his hand resting on the mantel. *Strange.* He didn't usually move during a vision. He always dreaded putting Necro into that state himself. He couldn't imagine what it would be like to regularly lose control of his body.

Abandoning your own flesh was practically begging for someone else to take it for a spin.

Nox didn't like it, even for a minute.

He looked up from the grate, where the carved mantelpiece rose into a ceremonial coat of arms over the center of the stone hearth.

He traced the emblem of his house with his fingers. A bird and a snake, flying directly toward each other. It was the same emblem he'd seen in the last moment of his vision, carved into the burning wood.

The same wood he was touching now. It was a repeating pattern, carved at least once in nearly every room, throughout the paneled walls of Sirene.

It's possible that the Siren is going to die in this very club, he thought with a pang.

A pang of what? Guilt? Remorse? Curiosity?

She will die. By fire.

His last thought scared him: *Because of me.*

It was the most likely scenario.

Nox couldn't be sure; he could never see his own future. But if she were to die in this room, it would probably be at his hand.

It was the way the Wheel of Fate was rolling. There was nothing he could do to stop it....

For the first time in his entire life, Lennox Gates found himself wondering if he could be wrong.

Or if he just wanted to be.

⊰ CHAPTER 21 ⊱

Expendable Youth

The next day, Lennox stared at Necro across the subway tracks. He needed her one more time. It was cold and damp in these tunnels, yet there she sat in a tattered white T-shirt and ripped jeans. A tattooed coil of barbed wire snaked its way up and down her bare arms. The chain-bound combat boots recalled her inner Necromancer.

Good. I want her to be tough.

Nox didn't take threats from the Otherworld lightly, and that was precisely what he was dealing with here. Even dead Incubuses tended to have friends in low places. Lately, he had taken even greater precautions. He made sure Necro hadn't been followed. He had sealed off the Underground stop, even from Casters. He'd dragged a broken-down bench over for her to sit on.

Then he'd compelled the Necromancer out of her warm bed and guided her here.

He didn't feel any better about it, but he didn't have a choice. Who was he to mess with things like vengeance and fate?

Destiny. There is an Order of Things, even now.

When the dead called for you, you had to listen. What often started with a message from the other side quickly became a premonition and then a hallucination. By the time the nightmares began, nothing good followed. After his last night, he knew it was time to talk to Abraham. The Otherworld had a thousand powerful connections and reconnections to this one. It wasn't like Nox could ignore the call, no more than it was his fault that Necro had to take it. There wasn't another Necromancer in his employ. And she'd displayed an uncanny gift for channeling the Ravenwoods in particular. Not to mention, a willingness to do it, so long as she didn't have to carry the Ravenwoods around with her, in her conscious mind.

Nox didn't know why, but he depended on her.

The candles were smoking. Halfway melted, down to inch-high stumps of white wax. Necro's head tipped back, exposing her pale neck.

Necromancers happened to be the most valuable when they were the most vulnerable. Sleep created the clearest connection.

He was running out of time. He could only have so many of these conversations before Necro would remember. Besides, the Royal Barbados cigar box on his desk at Sirene was almost empty now.

His mother had always kept the box full, for those times when Abraham visited, which was probably the reason the cigars were such powerful conduits now. Nox could still recall Abraham sitting on the creaking settee on the veranda of his family's island home—hovering like a threat over his parents, like the dark cloud Abraham had been for as long as Nox had known him.

He was the one family friend who most often dropped by, to be anything but friendly. Which was understandable, considering Abraham Ravenwood was so busy being too many other things.

Say, for example, an extortionist. Or a thief. Or a prison guard. Sometimes even an executioner.

All the while savoring these nasty cigars.

Nox stared at the golden cigar paper and touched the tiny crown stamped on its side. Lost in another time.

If my mother had only listened. If my father had only believed me. If only Abraham hadn't had the whole Dark world wired to his own puppet strings.

Even from the Otherworld.

Hopefully this business would wrap itself up soon, one way or another. Nox needed to move on. There was only so much living in the past a person could stand before they started to lose their mind.

Particularly when the past was this toxic.

There was no putting it off any longer. Nox lit the cigar and looked away.

Better get this meet-and-greet started.

Almost instantly, Necro's eyes opened. "Boy," the voice bellowed out of her limp mouth.

"I'm right here." Nox nodded across the tracks. "Like I said I'd be, when you sent that posse of Vexes to rattle around at my place last night. Message received, old man."

"You talk a big game, yet you continue to be a disappointment." Necro's gold eyes rolled up as she spoke, leaving the glowing white that always made Nox think of the inside of an oyster.

"You're still singing that same song, Mr. Ravenwood." Nox flicked ash from the cigar. The smoke burned in his nostrils. "The song of a dead man."

"I'm done singin'. Like I'm done waitin' for you to fight my battles."

"Good. I was getting tired of fighting them. Unlike some of us, I have a life to live."

"I said I was done waitin'. I didn't say I was done with you."

"I thought—"

"You don't think about anything but yourself and your idiotic clubs. You're a stain on the Caster race, Lennox Gates. Come to think of it, you have been since you were a little boy." Necro gave him an angry smile.

Nox snapped. "If that's the case, then why I am the one you're talking to? Where are your own beloved grandchildren now? Because I'd be happy to leave your nasty affairs to them."

Necro shook her head, swinging her wild blue faux-hawk. "None of your business. Not anymore. Now that you've outlived your usefulness."

Nox averted his eyes and blew on the cigar ash, holding it away from his face. "Name one person who still visits your grave. Even one, Abraham." Nox waited, and smiled. "That's what I thought."

Then the word came, suddenly and improbably, flying at him from out of the blue. A brick through an unsuspecting window.

"Silas."

Necro smiled as she said it, all teeth.

The cold seeped through Nox at the sound of the name. He

183

started to say something—most likely, something as bitter as he felt—but caught himself.

Careful. Silas Ravenwood is nothing to joke about. Watch yourself.

Nox cleared his throat and began again. "Silas Ravenwood is a busy man. And from what I hear, he's a whole lot Darker than his son, Macon. More like his grandfather, wouldn't you say?" His heart pounded. He needed to get out of this conversation, fast.

"Silas has always done me proud."

"That criminal? I hear he's too occupied with building the biggest Blood Incubus syndicate in the Underground to visit anyone's grave. If he had time for you, why hasn't he been dealing with your business instead of me?"

The answer was a slow, low drawl. "Not everyone has a Necromancer in their employ, boy. Makes you easier to reach than most, from where I sit. You've always stood too close to this side of the veil, like you already knew you were a dead man." The old man's laughter echoed through the tunnel. "Don't you worry about Silas. He has a part to play in all this. Unlike you, he'll be ready to play it when the time comes. In fact, he'll be stopping by Sirene to give you my regards."

The thought made Nox's stomach twist into a knot. He tried to sound like himself, but he was suddenly having trouble remembering what that was supposed to sound like. "I look forward to it."

"If I wasn't clear enough, boy, that was a threat."

"I picked up on that."

"You know what you have to do. Make sure you do it, or Silas will."

"Another threat?" Nox asked.

"Your choice. Your coffin."

"I'll take your word for it, dead man. Considering I don't actually own a coffin, myself."

Necro growled. "You will, unless you hand over the people who put me here, boy. Especially the Siren and the hybrid Incubus."

"So you've said." Nox had to keep stalling. He'd already survived this long. He just needed more time to figure out his end game. It was one thing to pretend to do business with Abraham Ravenwood. It was another thing to spill blood on his behalf.

Necro grunted. "It's not a request."

Nox drew a breath. "Don't be so dramatic. When haven't I done everything you've asked?" It was true, as much as Nox hated to admit it. It hadn't been easy, but he'd made a few suggestions here and there. He had delivered both the Siren and the Incubus, at least as far as the club. His form of Persuasion wasn't as obvious as a lollipop, but it was infinitely more powerful. Not even the most powerful Natural in a millennium had seen him coming.

"If you had done everything I'd asked, you'd be digging graves by now." Necro-Abraham did not look impressed.

"It's happening. The plans are in motion. I can give you both of them if you give me enough time." Just because Nox hadn't decided what to do didn't mean he couldn't do it. He was his mother's son. He believed in options.

"Then why are they still alive?"

It was a legitimate question. Nox had been wondering how to answer it. Stalling would only buy him a little time. Eventually, it would run out for everyone, and heads would roll.

His and theirs.

He gazed across the tracks. "You're a greedy old man, Mr. Ravenwood. Greedy and impatient."

"I'm a dead man, Lennox. You know what the problem is with dead men? We've got nothin' to lose."

"Sometimes," Nox said, "neither do the living."

Necro drew her switchblade out of her pocket, moving it up to her neck, guided by Abraham Ravenwood, the monster inside her.

She pressed the blade so hard against her skin that Nox was sure she was going to cut herself.

"Is that so, Lennox?" Abraham's voice rasped from her lips.

Nox froze.

The point pushed deeper.

"I've made contact with Silas now. There are other Necromancers. I don't need this one anymore. But you seem mighty fond of her."

Do not react. Do not let him see you flinch.

The skin was beginning to separate beneath the point of the knife. A thin trickle of blood was racing down the pale skin of her neck.

If he thinks you care, she'll be dead. You can't do that to her.

Nox sighed. "If it means less time spent talking to you, I'll slit her throat myself. Obviously."

"Obviously." Necro pulled the knife away from her skin and held it out to Nox with an eerie smile. "Be my guest," she growled.

Nox stood there for a long moment. Then he tossed the cigar down onto the tracks.

The longer he stayed, the more danger his Necromancer would be in. He was powerless; all he could do was go.

It wasn't a feeling Nox Gates liked.

As he walked away, all he could hear was the sound of bitter laughter echoing through the tunnel behind him.

◄ CHAPTER 22 ►

Damaged Soul

How's it going, Rid?" Lena's voice crackled over the speaker of Ridley's new cell phone. Nick the Nerd Warrior was a good friend, and she had the reception to prove it.

Aside from that, there wasn't much to feel good about. It had been a long day of work for Ridley, who, though no closer to finding her dream than before, had at least determined it did not involve Mortal hair.

Ridley sighed. "Great. Perfect. Like a dream come true, Cuz."

Monday Tuesday Wednesday Thursday Friday. So many days for nothing but work. Why do there have to be so many of them in a row?

Her feet hurt. Her hands had some kind of itchy rash, probably from disgusting scalp fungus. The heel had snapped off one of her black Louboutin ankle boots on the subway. Talking to her cousin only made it worse.

"Is New York amazing?" Lena asked.

"The most." Ridley tried not to let Lena hear her sniffle. She held the phone away from her face and then brought it back to her ear again.

She caught a glimpse of Lucille Ball sitting in the doorway of the kitchen, judging her. Ridley made a face at the cat, but Lucille didn't so much as move.

"Have you seen all the sights?" Lena sounded excited. It only made Ridley feel guiltier, like she should have returned one of her cousin's fifty messages before now.

"Yep. That's why they're called sights, L. You see them." She didn't elaborate on what glam sights she had managed to see. *Like the dirty subway tunnels, the old diner. Oily ladies' scalps, reeking trash cans in the streets.*

"What about the club scene? Charming your way into fabulous restaurants and amazing boutiques?"

"You know me. I'm practically out of lollipops."

"I'm so jealous. All I do is study, study, study," Lena complained. "Although I got into this writing class. It's a poetry seminar, actually, and the professor is really great. I didn't think..."

Blah, blah, blah.

The conversation faded into a strange collage of images Ridley couldn't—and to be fair, didn't really want to—process.

Red cups and college sweatshirts and late-night pizza and dorm restrooms. Football games. The dining hall. *The Creation of Adam* and *Guernica* and Hopper's *Nighthawks* and the life of Buddha.

Did she really say public restrooms? With the kind of showers that you have to wear shoes in?

The conversation ended when Lena had to go to something called a study group to talk about things called handouts—or something like that.

What could Ridley say?

There was no way to explain the jam she'd gotten herself into, or the mood she was in.

How could someone as Light as Lena understand cheating at a card game and losing a marker, let alone two? How could Lena believe that someone was controlling Link and his stupid band, and using them for their own secret agenda? Worst of all, how could her cousin hear or solve or even understand the one problem that loomed over all the others?

Him and his stupid club. His threats and his lies.

Ridley herself could hardly stand to even think his name.

The phone crackled. "Are you listening, Rid?"

"Yeah, of course. I'm here. I'm just tired."

"I'm worried about you. Every time I think of you lately, my ring turns bloodred. Like fire. Sometimes it even burns my finger."

Red? Ridley's ring always turned green.

"I'm sure it's nothing." Ridley glanced down. Now Lucille Ball was sitting at her feet, looking at her with enormous cat eyes, as if to say *Red? Really?*

Lucille Ball was not pleased.

"I asked Ethan, and he said Link never has time to talk," Lena said.

"Well, you know. Rock stars."

Lucille thumped her tail. *Tell her.*

"You'd tell me if something was going on, right?"

Lucille thumped her tail again. *Tell your cousin.*

Ridley ignored the cat. "Of course."

"Anything the least bit out of the ordinary?" Lena asked.

"I'm fine. Everything's fine. Honestly, I've never been happier. Or more ordinary."

Lucille howled, stalking out of the room.

By the time Ridley hung up the phone, she'd told so many lies she could barely remember her own name. She knew that her life in New York was nothing close to regular, and more importantly, nothing close to a success. She had lied on the phone to her cousin, and she had been lying to herself. She was not cut out for this. It wasn't who she was.

Link was right. She didn't belong here. Maybe the two of them really were through.

Maybe this week's breakup was for real.

She couldn't ask him, though, because he was avoiding her, spending all his time with Floyd in the practice room.

By the time she went to bed, she felt like crying. By the time she fell asleep, she was. Even in her dreams.

"I told you not to wear that old thing. You look like a hair ball some cat vomited up."

Ridley pulled on her cousin's sleeve, twisting the knit sweater out of shape. She knew she was being mean. She even felt mean, but she didn't care.

Her cousin might as well be walking around with a big old target on her forehead.

"Shut up, Rid." Lena looked like she wanted to shrink back into her locker.

"That sweater says Kick Me." Ridley pinched her harder.

Lena was standing by the lockers, because Lena was always standing by the lockers. It was as far as she'd venture into the open waters of middle school.

Ridley had no problem venturing anywhere, on the other hand. It was just the trouble that ventured with her wherever she went that was the problem.

"Did you even do your geography homework?" Lena asked with a sigh.

"Why do you care?" Ridley sighed back, one hand on her hip. She was wearing her favorite outfit: a kilt she'd cut off short with her Gramma's scissors, a T-shirt with the neck ripped out, and a pair of old black boots she'd found in someone else's locker, two schools ago.

Her first heels. They made her feel good. Tall, like she could look down on everyone in the whole world, the way she liked it.

Lena handed her a piece of paper covered in pencil scribbles. "Here."

"Aww, you doing my homework now, just in case?"

"Someone has to."

Ridley held up her hands, refusing to take the paper. "Has it ever occurred to you, L, that what happens at this miserable little Mortal school doesn't matter?"

"Stop." Lena was embarrassed.

"None of these stupid little brats—" Ridley raised her voice even louder.

"They're not brats. Not all of them." Lena looked around uncomfortably.

"Or their stupid teachers."

"I like my teachers."

"Or their stupid history. Their stupid laws. Their stupid sciences."

"Rid."

"It doesn't matter. Not for us Casters. Not where we're going. Not with the kind of life we're gonna have."

"It matters to me."

Ridley slammed her cousin's locker shut. Lena could just make her so mad sometimes. She was a punching bag for Mortals. She had begged to go to Mortal school—she tried so hard to please them, all the time. And she was just so bad at it.

Better not to try.

Better not to expect to be invited to their birthday parties and their trips to the mall.

Better to know the teachers weren't going to call on you.

Better not to care.

But as soon as Ridley slammed the locker door, she regretted it—not only for the look on her cousin's face, but for the crowd it attracted.

She had forgotten the first rule of going to Mortal school: Lay low.

Even for a girl who hated rules, that was the one rule Ridley had the hardest time with. Who wanted to lay low when you had it in you to fly high?

Only Lena.

Who was now being circled by a crowd of girls so skinny-legged and straight-haired and mean-spirited that they made their own mothers look friendly.

"Cute sweater, Lena. Where'd you get it?" The girl closest to her, Caitlyn Wheatley, purred. She pinched the greenish-gray sleeve. Lena just stood there letting her do it. She always let them do it, which was why they did it in the first place.

"I don't know," Lena mumbled.

"Maybe your mamma knitted it for you from prison?" That wasn't Caitlyn. That was Sandra Marsh, who never could resist a good whupping, so long as she wasn't on the receiving end.

Lena didn't say anything.

Ridley sighed.

"Maybe your old granny knitted it for you in the old folks' home? Isn't that where you live with her?" Caitlyn moved closer. The rest of the hallway began to look on with interest. It was a familiar scene. They knew they were just getting to the good part.

Lena tried to walk away. The little posse of girls followed.

Caitlyn raised her voice. "You look like cat puke, you know that? Like a big old hair ball my cat just threw up onto the carpet."

That was it.

Ridley slammed her own locker door, and Caitlyn stopped in her tracks. "I'm the only one around here who gets to say what looks like cat puke, and I say it's your face."

The hallway started to laugh.

"Don't," Lena said, looking at her cousin.

Ridley shrugged as she slipped a piece of bubble gum out of her bag and unwrapped it.

"And you want to know why I say that?" Ridley kept on going. "Because I was there, Caitlyn, when your own cat puked it up, and I was there when you ate it."

More laughter.

Ridley popped the pink square of gum into her mouth.

"Shut up," Caitlyn said. "Liar."

"Yeah," Sandra said. "You're makin' that up, and it's disgustin'."

"Am I?" Ridley asked. She looked from Caitlyn to Sandra. "Caitlyn, tell Sandra the truth." Ridley began to chew.

"What are you talkin' about, freak?" Caitlyn glared.

"Tell Sandra what you did at your house yesterday. Right in front of me." Rid looked encouraging. She chewed harder.

"Rid," Lena pleaded. It was the same warning she always gave, and the same one Rid always ignored.

"Tell all of them." Ridley smiled, blowing a round, pink bubble.

Caitlyn had a strange look on her face now. She looked up at Sandra like she herself was the one about to be sick. Then she looked out to the sea of faces in the hall of Albert Einstein Middle School.

"I ate cat vomit." The words were strangled in Caitlyn's throat. Sandra looked at her, disgusted.

"She's just joking," Lena said. No one listened.

"And?" Ridley said, encouraging.

"I ate cat vomit, and I liked it," Caitlyn mumbled, looking stricken.

"And?" Ridley asked.

"And I'll do it again tomorrow." Tears ran down Caitlyn's face.

The laughter was so loud that it was hard to hear her.

Lena ran away, out the door of the administration building, through the gates of the school.

Rid didn't catch up to her for three more blocks.

By the time she grabbed Lena's arm and forced her to stop,

Lena was no longer crying. Her face was red and her eyes were flashing.

"Why did you do that?"

"Because," Ridley lied, "I can." It wasn't the only reason. It was just the only one Lena expected her to say.

Now she was holding her cousin by both arms.

"I can, and they can't. It will always be like that. You will never be one of them. Neither will I. They'll never be good enough or bad enough for either one of us."

"Why does it always have to be like this?" Lena looked as tormented as Caitlyn Wheatley, in her own way.

"Does it matter? You can't change the way it is. Stay away from Mortals. They bring out a bad, bad side in us."

At least, Ridley thought, in me.

Bad to the bone.

Bad to the bone and I haven't even been Claimed yet.

They never went back to that school again, but Ridley didn't care. She had already learned everything she needed to know.

Ridley woke up thinking about Caitlyn Wheatley for the first time in years. She wondered what had happened to her. Maybe she'd ask Nick the Nerd Warrior to find out. These days, she had much worse problems than Caitlyn Wheatley. Far more annoying Mortals were bringing out her bad side now.

Even if the one she was thinking about wasn't completely Mortal, and there had been a time, not that long ago, when he would've gladly said he'd eaten cat puke for her.

Just as Ridley had made Caitlyn Wheatley say it for Lena. And after Caitlyn Wheatley, so many others.

Ridley lay back in her bed.

She had been the one to do it. She had always been the one.

I had to be.

I was Dark so Lena could be Light.

It was who they were, but it was more than that. It was who their world had expected them to be. After a while, it was who they expected themselves to be.

Has it always been that way? Does it have to be?

Rid pushed the question from her mind. It didn't matter. She couldn't change the way these things worked. She should've remembered the basic rule of living among the Mortals: *Lay low or stay away.*

Otherwise they'd always burn you.

CHAPTER 23

Comfortably Numb

Sirensong was on their way to rock the house.

Ridley hadn't wanted to go back to Sirene. Link avoided her now, like she was worse than Emily Asher, but Rid refused to send him into Lennox Gates' club alone and unprotected.

So she was Sirensong's first groupie.

First, and most hated.

This is not how I imagined my "regular" life, Ridley thought.

"I don't feel so hot," Necro said. She leaned her head back against the rough stone of the Underground. Her face was pale, and as she closed her eyes, she looked weaker than Ridley remembered.

Floyd looked at Necro sideways. "You want to go back?"

"I can take her," said Rid quickly, fidgeting in her sixties silver shift dress. She and Necro hadn't exactly been speaking lately, and it bothered Ridley more than she cared to admit.

Besides, Sampson and Link were already at Sirene. Floyd could still make it.

Necro shook her head. "No way am I going to not show for my own gig."

"What's that?" Ridley reached for the collar of Necro's leather jacket. Necro yanked her hand away before she could even touch it.

"Personal space, Siren." Necro glared.

"Wait, you're bleeding." Rid moved Necro's collar down. Blood was spotting the white tank beneath Necro's black leather jacket, and Ridley wondered why they hadn't seen it before.

Necro touched her neck, and her fingers came away a deep, dark red. At least, that was what color Ridley thought it was, though it was more deep and dark than red. "It's nothing."

"It's not nothing. You're hurt. What happened?" Floyd looked worried.

"Nothing happened." Necro stared straight ahead, as if she was willing her friends to disappear.

But they weren't about to, Floyd in particular. "Nec."

"I don't know, okay? I went to sleep. I woke up. My neck was bleeding." Necro pulled a dirty black scarf covered in white skulls out of her pocket. She tied it around her neck.

"Where?" Floyd was somber.

"In the neck, brainiac." Necro was as grouchy as she was ill.

"Come on, Nec. Where did you wake up?" Floyd sounded anxious.

Rid interrupted. "Um, I'm guessing she woke up in her bed? What the hell kind of question is that?"

Floyd raised an eyebrow. "Necro's a sleepwalker."

"What?"

Necro shrugged. "I wake up in strange places sometimes. I think it has to do with being a—you know. Being me."

No Necromancer ever wanted to say the word, as if death was catching. Not even Necro said the whole word, usually.

She went on. "I have horrible nightmares, I wake up, I feel like total garbage, and I find my way home. Sometimes I stink like smoke. But I've never been actually hurt before."

Ridley shook her head. "That's not good."

"No kidding," said Floyd. She wasn't joking around anymore.

"It's no big deal," Necro said, stumbling down the length of the tunnel. "Really, guys."

It was a lie. Ridley had told enough of them herself to recognize a lie when she heard one. She wondered what had actually happened. If Necro was anything like her, she'd never tell.

She held out her arm to help Necro walk, but Necro didn't take it.

They were more alike than Ridley had thought.

It wasn't even four o'clock. They still had hours until the gig began, but Link and Sampson were already messing around onstage. From the moment Ridley passed through the door—the bouncer offering no complaints this time around—the music crept toward her. The music and, carrying with it, what it meant.

Who she would have to deal with—or what she'd have to say. That she was sorry. That she was worried. That she cared about him. Them.

Not that she would say it.

Not that anyone would listen.

She stood there watching, from the back of the main room, which would stay closed off to the general public for three more hours, as it did every afternoon. The stage loomed on the far side of the cavernous space, lights up and sound system live, as if the show was about to start—which it wasn't. They still had time to warm up.

Not that they needed it. Things had been pretty warm this past week. At least, that was how it looked to anyone but a Siren. The lines were long and the crowds were raving, and Ridley still had no idea why or how.

She had an idea but was minus the facts to back it up.

It wasn't because of the music. Link's musical taste had gone from bad to worse, as if the whole band was infected with it now. Link was trying out new lyrics while Ridley stood there, and when she could make out the words, they were so bad she wished she couldn't.

> *"My Chicken Wing / You make my gut sing*
> *You make everything / Really swing.*
> *Dipped in batter / Heart goes pitter-patter*
> *Do your wild thing / My Chicken Wing."*

He continued the set, singing, *"Cole Slaw / Get under my craw,"* and *"Fried Pick-le / Love how you rib tick-le."* Pretty soon there would be no major food groups left to write about, and he'd have to get a new muse. The way things were going, though, Ridley was fairly confident it wasn't going to be her.

She sighed, leaning against the doorway as she watched her not-quite-boyfriend rock out on the stage. Within minutes,

Necro and Floyd would join in, and soon the whole band would be singing about whatever picnic basket of nonsense Link had decided was worth their time.

And a few hours later, for unseen and unknown reasons, the crowd would be eating it up. Wesley Lincoln, formerly of Meatstik, and of the Holy Rollers and Who Shot Lincoln before that, was making it big-time as Sirensong. The hottest new indie act of the Caster Underground club scene.

Wesley Lincoln, a quarter Incubus and the worst drummer in five boroughs, above or below the ground. *Him, and his cole slaw, and his fried chicken, and his sweet meatballs.*

Ridley shook her head. She should text a picture to Ethan and Lena. They'd never believe this. Lena had already thought Ridley was kidding when she'd told her about it on the phone. Talk about being on the lookout for something out of the ordinary. The success of Sirensong should've been the first clue.

"Do you mind if I ask you something?" The voice caught her off guard, but she recognized it before she turned to see him.

"Would that stop you from asking?" Ridley looked at Nox.

He shrugged. *Not really.*

"Why are you with him? Why bother?" Nox stood next to her now, watching the band.

"What are you talking about?" Ridley moved closer to the stage, ignoring Nox as best she could. What she was or wasn't actually doing was no business of his, she thought.

"Not meatballs," Nox teased. "I promise you that much."

Link was prancing around on the stage, playing the air guitar. At least, Ridley thought it was an air guitar. From the looks of it, it also could have been an air accordion or even some kind of air DustBuster.

Ridley tried not to appear openly annoyed, but Nox just laughed.

"Look at him. The big lump of idiot Incubus muscle and Mortal mental limitations."

She glared at him. "I'm sorry, are you talking about my boyfriend?" *My almost-ex-boyfriend. But Lennox Gates doesn't need to know that.*

"Am I? I'm not sure, to be honest." Nox looked at her over his glass, amused. "Is that what he is? Really?"

"Do you speak English?"

He laughed. "English, not Idiot." He gestured toward the stage. "Speaking of which, some of his lyrics I find hard to understand."

She raised an eyebrow. "That's funny, because every time you open your mouth, Idiot is all I hear."

"You and him? That's not a relationship. If you think it is, Little Siren, you're in worse shape than I thought. Or should I call you Little Chicken Wing?"

"You could. But then I'd do this." Ridley slapped him as hard as she could.

Nox winced, rubbing his jaw. "All right. Okay. Truce."

She ignored him.

"You know why I make you so angry? Why I get right under your skin? We're two of a kind, you and me." He dropped his hand. She could see his eyes pulling toward her. She looked away.

"Don't flatter yourself."

"Birds of a feather. Peas in a pod. Casters out of the same Dark handbook." Nox winked. Ridley wanted to hit him even harder than she had before.

"You are so, so wrong."

"Am I? And here I thought we were so simpatico."

Her temper flared. "Simpatico? How? There's nothing likable about you, and barely anything likable about me. In fact, we're just about the two worst people I know." It was how she felt about herself lately, and it made her feel a little better to finally be able to say it out loud.

Because it's true, she thought. *And it always will be. No matter how many jobs I get or how hard I try. No matter how badly I want to change.*

How regular I want to be.

Nox nodded agreeably. "The worst. Exactly. Maybe we got off on the wrong foot and we were meant to be friends, in our own twisted way. Just like, I don't know, *Link Floyd*?"

She swung up her arm to slap him again, but this time he caught it.

Nox shrugged. "We are who we are. I'm a Rolls, he's a— what does he call it? A Beater?"

"Maybe," Ridley said as she pulled her hand away. "But if I wanted a Rolls, Mr. Gates, don't you think I'd just Charm a chauffeur?" She examined her silver nails.

He ignored her. "I own the club, which means I own your little boyfriend, too."

Ridley twisted the pink streak in her hair expertly. "And if I wanted a club, Mr. Gates, don't you think I'd just Charm the club owner?"

"Who says you haven't?" He smiled. "Now that you mention it, who says he hasn't Charmed you?"

She rolled her eyes. "In your dreams." Now Ridley's hand was at her tiny silver clutch, casually flicking the lock, casually drawing her fingers inside.

"Would you like to be?" His voice dropped, dark and husky.

She laughed. There was some new angle to this game, and it wasn't lost on her. Ridley was an expert at playing the angles. "Why are you trying so hard, Mr. Gates? I'm flattered, but we both know this isn't about me."

"You're a Siren. I thought everything was always about you."

"No, really. What's changed since our last conversation? Why don't you just tell me what you want from me?" Ridley leaned forward. "Can't take the pressure? Your goons coming for you? Let me guess—I'm not the only person who owes someone a little something-something around here?" She leaned closer. "Maybe you owe a few markers of your own?"

"You have no idea what you're saying." Nox was annoyed. "So try shutting up about it."

Bull's-eye, she thought.

Ridley reached out to smooth the lapel of his coat with a tiny, victorious smile. "Gladly, Mr. Gates. And here's a little good-bye for you: Whatever it is, I'm not helping you do it, find it, or get it. If it has anything at all to do with that *lump of Mortal mental limitations* up on that stage, you can forget it."

A moment of anger lit his face. "For a Siren, you're really not all that enthralling."

"And you're nobody's sweet meatball," she said, patting his cheek. "Poor thing."

He covered her hand with his, leaning toward her to press his lips briefly against hers. She was breathless, and he took full advantage, biting her bottom lip. A surge of raw energy hit both of them. Ridley pulled away, gasping.

Then she kissed him back, pressing toward him like she was

falling. She couldn't help it. His kiss was like a Cast, and she was the only person Bound by it. Her lips were burning.

I want to slap him, but I want to kiss him. And I want him to kiss me.

As soon as she thought it, Nox pulled away from her, studying her eyes.

"Mmm-mmm," he said. "Just like I thought. You're sweet enough for both of us." Then he stepped through the crowd and was gone.

No.

Ridley backed away, speechless, and fled to the front of the stage, her hand pressed against her lips as if she wished she could rip the kiss right off them.

Too bad she couldn't.

Too bad she had lost control and kissed him back.

Too bad it was at that precise moment that Sirensong's lead Linkubus happened to look up from his drum kit, center stage.

Watching your girlfriend—whether or not you'd broken up—kiss another guy always made something in a guy's head snap, free and clear. Whether you were a Mortal or an Incubus.

Ridley could almost hear it snap, and she could tell from the look on Link's face that there were no questions left. Not for him.

Link was out.

Ridley's eyes blurred as she fought back tears. She could see it in Link's face, even though he wouldn't look at her.

Even though they hadn't said a word to each other.

They didn't need to say anything.

Link's hand was glowing, as red as blood. The ring. Just like Lena had warned her. Ridley had never seen it that color before.

He wasn't singing, but he was pounding on the drums as if he wanted to smash them.

Then he did.

"What the—" Floyd backed away as drum skins and metal and drumsticks and cymbal brass went flying.

Sampson dropped the mic stand.

Link picked up the bass drum and hurled it off the stage. The music stopped. He kicked over the keyboard, smashing it to the floor. It was like watching the Hulk on fast-forward.

He was done.

The stage had become a dark place.

But it was Necro who seemed to be feeling it most. When the bass hit the floor, she hit the floor with it, passing out into a crumpled pile of arms and legs and black leather.

Link looked down at his blue-haired bandmate, panting for breath, his voice raspy. "You okay?"

By the time Ridley pulled herself up onto the stage, Necro was out cold. Rid bent down and caught a glimpse of the girl's neck. The cut was festering, a dark liquid oozing from the wound.

Black blood.

⊰ CHAPTER 24 ⊱

Wish You Were Here

It only took a few seconds for Link to pull off his sweat-soaked T-shirt and wrap it around Necro's neck. Floyd held it there, but the blood kept seeping through.

"That's not a regular cut," Ridley said, hovering. "It wouldn't be bleeding so much."

"Don't you think I know that?" Link snapped.

"Somebody," Floyd said, her face pale. "Somebody help us."

"Link—" Ridley began.

He looked up at Ridley, his hands streaked black with blood. "No. Not now."

"What can I do?" she asked.

Floyd stood up. "Leave."

"I want to help." Ridley was shaking.

Floyd looked like she wanted to slap her. "Nobody cares what you want."

"I didn't mean—"

Floyd's voice rose. "For once will you shut up? This isn't about you."

"Just go," Link said again. "Please, Rid."

Then he scooped Necro up, as carefully as he would one of the Sisters' baby squirrels, and carried her off the stage.

I really am the worst person in the world. Worse, even, than a Mortal. Worse than Lennox Gates himself.

It didn't even take the whole cab ride for Ridley to come to that conclusion.

Link had told her to go, and so she'd gone, with nothing except the clothes on her back and a pocketful of lollipops. She'd Charmed the first taxi she saw and asked the driver to take her to the nicest hotel in New York City.

For once in her life, Ridley wanted to help. And she didn't feel like abandoning all the inhabitants of apartment 2D, which was a new thing for her. And it was ripping her up inside that something was wrong with Necro; even she hadn't seen anything like that before.

And Necro was the only person who had actually been nice to her since she'd gotten to New York.

Ridley felt terrible. She felt responsible. She felt worried. She felt anxious.

These were all unusual feelings for Ridley.

But Link didn't want her around, and Floyd and Sampson cared more about getting Necro back to the apartment than anything else. The best thing she could do for all of them was leave and let them try and help Necro.

She had made this mess that night at Suffer, and she'd only made it worse since then.

It was time for her to go, and it was what Link wanted.

So she left behind Sirene and Marilyn's Diner and apartment 2D and the Brooklyn Blowout. She left behind a sick Necromancer, an Illusionist with eyes for her ex-boyfriend, a highly questionable Darkborn, and a betrayed, brokenhearted quarter Incubus.

Ridley didn't know where she was going, only what she was leaving behind. Which was everything.

When she looked out the window, there was nothing familiar. The city was changing in front of her eyes—the buildings getting taller, the window boxes getting watered, the streetlights getting brighter. This wasn't Brooklyn. New York was the toughest place in the world if you couldn't afford your rent. On the other hand, if you could afford not only your own rent but the rent of a thousand other people, New York was the greatest city in the universe. That was the part of town where Ridley was headed. She couldn't afford it before, but if Link was the only reason she wasn't using her powers, and he didn't want her, there was nothing holding her back.

Seeing as Ridley herself had no interest in being a regular person.

Then again, nobody in this neighborhood was a regular person.

That was all she could think about as she walked into the lobby of Les Avenues Hotel. Seventy-Seventh and Madison, in the heart of Manhattan's Upper East Side, was as far away from Bushwick as Gatlin.

Maybe farther, she thought as she stood looking at the lobby floor of black and white inlaid marble tile, dotted with love seats so modern that you would have to be a gymnast not to roll right off them.

A man in a fedora sat reading a paper on one of them. As he turned the pages, she noticed a glinting signet ring on his finger.

He looked up.

She looked away, her breath catching in her throat.

What is it?

There was something about him that looked familiar, but he was gone before she could think why. Only the paper remained behind, folded on his chair.

Strange.

As Ridley leaned against the front desk, she realized she was exhausted. Exhausted and overwhelmed. *All I want to do is collapse into a bed.* Luckily, a desk clerk appeared as soon as she had the thought.

"Good afternoon. Can I help you?" Even the desk clerk looked more sophisticated than Ridley felt at the moment. Ridley couldn't help but notice the high quality of her blowout. *Glossy ends. Good conditioner. None of the cheap stuff we use.*

"Yes. I have a reservation. Ridley Duchannes." She smiled her best *How little you understand can't you tell by the way I say my name how much it means* smile. It was a new one, one she'd perfected since coming to New York. It worked better if she did the eyebrows with it, but Ridley was too tired to move any other part of her face right now.

The clerk had a smile of her own, and it was nasty stuff. "Did you make it recently? You're not showing up in our computer." She raised a tiny *Do you think I care who you are* eyebrow right back at Ridley.

"That's strange," Ridley said. *Not that strange, since I don't have a reservation at all.*

She waved her hand at the computer. "Can't you do a little something with that thing and fix it?" *Nick the Nerd Warrior would have come in handy right about now.* She eyed her phone wistfully.

"What *little something* do you suggest I try, madame?" The desk clerk raised both eyebrows.

It was no use.

Ridley sighed, unwrapping a cherry lollipop. She didn't want to do it.

Still.

She gave it one last halfhearted try. "I know you have a room for me, Sweet Cheeks. You e-mailed me saying I had been comped for the weekend."

"This isn't Las Vegas, madame. We don't customarily *comp* people." Now the desk clerk allowed her eyes to flicker up and down Ridley's outfit.

It wasn't a compliment.

Ridley sighed again, inserting the lollipop into her mouth. As she did, the flecks of gold in her eyes intensified, until it almost looked like they were glowing with light from within. She could feel the power surging up and out from her body, emanating from her on all sides until the lobby itself seemed lit by a slight golden haze.

"Why don't you look again?"

The woman scrolled down her computer screen. "Sorry. It—it sounds familiar. But I don't have you in the computer."

Ridley raised an eyebrow.

Interesting. She's one tough bird.

"Did I say weekend?" Ridley began. "Because now that I think about it, the letter only said that you had a room for me and I could stay as long as I liked. Free of charge. I think it was something about my fans? Wanting them to know that I had chosen you."

Those were the fundamental rules of Persuasion: Bluff. Never back down. Believe what you're selling. The bigger the ask, the more likely you'll get what you're asking for.

Just not this time.

"I don't have a note of that in my computer. Are you in the entertainment industry?"

"In a manner of speaking."

"Would you like to give me a credit card? I could book you a standard room overlooking the construction on Seventy-Seventh Street. It's a bit smaller than—"

"Did I say room? I meant suite." *Raise the stakes, Siren.*

"We don't have a suite available right now—"

"Did you hear *suite*? I said *penthouse*." *Believe it. You deserve that penthouse. You can't imagine not having that penthouse.* Ridley removed her sunglasses, looking at the woman with the full power of a Siren's eyes.

"She's with me, Penelope."

Ridley was spluttering and infuriated when she turned to see Nox standing behind her, his black leather jacket slung over one shoulder.

Not him. Please. Not now.

"I'm so sorry, Mr. Gates." The clerk was flustered.

"Please, call me Nox." He leaned over the counter, winking at the woman. "Seeing as we're all such close friends here."

"Of course, Mr. Gates."

"You can put her in my sister's rooms. She's away for the moment." He looked at Ridley. "We keep a few apartments here. You never know when they'll come in handy."

Ridley didn't respond.

"Very good, sir." The desk clerk averted her eyes.

Nox smiled at her encouragingly. "Maybe Frederico forgot to give you the message when I called earlier to tell you to expect Ms. Duchannes."

"I do apologize, Mr. Gates. Er, Nox."

Ridley watched the cold-hearted front desk agent melting.

He was good.

Whatever he was, he didn't need sugar. Not a lollipop in sight. He didn't have a tell, as far as Ridley could see. But he had all the power of a Siren.

Did he always? Was he using it on me? Was that why I kissed him? The thought was too unsettling for Ridley to process.

But the evidence was clear. He had some kind of power.

Whatever Lennox Gates was selling, this woman wanted it.

Ridley had never hated him more.

"Are you stalking me?" she hissed at him. He held up a finger. *Not yet.*

Nox motioned toward a bank of elevators. As they walked away from the front desk, Ridley's blood was boiling so loudly she couldn't hear the click of her heels on the black and white striped marble flooring. "What was wrong with that woman? I felt so—so—Mortal." She shuddered.

214

"Welcome to New York."

"You know, every time someone says that to me, I'm starting to understand they mean the opposite." She didn't know why she was talking to him. She shouldn't be. He wasn't worth it.

"Not me. I mean exactly what I say, every word of it."

Liar. Ridley looked at Nox. "The Power of Persuasion couldn't move a hair on that woman's head."

"You should probably consider Les Avenues immune to your powers."

"Immune? As in, I'm nothing here?" The idea was staggering.

"Says everyone who has ever ventured into this neighborhood." Nox laughed at his own joke. Then he gave up. "She's a Darkborn."

"What?"

"The top three floors of this building? All Casters, all powerful, and not exactly the Light variety." He shrugged. "So the bottom floor, the staff? Darkborns. Ultimately impervious to power of any sort. The latest thing in Caster security." He shrugged again. "It works."

"But you could control her."

"Of course. I've got the oldest power of all—an obscene amount of money. My father had the Sight and couldn't resist the Mortal stock market." Nox pressed the elevator button and held out a key card. "Take the room. My sister never uses the place."

Ridley frowned.

"Take it. Think of it as a peace offering. I'm sorry about what happened back at the club. I shouldn't have done it."

The kiss. Even he can't bring himself to say it.

"And I thought you meant everything you said."

"I do." He looked up at the mirrored glass ceiling. "At the time, I meant that, too. I just don't know why I did it." It sounded like he was being honest, but she'd given up on judging Nox Gates by how he appeared.

They were alone in the elevator now. Ridley stared at the elevator buttons. It was the safest place to look—until the elevator lurched to a stop.

Nox watched her face as the elevator door opened. He held it. "I'm starting to think that something in you brings out the very worst in me." The words were painfully familiar. He shook his head. "Or maybe it's all for the best. It's hard to tell lately."

Ridley took a step from the elevator to the hallway beyond the doors. "You don't exactly make me want to be a good girl, if that's what you're saying."

She didn't mean it as a compliment, and she hoped he knew it.

"Fire," he said as she moved past him.

"I'm sorry?" She paused.

He sounded strained. "When I kissed you, I tasted fire. I don't know what it means. I thought you should know." He was rattled.

Curiously rattled, she thought.

"I'm sorry, that probably sounds insane." He looked away.

"Not at all." Ridley shrugged. "That's what all the boys say."

Then she moved down the hallway without a word, and the elevator door slid shut between them.

The black lacquered door waited for her at the far end of the hall. The moment Ridley waved the key card over the lock, she suspected that what lay behind the door would not be anything like apartment 2D.

She was right. Lennox Gates and his sister apparently lived like Prince and Princess Charming.

Or Charmless, she thought.

At least, when they were staying at Les Avenues.

The entry door swung open into a wide foyer. Just as in the lobby, there was a black and white inlaid marble floor, which extended into a living room with a panoramic view of the city. The floor-to-ceiling windows were dizzying. Every surface in the room was reflective—from the polished bamboo cabinets and the massive globe chandeliers suspended from the ceiling to the silver edging on the slab of white marble that served as the coffee table. Low black leather couches surrounded the table, where there was a massive display of white orchids. The remaining surface was occupied by dish after dish of candied fruits and chocolates.

She kicked her shoes off and leaned back on a couch, picking a candied sea horse from a dish. Candied sea horses were her childhood favorite.

Strange.

How could he possibly have known? How could he have been expecting me? Even I didn't know where I was going.

She reached for a cream-colored card, folded in the middle of the dish of candy. *"If you need anything, R, ring the bell. The bath should be almost full by now. Clothes are in the closet."*

Cocky little son of a witch.

The note confirmed what she had already suspected. Lennox Gates had known she was coming, which meant he had some kind of foresight, more even than just a Seer. Reading the future was a rare and limited gift. Reece could only read faces, and she had become completely insufferable. Nox had teased Ridley

217

about her future before, but only in the way that anyone with half a brain could.

If Nox had foresight as well as his other abilities, Ridley had to admit he was one of the most powerful Dark Casters she'd ever encountered. She had known that he could manipulate material objects, that he had some kind of control over the material world. Aside from an Illusionist like Larkin or Floyd— who could only appear to have that sort of gift—the only person Ridley knew who could really do something like that was Lena. Or Sarafine, but she was truly out of the picture now.

At least, that's what Ethan had insisted, ever since he had returned from the Otherworld.

She stared at the card in her hand. The note left Ridley no choice. She had to accept that there was more to Lennox Gates than a love of gambling and nightclubs. There was too much—his powers of Persuasion, Manifestation, and Temporal Distortion—it was too much for one Caster, and she didn't know how or why he had come to be so powerful.

But it was something.

Something that made him either potentially dangerous or potentially useful.

It was an interesting thought.

Ridley leaned back against the couch. She felt awful about Link and worried about Necro.

No wonder they had kicked her out.

She heard the water running in the other room. The bath. She stood up, feeling the soft pile of the thick white rug beneath her feet. Maybe a bath would help her calm down. Think more clearly. Figure out what to do now.

A few bubbles couldn't hurt.

She tried not to look at the enormous bed as she wandered through the bedroom. All she noticed was the circular skylight cut into the ceiling and roof above it. She imagined lying there, studying the stars.

Princess Charming had one hell of a view.

Ridley found the door to the bathroom and shut herself safely inside, where the massive tub was filling itself with rose- and lavender-scented water. Exactly as Lennox Gates had promised it would.

Only then did she let herself cry.

She told herself it was the soap burning her eyes.

Three thick white towels later, Ridley felt like a new person. Wrapped in a plush robe, she toweled dry her long wet hair.

She lectured herself as she stared in the mirror, brushing out her tangled curls.

Pick yourself back up. Get it together, Siren. This is what you do. Stop acting like you care about them. Stop acting like Uncle Macon.

Like you can't accept who you are, how Dark you are. Like you have a choice. Like you have a home.

Like every other door wasn't slammed in your face on the night of your own Claiming.

Let it be.

Ridley put down the brush and stood up, before the face in the mirror revealed anything to the contrary.

The apartment unfolded into a kind of luxurious stillness in front of her. She padded through the halls in bare feet, wandering into the living room to investigate. Beyond the foyer, the apartment was divided into a living room, a bathroom, a massive closet area, and a bedroom. The living room was framed by a wall of windows, with a marble fireplace dominating the far end of the room.

As she stood in front of it, the fire lit itself, crackling to life.

Nice touch, Prince Charming.

Above the fireplace, Ridley noticed a framed piece of parchment, old and yellowing. It was a passage from Homer's *Odyssey*, familiar to all Sirens: "The Song of the Sirens." She knew the words almost by heart. Uncle Macon had a similar page in his library. The pages were rare, but important.

A Siren relic, if such a thing existed. How weird to find it here.

Come hither, come, Odysseus, / Whom all praise, great glory of the Achaeans!
Bring in your ship and listen to our song. / For none has ever passed us in a black-hulled ship
Till from our lips he heard ecstatic song, / Then went on his way, rejoicing and with larger knowledge.
For we know all that on the plain of Troy / Argives and Trojans suffered at the gods' behest.
We know whatever happens on the bounteous earth.

Ridley stared at the words, remembering what they had first meant to her. Being Dark was hard to accept at sixteen; knowing that it was her destiny made it easier. For centuries, Siren after Siren had shared her fate, just as sailor after sailor had shared the rocks.

Why should I be spared?

She touched the parchment gently. The world was a cruel place, but at least it was consistent. Ridley understood who and what she was.

Ridley understood destiny.

She moved along the wall, looking at paintings and photographs and other Gates family memorabilia—until she came across a childhood photograph of Nox and his baby sister, sitting in a woman's lap.

A dark-eyed man stood behind them. He looked familiar.

Even though it was only a photograph, she could feel the unmistakable power resonate through the room.

The Power of Persuasion.

Here.

Now.

Sirensong. Sirene. Everything Ridley had felt in the club. Suddenly, it all made sense.

The woman in the photograph was a Siren. The woman in the photograph was also, most likely, Nox's mother.

Lennox Gates had Siren blood running through his veins.

CHAPTER 25

Knockin' on Heaven's Door

Link didn't have time to pick up the phone. To be honest, he didn't have time to think about Ridley. He didn't have time to do anything but freak out.

In a big way.

A hybrid Incubus–sized way.

More than anything, Link hated it when girls cried. He hated it when they cried or when they were mad at you or when they just gave you those big old eyes so wobbly that they made it seem like they belonged in a basket of puppies.

But this was worse.

Necro wasn't doing any of those things. She was just lying there—not moving. She didn't even look like she was doing all that much breathing. She didn't look all that different from the dead she was supposed to be talking to, Link thought.

Her skin was pale to the point of near greenness. Shadows

had emerged under her eyes. The gash on her neck almost seemed to be growing, from the looks of it.

It was a mess.

All three of them had taken turns trying to bandage her neck. The results were pretty shoddy, but it didn't matter. The black ooze seeped through, no matter what they tried.

Even Lucille Ball sat on the foot of the bed, staring.

"That can't be good," Floyd said. "It should've stopped by now."

"You think Necro hit an artery or somethin'?" Link asked. "Do you have arteries in your neck?"

"I don't know." Floyd looked at him. "You think she's going to bleed out?"

"No." Link shook his head. "You can lose up to one-third of your body's blood before you die. But we need to suture her."

"What?" Floyd looked at him. He didn't sound like himself to her, but that was probably only because she hadn't known him during Shark Week.

"Sew her up." Link shrugged. "I saw it on the Discovery Channel."

"Hold on. Let me get my needle and thread." Floyd was losing it.

"That only works if it's sterile," he informed her. "You guys got a Insta-Clinic Super 24 around here?" Link tried to think what the New York version of that would be.

"You want to take her to a Caster emergency room or something? Because, guess what? They don't exist." Floyd sounded desperate.

"She's probably going to die," Sampson said from the other end of the room.

223

"Shut it, man," Link practically shouted.

"Please." Floyd shook her head.

"Let's face facts." Sampson paced across the room. "I don't know how long a Necromancer can stay like this before the effects are permanent. Not long. She spends enough time in contact with the Otherworld as it is. All it takes for someone like her to cross over is a little shove in the Other direction—"

"You think?" Link snapped, and bent over her bed. "Hey, Necro. Wake up, man. That was a killer gig. You gotta wake up so we can talk about it." He shook her arm. He was desperate, and he couldn't think straight.

What would Ethan do in this situation? What had Ethan done, seein' as everythin' that could go wrong in the whole universe had already gone wrong for him? Why is my finger burnin' like crazy where that stupid ring is?

But it didn't matter who tried, or what they said or did. Necro didn't respond. She looked pale and small, lying half under the blankets. Floyd sat next to her on the floor.

"Esperanza," Floyd said.

"What?" Link looked down at her, confused.

"Her real name's not Necro. It's Esperanza."

Link looked at the sleeping punk. "Are you sure about that?"

Floyd smiled sadly. "She hates it, and she'll kick your butt if you call her that. But sometimes she still seems like an Esperanza to me."

"You guys have been friends for a long time, haven't you?" Link suddenly felt almost as bad for Floyd as he did for Necro.

Floyd shrugged. "Yeah, I guess. She's all right. For a Necro."

"Who did this to you, Esperanza?" Link leaned closer to her face. "Esperanza? Wake up and kick my butt."

It was no use. The blood was seeping from her neck, turning the whole bandage black and green.

Link gave up. "How did this happen? We would've seen it if she was in a fight."

"Not in the night, when she's sleepwalking." Floyd looked stricken.

"And I don't sleep, remember?" Link said. "I shoulda seen her, comin' and goin'."

"Not if someone didn't want you to see her." Sampson looked up from where he stood, leaning against the doorframe. "Not if the right Cast was in place."

Now he was next to them. "Not if the right Caster was behind it."

"What the—" Ridley fumbled for the clock on the bedside table, barely registering that it was a carved silver elephant and the clock was resting on its trunk. She sat up in the middle of Nox's sister's otherwise empty bed, completely disoriented. The skylight overhead had turned orange pink. Almost sunset.

Then she remembered how she'd gotten there.

Ridley turned and pulled the pillow back over her head. Everything had caught up with her, and she was exhausted. She'd collapsed into bed, dreaming about ships and Sirens and gardening shears. Odysseus and Abraham Ravenwood and Link and Necro. She was still wearing her bathrobe, and the damp towel had tangled its way into the sheets.

Necro.

Ridley held up her phone. No calls.

Necro might be better by now, or she might be worse. Either way, Floyd and Link weren't about to pick up the phone. Not if it was Ridley on the other end.

Still.

She sighed, pushing the call button.

The phone started to ring and ring and ring.

Nothing.

The doorbell chimed in the other room, startling her.

Ridley was spooked. She hadn't figured out what to say to Lennox Gates when she saw him again. Not about the photograph, or the Siren, or *The Odyssey*. But when she pulled open the door, it wasn't him.

"Oh," said Ridley, strangely disappointed. "It's you."

The Darkborn desk clerk held a silver tray with a single card balanced on it. Ridley took the card and slammed the door in the clerk's face.

Dinner at eight? Three words. That was all that was written on the card, in spiraling calligraphy.

Really? He thinks he can snap his fingers and I'll jump? I won't. I don't jump for anyone.

Ridley looked down at herself in the robe, her stomach rumbling.

I'll think about it.

A girl really does have to eat. Even a Siren.

And I have to talk to him.

If I could get him to open up to me...

I could find out what the Siren in the photograph has to do with Sirene and Nox—and Link and me.

The more she thought about it, the more she was convinced of what she had to do. But first things first.

Like the fact that she was wearing what was basically a glorified towel.

What had Nox said about clothes? Ridley investigated the apartment until she found a large bamboo wardrobe built into the bedroom wall. When she pressed against the doors, they folded open, but the closet was empty.

"Great."

So much for Caster magic. Apparently the Charmings needed to spend a little less time in the throne room and a little more time at Bloomingdale's.

She reached for one sad-looking, empty hanger and pulled it from the silver bar that ran the length of the closet.

As she lifted it higher, though, she could see it wasn't empty at all.

Now a dress hung on the hanger.

Not just any dress, but a black leather Gucci shift, cut like a knife—the one Ridley had admired in a Milan store window last summer.

It was more than a dress.

It was Ridley's weapon of choice.

Siren battle armor.

She tossed the dress on the bed and stuck her hand in again, this time pulling out a pair of sky-high, or at least thigh-high, calfskin boots. Prada.

She went back in for a bag—a soft suede envelope, in a sort of metallic gray. Chanel.

Earrings? Tiffany.

Bangle? Cartier.

Necklace? Harry Winston.

Diamonds really are a Siren's best friend.

She could've gone on like that all night, but she only had one body to put it all on, and it was nearly eight.

She resolved to come home early and play dress-up with whatever else the closet would cough up after dinner, which was the first moment she admitted that she really was going through with it.

She was going downstairs to meet Lennox Gates.

Ridley was determined to uncover the reasons behind the photograph on the wall, no matter what.

By the time she had squeezed into a dress that would stop traffic, she was ready for more than dinner.

She was ready to face Nox Gates.

He was waiting for Ridley in the lobby, looking less like he owned an Underground nightclub and more like he owned the world.

Worlds, Ridley thought. *Caster and Mortal alike.*

He rose from one of the sculpted horsehair lobby chairs as soon as he saw her, buttoning the center button on his tailored jacket. His long hair hit the starched linen collar of an equally well-cut shirt, but he wore the whole look as easily as he had his old leather one at Sirene.

Underworld and upper class. Another clue to the mystery of Lennox Gates.

"Nice threads." Ridley smiled. "Wait, are we playing polo with your butler tonight? My valet didn't tell me." Her voice sounded surprisingly light, under the circumstances.

Strange.

It didn't make anything easier that Nox was so good-looking, especially tonight. She couldn't help noticing. There weren't many guys who dressed like that in Gatlin. *Or any.* She couldn't imagine Link in that kind of getup. *That's what he'd call it. A getup.*

"Polo, yes, of course. At my country estate. We can take my yacht—I parked it around the corner." Nox looked her up and down. "Though I'm not sure you're dressed for anything as innocent as sailing."

It was true. Ridley did look like a bad girl tonight, even for a Siren. The way her leather dress hit certain places and skimmed others was practically criminal. *That really is some Caster closet,* she thought. *All the better for making a Dark Caster talk.*

She batted her eyelashes. "How ironic. Innocent is my middle name."

Ridley let Nox help her into his black Lincoln Town Car. As the door closed behind her, she settled into her seat, feeling guilty, like a princess going off to a ball. Battle armor notwithstanding.

A wicked princess crashing an evil ball, but whatever.

Charming was Charming, whether you were talking about Mortal royalty or a Dark Caster and a modern Siren. And whether you had a secret agenda or not.

You say glass slipper, I say calfskin stilettos.

She'd never left a shoe behind for a guy before. She supposed there was a first time for everything.

Stop it, she reminded herself.

This is war.

Nox Gates is the enemy.

And I'm keeping the shoes.

Dinner was private, as private as two people can be in a sprawling city of millions.

On this particular rooftop—the garden of an immense stone building—they were very intimately alone.

Alone with a chef and a violinist and a waitstaff, but still.

They sat at a small round table overflowing with white linens and white flowers. *Gardenias*, Ridley thought. The smell was as sweet as the city was gray. Instead of stars there were city lights. Instead of mountains there were high-rise buildings.

"Try a Metropolitan Cosmopolitan," Nox said, pouring a pink drink from a tall crystal carafe into a sugar-rimmed glass.

It smelled like the flowers in the islands, Ridley thought.

"Sort of a house specialty," he added.

"Big house," Ridley said, sipping from the glass. The sugar rush was intense. She could feel her heart pounding, so she put down the glass.

She needed a clear head tonight.

Nox shrugged. "Big? You could say that. It's called the Met."

"The museum?" Even Ridley had heard of that one, and she went out of her way to avoid museums or any place where people stood around looking at things other than her.

He nodded.

Rid picked up the glass and put it back down again. *Nervous? Am I nervous? Is that what this is?*

She cleared her throat. "Where is everybody?" They had come straight from a side entrance to a service elevator, and until they had reached the rooftop, Ridley hadn't seen a person except for the occasional security guard.

Nox sipped from his glass. "Let's just say I gave them the night off."

The view from their table was breathtaking. Puffs of green trees were still visible in the fading light, even with the concrete jungle rising between them. Ridley understood why Sirens throughout history had been drawn to this city.

"This is beautiful," she said, feeling very small. It was a new feeling, and she filed it away. There had been so many new feelings lately.

He shrugged. "It's a beautiful city. I don't know why I spend so much time in the Underground, when it's so incredible up here."

"You love Sirene." She smiled at him, pushing the conversation where it needed to go.

"I do."

"Why?" She tried to sound casual.

He studied the view carefully, as if it would disappear the moment he looked away. "I love all my clubs."

"Because they're Dark?" She looked at him. *Like the Siren in the photograph? The one you named the club after?*

But she didn't say it. Not yet.

A man like Nox Gates wasn't stupid. He wouldn't come clean that easily. Not to a Siren he barely knew—and certainly not about his connection to another Siren.

Nox studied the view. "No. Because they're home. Something I never had."

Ridley smiled, almost involuntarily. "You and every other Dark Caster in the world."

"Does it feel like home to you? New York?" He looked back at the city. "All this beauty?"

Ridley made a face. "Not so much our apartment. Or my

job. Or the subway. Let's see—yep, those are the parts I get to visit." She laughed.

He didn't. "There are others. Let me show you."

This is it, she thought. "Show me what?"

"New York, the way a Siren is supposed to see it."

Exactly. "A Siren? How would you know?"

He didn't say anything.

Ridley shrugged. "You know, I think I've probably seen enough New York for a while." *Not too fast. Make him work for it.*

"You haven't seen anything." He touched her hand.

She pulled it back, startled by the feeling of his skin on hers. *Watch it.*

He smiled. "One day. Just one. I'll be a good boy, I promise. Then, if you still want me to, I'll bring you back to your friends and demand that they forgive you."

"You think they care what you think?" Her face clouded at the thought of what was going on back in their apartment. *You think they're my friends?* She put down her glass.

"Of course they care what I think. Everyone does." He smiled.

"Don't flatter yourself," Ridley said. "If anything, they're scared of you."

"Like I said." He shrugged. "They care what I think. Does it really matter why?"

"It does," Ridley said, and she realized as she said it that she meant it. "It's taken me a long time to figure that out, but it does."

Nox raised an eyebrow. "You don't say."

Rid kept her eyes on the skyline in front of her. "It's nice to have people care what you think and laugh at your jokes. And notice when you say things, and when you don't." She smiled at him ruefully. "At least, it *was* nice."

Don't get distracted, she told herself.

"Just one day?" Nox pressed again. "Let me show you."

"One day is a long time." Rid hesitated. "A Siren's view of New York?"

He nodded.

"That's it?" Just a day? Was that all it would take to unravel the mystery that was Lennox Gates? Wasn't that what she wanted?

Ridley thought about the unanswered rings when she'd called the apartment earlier. Necro was hurt. What if they needed Ridley? What if there was something she could do?

It's not like they want me back. It's not like they'll let me back. They won't even pick up the phone. And at least this way I could get him to open up about the Siren in the photograph.

"One day. I promise." Nox crossed his heart playfully.

"And no trying to trick me or game me into staying?" Ridley looked at him, crossing her arms. She'd made and lost a bet with him before. She wasn't going to make that mistake again. "No house rules? No party tricks?"

"Nothing underhanded at all."

War, she reminded herself. *Answers. The Siren in the photograph. That's why you're doing this.*

The way he smiled, she felt like she could trust him.

And the way she fell for his smile, she felt she couldn't trust him at all.

As Ridley crawled into the massive circular bed that night, she stared at her phone. Still no calls. Not even Lena was picking up tonight.

No calls...and no friends.

Nothing.

Necro and Floyd and Sampson didn't want to have anything to do with her.

They didn't, and Link didn't.

It was bound to happen. It had only been a matter of time. Ridley had always known it.

You couldn't fight destiny. Not when destiny was just another door slammed in your face, whether you deserved it or not.

Not when destiny was just you sitting alone on the curb, whether you wanted to come inside or not.

Frustrated, Ridley pulled the covers around her.

But this isn't just about me. Necro could be really sick. Black blood. That's some bad mojo.

She had to try.

Even if no one cared, and even if no one wanted her to.

This time, Ridley let the phone ring over and over. Then she called again. And again. She counted the stars overhead until the ringing stopped and her cell phone ran out of power.

By then, she was asleep and dreaming of curbless streets and cracked stone walkways—of smiling mothers and endlessly open doors.

⊰ CHAPTER 26 ⊱

Back in Black

Looks bad. Worse, even. You think there's some kinda hex on her or somethin'?" Link was wide-eyed, staring at Necro as she lay on the bed. He looked horrified.

Lucille Ball, circling him, looked even more so.

Floyd scrambled to her feet to look at the wound. She nodded. "It looks way worse than yesterday."

"Bigger. Blacker." Sampson nodded. "A hex would be my bet." He examined the wound more closely. "I'm guessing the blade that did this was Charmed. And that the cut isn't what's making her sick. The Cast is. All it would take would be a nick."

He shrugged. Floyd and Link looked at each other.

"He's got a point," Link said. "Nec might not have noticed an itty-bitty cut. She probably would have noticed slittin' her own throat, if it had looked like this when she first got it."

"Either way, we can't help her until we know what's wrong with her," said Floyd.

"But if she's all hexed up, how are we goin' to be able to figure it out?" Link glanced over at Sampson. He didn't like the guy, and he didn't understand him. But he was in the band, so as far as Link was concerned, he was one of them.

Wasn't that how it worked?

"You got any ideas, Sammy?" Link asked the Darkborn. "If you do, speak up. 'Cause I got nothin'."

Sampson's eyes flickered from Necro to Link. "I don't get involved with Caster business."

Link was flabbergasted. "But she's your friend."

Sampson stared straight ahead. "Not really."

Link shook his head. "What's wrong with you, man?"

Sampson shrugged. "It's the Darkborn way. We aren't Casters."

"Yeah, well, your way sucks." Link was pretty clear on that point.

"You can say whatever you want, but I know you're my friend," Floyd said. "I know you're Necro's friend. You've been with us for too long, at too many clubs now—"

"Two. It's been two clubs," Sampson corrected her. He folded his arms, obstinate.

"It doesn't matter. She'd do it for you, and so would I." She glanced at Link. "And so would Link."

Link looked at her. "That's right. I'm here for you, man. And I'd do just about anythin' if you were the one lyin' on that bed."

Sampson didn't say anything.

Floyd nodded at Link.

He tried again. "Yeah, so. There's that. And…you know… whenever this world is cruel to me, I got you to help me forgive."

Sampson raised an eyebrow. "Says Queen. Now you're just quoting song lyrics."

Link clapped him on the back. "Awesome. You got it. And that, my main man, is why we're in a band together."

Silence.

Floyd nodded again. *Well?*

Link shrugged. *I got nothin'.*

Sampson sighed. "Fine. But don't get me involved. You don't owe me, and I don't owe you. And we aren't friends."

"Fine." Link held out his hand. "We aren't friends. Let's shake on it."

Sampson ignored him and glanced back at Necro. Then he looked Floyd dead in the eye. "I don't know how to help her. But I can tell you who did this to her."

"Who?" Floyd swallowed.

"More like what," Sampson said. "I might be immune to Incubus and Caster powers, but I can still feel them. Your powers make you all feel different, and I can sense it."

"What are you talkin' about?" Link frowned.

Sampson nodded at Floyd. "Floyd feels like a roller coaster. If I pick up something she's touched, I feel sick to my stomach. Dizzy."

"Gee, thanks. I love you, too, Frankenstein."

"Link, you feel more like a bad rash."

Floyd's mouth twisted into a smile, short-lived as it was. Link glared at her.

Sampson ignored both of them. "You make me itch—it's uncomfortable. Like poison oak. I think it's the clash between your powers and your powerlessness. Hybrids always feel like that."

"Maybe you're just allergic to good looks and musical genius?" Part of Link wanted to beat the guy up. But the rest of Link wanted to hear what he had to say, even more.

"Maybe." Sampson shrugged. "I don't like Incubuses much, either."

"Okay. We're gettin' somewhere."

"What about Necro?" Floyd asked.

Sampson reached for her hand and took it. "She feels still and cold, usually. Calm. It's not a bad feeling. More like floating, maybe in a lake."

"Have you ever been in a lake?" Link looked at him. "Because it's pretty much none a those things."

"Let the man talk," Floyd said. She looked at Sampson. "What do you feel now?"

"She's still there, cold as the Underground. But I can feel the Charm. It's heat and fire—sharp and strong. And something else."

"What?" Floyd sounded anxious.

Link reached out his hand and put it on Sampson's shoulder. "Seriously, man. You're killin' us. Spit it out."

"Sweet," Sampson said. "It's sweet. Like burning sugar. I think—"

"Don't say it." Link sounded grim. "You don't have to say it."

"A Siren," Sampson said. "And we've only been around one of those."

"That we know of," Link snapped.

"Would she do something like that?" Floyd was wide-eyed.

238

She stepped away from Link, as if the fact of his knowing Ridley was itself somehow contagious.

"No. Never." Link was sure of it.

"Your Siren's never hurt anyone before? Even if she didn't mean to?" Floyd looked doubtful.

Link didn't answer.

She never means any harm.

Much.

"Because if that's true, Link, she's the first Siren in the history of the world who could say that." Floyd sounded bitter.

"It wasn't her, Floyd, I know it. She wouldn't have done it."

"You're just whipped. You can't even see it."

Link brushed her off. "What does it matter, anyway? Rid's gone now. Knowing if she did it doesn't help Necro."

"Of course it matters. I need to know whose ass to kick," Floyd snapped.

Sampson shook his head. "Floyd's right, Link. You don't get it. Only the Siren who did this to Necro can undo it. You can't save her if you can't find the person who tricked out that knife." He looked at Link. "Necro's running out of time."

"You think you can find her? Ridley?" Floyd asked.

Link looked bummed. "She just took off. I have no idea where she is. But I'm telling you, it wasn't her."

Sampson practically growled. "You're sweet, Incubus."

Link grabbed Sampson by the collar of his shirt. "Listen up, Maybelline. I know Rid, and she didn't do this. I swear on my life."

Sampson looked at him calmly. "Let's hope it doesn't come to that."

Link flexed his hands, releasing Sampson's shirt. "Sorry, man."

As he pulled his hand away, his Binding Ring began to glow again—this time turning from red to a pulsing golden color.

Link stared at it, holding it in front of his face. Floyd and Sampson watched the ring change colors.

"What's that?" Floyd reached out for it, letting pink glow spill across her fingers. "It's sort of beautiful."

"Old magic," Sampson said. "And powerful. It doesn't feel like anything else. Not that I've encountered."

Link held up his hand. It glowed color after color, as if it had suddenly come to life. "I think this thing is tryin' to tell me somethin'. That, or it just wants to burn my finger off."

"Let it tell you, whatever it is." Floyd stared at the ring like it really was made of fire.

Link held his arm with his other hand. "It's pullin' me out the door."

"Whoa," Floyd said.

"Then follow it," Sampson said as the ring lit up the room.

"I think I know how to find Ridley," Link said slowly. "Or at least, I think the ring does."

Floyd turned toward the bed. "Don't worry, Necro. We'll be right back." She straightened Necro's blankets, then grabbed her leather jacket. "Let's go."

"You'll stay with her?" Link looked at Sampson, who nodded.

"One thing." Floyd stopped Link when they got to the door. "I don't care if she's your girlfriend or not. We're going to find that Siren and kick her ass."

Link didn't say a word.

He didn't have to.

If Ridley had anything to do with this, it wouldn't be Floyd who dealt with her.

"Hold on."

Link stopped for his backpack. He just needed to get one thing. Burning ring or impatient Illusionist or wounded Necromancer—or not.

A rusty old pair of gardening shears.

If Ridley was involved in something this Dark, there had to be a reason. And if there was a reason, well, it wasn't likely it was a good one.

Better to be prepared.

CHAPTER 27

Fly to the Angels

Ridley's phone was dead, along with her resolve. Lost phone chargers notwithstanding, no one accidentally missed a hundred calls, not even Link.

Message received, loud and clear.

She had promised one day, and Nox could have it. *Nox and his mysterious Siren*, she thought. If Ridley knew more about the Siren in the photograph, maybe she would understand the secret behind Nox himself.

Her battle armor was simple enough: The closet had offered up a vintage floral slip dress, along with chained and studded black leather ranger boots and a matching studded jacket.

The closet, it turned out, was partial to Saint Laurent. *Go figure.*

The sun rose leisurely, like it had nothing better to do. The day started late and continued with tea in the lobby and a tower of *macarons*, brought in from Ladurée, Madison Avenue's own Parisian tea shop. Rose, strawberry candy, and of course chocolate, and maybe the melon. All the best flavors.

In another lifetime, Ridley would've thought it was perfection.

Nox drank tiny cups of espresso as if they were hot chocolate. Ridley couldn't stand coffee. "The world is already a bitter enough place," she said. "I'll stick to chocolate."

"*Chocolat chaud*," said Nox.

"That, too. Now hand me the good stuff." She reached for the nearest plate of cookies.

"*Un de chaque*, that's what you want." Nox smiled, offering Ridley half a salted caramel *macaron*. He looked particularly out of place in his club clothes—black jeans, a vintage black jacket, and a skinny black tie—surrounded by pink and purple pastel cookies and pastries.

"What's that?" Ridley popped the *macaron* into her mouth, making a face. Salty sweet wasn't so much her thing as sweetly sweet.

"Well, in Paris they're not quite as indulgent, but the Italians get it. *Uno di tutti*. That's what I say when I walk into a Roman bakery. One of everything. Try the coconut."

She had.

Then she tried it again. And again and again, until the tower of plates was empty except for crumbs. With her mouth as full of sugar as it was, she hadn't had much time for questions. *Not yet*, she thought. *Soon.*

After breakfast, they wandered down Madison to the Whitney. Construction crews had ripped open the sidewalks, taxis were honking and screeching, fast-walking people were jabbering on phones.

It was a perfect New York City morning. At least, it should've been—and if things had been different, it would've been.

"It's only one day. Why waste it in a museum?" Ridley argued. "Is that what a real New York Siren would do?"

Now. Show me what you're about.

"It's not just a museum. It's my favorite of all the New York museums," Nox said.

"A *favorite* museum?" Ridley shook her head playfully. "Really? I don't believe you just said that. *Favorite* means you've gone to more than one."

"I have. So should you. Think about it. Andy Warhol did Marilyn and Liz. If they weren't Sirens—"

"They weren't." Ridley rolled her eyes.

"They should've been." Nox laughed. "Show me a great artist, and I'll show you—"

Ridley cut him off. "A gift shop and a snack bar."

"A great Siren." Nox grinned.

"Is that it? Marilyn and Liz? No other great New York Sirens you want to introduce me to?"

He looked at her, his smile faltering.

She met his eyes.

Now. The woman in the photograph. Tell me.

But Nox's phone buzzed, and he pulled it from his jacket, frowning. "Sirensong pulled out of a sold-out gig for tonight. What's going on?"

The moment had passed, and with it the light and the laughter of the morning. Nox's face was once again dark and impenetrable.

Ridley couldn't worry about it, though, because once again all she could think of was Necro.

Ridley pulled his wrist toward her and looked at his watch. "I'm sorry. I need to get back."

There. She could stop pretending it wasn't on her mind.

"To your friends?" Nox asked. "I thought they were the ones who kicked you out."

"They were, I mean, Link was. But my—" *What was I going to say? Friend? Was that what this was?* "Necro's sick."

"Necro?" Nox pulled his arm back, straightening his shirt. "What kind of sick?"

"She passed out onstage. Didn't you see it? Yesterday, just before I came to the hotel?"

He shook his head. "I left as soon as we—you know." A shadow crossed his face. "I'm sorry to hear that. I should call someone. Send a doctor." He felt for his phone.

"I'm not sure they want anything from either one of us right now." Ridley said the words slowly. "In fact, I'm pretty sure we're the last two people on earth that Floyd or Link or Necro want to see."

Nox lowered his cell back into his pocket.

"You think so?"

She raised an eyebrow. "You were there." *When you kissed me. In front of him. While they watched.*

"What do we do?" He sounded genuinely worried.

"I've left a thousand messages. All we can do is wait."

"Until what?"

"I'm not sure I know," Ridley said.

He sighed. "Fair enough."

"Sirens." Ridley looked up. *I'd better get on with it. The Siren in the photograph. A plan is a plan.* "You were going to show me a Siren's view of New York."

245

"First the museum. I think we've got to expand your definition of what a Siren is."

"Enlighten me."

Nox smiled. "Look, I'm not saying I know you better than you know yourself. I'm saying that if you open your eyes, you'll figure out you're not so alone. Or at least, you don't need to be."

"I'm not alone. I have—" Who? Not Link. Especially not after yesterday.

Not anymore.

"Well, I have my cousin, Lena."

Nox nodded. "The Natural. And you have your sister. The little Thaumaturge."

"Sisters. Can't forget Reece, no matter how much I'd like to." She stopped. "Wait—how do you know Lena's a Natural?" She didn't like surprises, and she didn't know if she trusted Nox not to pull them on her.

"She's Lena Duchannes. You're Ridley Duchannes. I've known many Duchannes, and more Ravenwoods. You don't exactly keep a low profile."

They kept walking. "And Ryan? How could you tell what sort of Caster she was?"

"I could feel it. She's a powerful little girl." He smiled. "Like her sister, I think. I can tell you care about her. But you have to admit, you yourself? You're something of a lone wolf. Especially for a Siren. I thought you only traveled in packs? With whole boatloads of your adoring sailors?"

Ridley didn't say anything. She'd been alone from the moment she'd left home until she'd met Link. Ever since her own parents had kicked her out of her family home, after her Claiming. But even with Link, no matter how well things seemed to go for a while, she always ended up back where she'd started. Alone again.

Back on the curb.

"Maybe I want to be alone," she said finally, because everything else was too painful to say.

"Maybe you're as big a liar as I am," Nox said, holding out his hand.

She took it.

His hand was warm and strong, and she felt inexplicably better holding it.

Even if he was the second most horrible person in the world.

Even if she was the first.

Then he squeezed her hand, as if he felt it, too.

The museum became a picnic in the park and shopping in SoHo. An afternoon walk became delicate sushi. Dinner became dessert, caramel and crème fraîche, and cream puffs drowning in warm chocolate fudge. Waiters stood at attention as if they were bodyguards; doors were opened, cars were waiting, store clerks were doting.

It was like a popcorn wish-fulfillment movie of someone else's life. Ridley wished it were real. She wished it were hers. But even if she was only playing the part for today, it was better than nothing.

Still, there were no Sirens.

The day might have been charmed, and the prince might have been charming, but there was no evidence of any other kind of Cast or Charm.

Still, she savored every minute of it.

By the time they ended up back at Les Avenues, Ridley let Nox come up to the apartment with her.

"Just for a minute," she said.

He's not half bad, she thought, *as far as princes go.*

"Just to watch the sunset," he agreed.

He's not half bad, she thought, *as far as enemies go.*

"Just to see the stars," she conceded.

This isn't half bad, she thought, *as far as wars go.*

"Just one day," he said. "You promised."

And just to take another look at one small photograph hanging on the wall, she thought.

Lennox Gates, what is your Siren story?

CHAPTER 28

Fear of the Dark

How well do you know this guy?" Link was sweating. He shook his ringed hand. The whole thing felt like it was burning off.

"Who, Sampson? How well does anyone know a Darkborn?" Floyd was annoyed. They were stuck on the subway. Not the Underground, and not the Tunnels. The regular old subway. The one that smelled like stale cigarettes and adult diapers.

It was rush hour in New York City, which meant every time the subway doors opened, as many people got into the car as were already inside it.

The whole thing was a hopelessly broken puzzle.

Link and Floyd had been following the ring throughout the Underground, and as far as Link could tell, it was leading them both to nowhere and back again. Necro didn't have time for either. And Ridley...

Link had a bad feeling Ridley was in a whole lot more trouble than even he realized. *That second marker,* he thought. *That second marker means she's not in control. That second marker means Lennox Gates can make her do anything he needs her to. Even if that means hurting Necro.*

He didn't know what to think about Ridley, but any way you looked at it, he was worried.

Link tried not to think about it. He clung to the overhead pole, letting his long body sway with the motion of the car. Then he looked back at Floyd. "But for a Darkborn. You think he's for real?"

Floyd stood firmly planted against the side of the rattling seat. "Look, Link. Are you asking me if I believe him that your girlfriend could hurt my best friend in the world? Not to mention our keyboard player? Of course I do."

Link watched the tunnel pass by, through the flickering black windows of the subway car. *She's not my girlfriend anymore. But that doesn't mean I don't know her. And it doesn't mean she could do something like this. Not on her own.*

His hand ached.

Floyd only watched him. "You don't think she could?"

He made a face. "Don't be stupid. Of course I don't."

She looked away, hurt. "All right, then. If I'm so stupid, then I guess there isn't much left to talk about."

"I guess not." Link didn't want to think about the gardening shears tucked in his back pocket. *If you're so sure, why did you bring them? Who do you think you're gonna fight? And what could she possibly have gotten herself involved in this time?*

After that, Floyd and Link rode in silence. But the silence only lasted for a few minutes, because then Floyd looked up at him and started talking, out of the blue. "It's none of my business."

"What is?" Link wasn't really paying attention. He was watching a guy at the end of the row of seats secretly pick his nose, which wasn't all that easy to do on a crowded subway car during rush hour.

"You deserve better. That's all I'm saying." Floyd looked away.

Link rubbed his hand through his hair, confused. "Better what? What are you talkin' about?" She wasn't being all that specific. Plus, the guy had his finger halfway up his nose now. If he wasn't careful, he was going to scratch his own brains.

"You know what I'm talking about." Floyd was irritated. Link could tell.

She sounds kinda mad.

"I really don't." Now Link was irritated. He flexed his burning hand against the safety pole he was holding on to.

Seriously. Not a clue.

"It's none of my business. I'm done."

See? She's ticked.

"Fine," Link said. "Be done."

Seein' as I have no idea what you're done with.

A man shoved between them. Floyd shoved back. She slid closer to Link. "Ridley treats you like garbage."

Here we go. "Rid treats everyone like garbage."

"Why do you let her?"

"Nobody *lets* Ridley do anything. That's just Rid. She's a Siren. She's..." He sighed. "Messed up."

Floyd folded her arms. "You deserve better. That's all I wanted to say."

251

"I know." He'd seen the kiss. There was nothing left to talk about. Not that Link wanted to talk about it with anyone, especially not Floyd. Ridley was done with him. You didn't let a guy kiss you like that if you were in love with someone else.

If she ever was.

"You don't understand. Any girl would be lucky to have a guy like you." Floyd was still going.

"Any girl?" A shooting pain pulsed from the ring through his hand. "Sweet Chees—" The subway pole jerked off its moorings on the ceiling, coming loose in Link's hand.

Link looked around in a panic, accidentally swinging the pole in a circle around his head. His neighbors in every direction ducked. "Sorry. No big deal. I'll put this thing right back where it belongs." He tried to shove the bar back up into the ceiling, but it didn't work. "Everything's fine."

He gave up and tossed the bar to the floor, kicking it beneath the row of seats next to him. Only the guy in the headphones standing closest to him seemed to care. "Way to go, jerk." The rest of the car didn't so much as look in Link's direction, now that the bar was out of his hands.

Link felt about as far away from Gatlin as he'd ever thought he could.

He felt a whole lot of things, actually.

His girlfriend had screwed him over, like everyone had always said she would. He'd watched her locking lips with another guy, who was—let's face it—almost as good-looking as he was. Someone in his band was probably dying. He couldn't eat. He couldn't sleep. His best friend was gone. His family was nuts. He wasn't even all that sure his music was any good, for some reason.

And I just broke the freaking subway.

As soon as he thought it, the car lurched to a stop.

The doors flung themselves open, and even more people flooded on.

Link's hand was throbbing. He felt like he could almost hear his skin sizzling. He was considering ripping the entire car apart.

Then he looked down at Floyd.

"This is ridiculous." Link grabbed her hand and closed his eyes.

She looked at him, confused. "Link? What are you—"

He pulled her closer.

Then it was silent, except for a familiar whirring sound, the sound of a Caster and an Incubus sliding out of a subway car, out of a crumbling tunnel, out of a rush hour crowd, even out of this dimension.

Ripping away.

Nobody else in the car even looked up.

❧ CHAPTER 29 ❧

We Are Stars

Ridley had never seen so many stars. Mortal constellations, as far as the eye could see. The Southern Star was nowhere in sight, but then, Ridley didn't have her mind on anything to do with the Casters, with the possible exception of the one there with her right now.

And the one in the photograph on the wall.

She sat next to Nox, staring up at the darkness from the very center of the penthouse garden, lit only by the candlelight that surrounded their shared chaise.

From the roof of the hotel, the night seemed enormous.

I will always remember this, she thought. *Prince or war. Good or bad.*

This night. How this feels.

How I feel.

The city below was a crazy crowd of lights beneath the dark wash of sky.

I can look down on everyone, she thought, thinking of the little girl who could never find heels high enough.

And it's still too low.

Ridley's jacket was long gone, and the evening breeze blew her hair off her bare shoulders. She shivered.

Nox slid his arm along the back of the softly upholstered chaise. An elaborate row of candles of every height flickered on the table in front of them.

"This is nice." Ridley spoke the words out into the darkness, where things like the truth could be revealed under the cover of night.

"Nicer than expected." He leaned his head back against the cushion. "Considering."

"Considering what?"

"One Wesley Lincoln, for starters. I'm assuming it's some kind of Southern fetish. Like fried chicken or pecan pie."

The joking annoyed her, and she sat up. "You assume wrong. He's a good person, and I—" The words trailed off. She didn't finish.

She didn't know what to say.

"You what?" he pressed.

"I care about him deeply." The way she said it made it sound like she was talking about one of her elderly relatives. She frowned.

"And does he *care deeply* about you?"

Ridley shook her head. "Not anymore." She leaned back. "I messed it all up. I always do."

Nox didn't smile. He sounded strangely serious. "Did he feel something more than that? Is that what he told you?"

"How did you know?"

"Let me guess. The word *love* comes to mind?"

"He didn't know what he was saying. I'm a Siren." She said the word carefully. Intentionally. "You know what that's like."

Don't you? Or does she, whoever she is? The woman in the picture?

"So?" Nox studied her face.

"So people can't help what they say to me. You know that." Regular people, Ridley thought. Helpless regular people.

"What if he did? Know, I mean. What he was saying? And what if he could help how he felt?"

"Does it matter? How will I ever know the difference? I have unnatural abilities that make people care for me. How can I ever trust anything anyone feels about me?"

"You can't," Nox said slowly. "Not the good feelings. Only the bad ones. Which is why you do half the things you do and say half the things you say. To provoke the feelings you know you can trust."

Yes. Exactly. So I know if something is real.

Ridley couldn't speak. This wasn't a conversation she had ever imagined having with anyone. The words were breathtaking. Exhausting. She'd never told a soul these things. Not Lena. Not even Link.

What does that mean? That I can have this conversation with Lennox Gates? That he knows my deepest secret?

She turned her face so he couldn't see the sudden shine in her eyes.

Nox turned to her. "You are such a Siren."

Ridley wiped her eye with a smile. "Am I? Like your mother?" she asked carefully. Because it was time. He would tell her now. He had to. He was as alone as she was. They were two of a kind, and this was their war. Their curb.

The same doors had been slammed in both of their Dark Caster faces—Ridley was sure of that.

Because Lennox Gates is Siren-born.

He has to be.

He's as far from a regular person as I am.

Ridley wondered how long she had known, in the back of her mind, and then she wondered what had taken her so long.

Nox looked at her, surprised.

Ridley took a breath. "Sirene? The Power of Persuasion, raging like fire through your club? Did you think I wouldn't figure it out?"

She shivered involuntarily.

"Come on," Nox said. "Inside."

The lights were low but the fire was high. Nox sat with his back to the flames while Ridley faced them. Beneath the two Casters, the thick rug was warm and soft.

Ridley watched him. "Why didn't you tell me?"

"That my mother was a Siren? It's not exactly the kind of thing you go shouting from the rooftops."

"Why not? Is it supposed to be a secret?" She bristled. "Are we really so bad?"

Nox leaned forward, looking disgusted. "It's not about her being a Siren. It's about her situation."

"Her situation?" Ridley shot the words back into his face. "Is that what you call it?" Her eyes blazed. "How about *affliction*? How about *infection*? Is that why you've never spoken of her? You're afraid you might catch whatever she has?" Ridley was shaking with anger.

"That's not what I mean." Nox put a hand on her arm, but she yanked it away. "You're taking this all wrong."

"I'm the wrong one here?" *Unbelievable.*

"No, I mean, I'm saying it wrong." He looked miserable. "Besides, I thought you knew. I thought everyone did."

Ridley softened a little. "Knew what? How could I know anything?"

"The fall of the house of Gates? Come on."

"Tell me," she said. This time she was the one who took his hand. "You can tell me, Nox."

He didn't say anything for a long time. "I don't know much. My mother died when I was really young."

"I'm sorry." Ridley could see the sadness in his eyes. *This is real. He's not playing you.*

Nox nodded, but his eyes were faraway. "You remind me of her. The way you always seem to know that you were meant for something more than an average life."

Regular, Ridley thought. *The word is* regular.

"My mother was meant for a better life, too."

"What happened?" Ridley didn't let go of his hand.

"She was taken from us and kept like a pet in a cage. She was never seen as a person, only as a power to be traded back and forth between powerful Casters and Incubuses."

As were so many Sirens before her, Ridley thought.

"It destroyed my parents. My sister. My life." He looked at Ridley. "How could anyone be that cruel?"

She took his other hand. Now, when their fingers touched, they felt light and warm, and she didn't look away.

"I understand," Ridley said. "I was kept in a cage once before. I'll never let it happen again." Her voice grew as dark as the expression on her face. "I'd die first."

Nox looked at her. "Do you love him? The hybrid?"

"What does that have to do with anything?"

"I need to know."

Ridley felt her anger flaring. "It's none of your business."

Nox was just as angry. "Was it a cage?"

Now she was furious. "What?"

He forced out the words, awkwardly, one at a time. "Love. Did it—does it—feel like a cage, too?"

She didn't answer. Slowly, he pulled his hand away, pushing to his feet. He stood at the long wall of windows, staring out at the city.

"Did my mother ever feel anything else but trapped? For my father or my family?"

Ridley stood next to him. "For you?" she asked, softly.

Now Nox was silent.

Ridley took a breath. "He loved me. Link. I mean, that's what he said. It's so—it was strange." It felt even stranger to try to put it into words, especially now. Especially to Nox Gates.

Did it feel like a cage? Is that why I ran? Is that what love is?

"No," she said suddenly. "It's not a cage, Nox." She put her hand on his shoulder. "Love is an open door."

She reached around him until her arms encircled his chest

and as much of his tall, broad shoulders as she could. He laid his head against her arms.

He didn't speak for a long moment, and when he did, his voice was muffled.

"Ridley Duchannes, what could have possibly convinced you that you weren't worth loving?" She could feel his heart pounding in his chest.

Curbs and cages. This is our world.

She didn't begrudge it. She understood it.

It, and him.

Ridley shook her head. "Love, Nox, is awful. It's painful and humiliating and it involves songs—horrible, sappy songs—about hearts breaking and tears falling and following people into dark places."

"Sounds pretty bad," Nox said. She couldn't tell if he was smiling as he said it. There was too much darkness in the room between them.

It's safer that way.

"It's like a disease, Nox. A Mortal disease. A complete loss of spine. The emotional equivalent of projectile vomiting. And way too much acoustic guitar."

He laughed, raising his head. "You're killing the mood, Little Siren."

"Exactly. But when you're in love, you're not in control of what you think or say or do. And there is nothing I love more than control, and nothing I love less than not having it. So you tell me—what is a person like me supposed to do with a feeling like that?" She felt her own eyes beginning to burn.

He sighed. "So you were lying. About the cage."

It was true, and it would always be the problem. Love was

the opposite of power, and Ridley couldn't stand to not have both.

She pulled her arms away from Nox, staring out into the night. The city was so huge and so far beneath her, she felt like she was flying. She wished she could. She'd fly away and this would all be behind her.

Nox followed her. Ridley felt him move closer to her, taking her hand in the darkness. He held it to his lips.

She pulled it away. "Didn't you hear a word I said?"

"I didn't have to listen. I could've given that speech myself."

Yeah, right, she thought. But she didn't contradict him. Instead, she looked up at him. "I hate it. Feeling so weak."

"And being so wrong."

"What?"

"Little Siren. Did it ever occur to you that loving someone powerful only makes you more powerful?"

She shook her head. "No. Love is love."

He pushed a curl behind her ear. "It's not." He tilted her face toward him, pressing his thumb against her chin. "It's so not."

His eyes were locked on hers, even in the darkness.

Dark eyes, Dark Caster, dark night. Not the safest of combinations, she thought. But she couldn't help it, any more than she could help herself.

There was something that connected her to Lennox Gates. Something powerful.

They stood together, looking out at the city, almost face to face. The lights sparkled in the distance, oblivious. He slid one hand down her bare arm. In that moment, she knew that she wanted him to kiss her more than anything.

Kiss me, she thought. *I want you to kiss me again.*

It was the feeling from the club, and it had returned full force. She felt dizzy and hot, and her lips began to burn, just as they had when he last touched them.

For our first real kiss.

It felt right. It felt like destiny.

And it felt strangely familiar.

Why?

"Nox." Her voice faltered. "Have we done this before?"

What is it about wanting Lennox Gates that makes me feel like I've wanted this all before?

Something about him.

His face. I know his face.

But then Ridley's eyes fixed again on the photograph hanging on the wall. On a different face. She could just see it over Nox's shoulder.

The Siren family. The sister. The mother. Nox.

She didn't know why she hadn't seen it before.

She hadn't been looking for it.

She hadn't known.

The dark-eyed man.

"I can't—" she began.

"Don't think about the hybrid. Leave him behind," he whispered in her ear. "Before it's too late."

Ridley wasn't listening.

I know that man.

In the photograph.

She took a deep breath.

Then she couldn't breathe at all, because she knew who the man in the picture was. It cut through her like a sharper blade than Necro's knife.

The man in Nox's family photo—right there, with Nox's mother and his baby sister—was a younger Abraham Ravenwood.

Abraham Ravenwood.

Dead by Link's hand, with my help.

Abraham Ravenwood is part of Nox's family.

Abraham Ravenwood is Nox's

Is Nox's

Nox's

She pushed away from Nox, moving directly in front of the framed photograph on the wall. "It's him."

Nox looked pained.

Ridley was stunned. "But Abraham only had John. John would have known you."

"Abraham wasn't my father. He could never be my father."

"And you know that because?"

"He's the one who kept my mother in a cage. He's the reason my father ended his life. Abraham Ravenwood destroyed my family, and now he's going to destroy yours."

Ridley wanted to rip the photograph from the wall. "I don't believe you. I don't know what I believe."

Nox grabbed her hand again. "It doesn't matter. You've got to get out of here before it's too late."

It sounded more like an order than a request, and Ridley didn't respond well to orders.

"Too late? Is that a threat?" She took a step back.

"I didn't mean it that way." He moved closer. "I only want you to get away from the hybrid before something happens to you. To both of you." Now Nox sounded as cold as she did.

"What are you talking about, Nox?" She took another step

back. "Link? Delivering a hybrid Incubus to your associates? Are we back on those threats again?"

"It's complicated."

"It always is with you."

"I can't explain it, but you have to trust me. Please. I can protect you. He can't." Nox extended his hand, but she didn't take it.

"Actually, I'm starting to get the feeling that you're the last person I should trust."

"You're wrong."

Ridley turned away. "Exactly. What's wrong with me? I don't even know what I'm doing here."

"You're a Siren. You're doing what you do best," Nox said bitterly.

"What's that supposed to mean?" Ridley didn't like where this conversation was going.

"*First you will meet the Sirens, who cast a spell on every man who comes their way.*" Nox was quoting Homer, his voice unmistakably dark.

He's starting to sound like a raving lunatic, actually.

"Stop it, Nox."

"*Whoso draws near unwarned and hears the Sirens' voices, by him no wife nor little child shall ever stand, glad at his coming home.*"

"I don't do that to people."

"*For the Sirens cast a penetrating song, sitting within a meadow. Nearby is a great heap of rotting human bones; fragments of skin are shriveling on them.*"

"Shut up!" Ridley shouted.

"*Therefore sail on, and stop your comrades' ears with sweet wax, kneaded soft, so none may hear.*"

"I'm not like that." Tears prickled Ridley's eyes.

Nox looked up at her. "But Odysseus was only a man, and we all know how that ends. Just ask Homer."

"You don't have to quote *The Odyssey* to me. I'm not going to destroy you. I'm not a monster," Ridley said.

Nox stared back at her, his expression unreadable.

"No. I don't think you are. But I am."

CHAPTER 30

Some Kind of Monster

A monster?" Ridley shrugged. She couldn't take her eyes off Abraham Ravenwood's face in the picture frame. "Like father, like son, I guess." She wasn't cutting Lennox Gates any slack. Not after he'd sprung something like this on her. *No wonder I never trust anyone.*

"Don't say that!" Nox was furious. He pulled the picture from the wall, throwing it to the ground. Shattered glass flew everywhere. "I told you. He's not my father."

"Right. And because you've proven yourself to be so trustworthy, Nox, I'll just take your word for that."

Nox walked to the window and stared out at the Manhattan skyline. "There isn't a Caster category for what I am. I can't just check the Siren box on some Underground passport."

"Why not? You've been as manipulative as any Siren. You're

Siren-born, no matter who your father is. And aren't you the one behind the Power of Persuasion at Sirene?"

"Ridley." He was pacing.

"Come on, Nox. Let's at least be honest with each other now."

Now that we have nothing left to lose, Ridley thought. *Now that I know you're in league with Abraham Ravenwood.*

She kept going. "Aren't you the reason Sirensong is doing so well, bringing in all the crowds, all the fans?"

Nox shrugged. "It's the name of the band. That should have been your first clue."

"How did you do it? A drink? Was it in the Nectar of the Gods?" It wasn't unthinkable.

He shook his head.

"No Siren can affect that many people that strongly all at once. The ventilation system? Amplified by some kind of Cast?" She'd heard of such a thing.

"No."

Ridley twisted a strand of blond hair around her finger. "Come on. It's tricks of the trade time. Tell me how you did it."

Nox was silent for a long time.

"The music," he said finally.

"What?"

"It's Sampson's guitar. It's actually more of a lyre. It belonged to my mother. I tweaked a few things, and there you go. Instant success."

Ridley shook her head. "Well, I knew it wasn't the lyrics. I guess I shouldn't be surprised. Why else would you name your club after a Siren unless you were planning on working a little mojo?"

"Trust me. The specifics aren't important. In fact, the less you know about me, the safer you are."

"And the Turkish Delight? The disappearing club? How do you explain the rest of it?" *How do you explain the way you make me feel sometimes? This war that is not a war?* She wanted answers.

"Liar's Trade." He looked at her. "What, you think yours are the only markers I have? What do you think happens to all those lost talents, favors, and powers?"

"Of course. The TFPs. You're a thief. All your power is stolen." It was so clear now. She couldn't believe she had missed it.

"Not all of it. You know my mother was a Siren. My father— my real father—was a Seer. Their blood runs in my veins."

"If you say so," Ridley said. She couldn't help twisting the knife. Especially when the knife was Abraham Ravenwood.

Nox stopped pacing. He was livid. "My family is my family. It wasn't perfect. In fact, it was hell."

Ridley nodded. "I'm beginning to get that."

"Exactly. But you know what else it was? My own damn business."

Ridley stepped in front of him. "Nox, calm down. What's going on? Why won't you tell me? One minute you're trying to scare me, and the next you're treating me to a New York City dream day. You're either a complete nutbag or a huge jerk."

"Thanks."

"Either way, I'd help you if you told me what was happening. I really would."

"No," Nox said. "You're in enough trouble already. You don't need me to drag you into any more. It seems to find you on its own, the same way it finds me." Nox looked more nervous than Ridley had ever seen him.

"So we're back to monsters again?" she asked, almost afraid to hear the answer.

"You don't know what it's like. I'm Darker than you." He shook his head. His voice was low and trembling. "When I think about what they wanted me to do to you…"

"Stop it," Ridley said. "You're a lot of things, Nox, but a monster isn't one of them. Trust me. I've seen my share."

"Like Abraham Ravenwood?" Nox asked. His tone was even darker now.

"I won't argue that one."

"He stole my father's Sight and used it for his own Dark purposes. Until one day, my father saw his own death at my mother's hand."

The man you hope is your father, Ridley thought.

"He couldn't handle it. He threw himself off a cliff in Barbados to keep the only woman he'd ever loved from having to live with that guilt."

"Nox." She didn't know what to say. He was every bit as broken as she was, just as she had suspected.

Maybe even more.

"I was raised by my grandparents, just like you. Abraham drove my mother to madness, and he made sure that my life was as pathetic as his twisted little Incubus science experiments."

Ridley knew all too well what Nox was saying. "No one has a run-in with Abraham Ravenwood without walking away with a scar."

Nox nodded. "Maybe that's why I hate the sight of your

hybrid Incubus boyfriend so much. I hate anything that reminds me of Abraham, or his labs."

Ridley reached for Nox's hand. She couldn't help it. He looked like a little boy, incapable of being consoled. "Not to state the obvious, but Abraham's dead. I should know. I was there."

Nox remained glum. "So I've heard. Gardening shears, right?"

Ridley nodded. "He took a pair through the heart. He's as dead as a doornail." She squeezed his hand. "What is it that you're not telling me, Nox?"

"I've been trying to tell you." He looked away. "The complicated side of the story."

"I'm listening."

"Little Siren," Nox said, "I'd give anything in the world to have met you some other way."

"I know." She held his hand even more tightly.

He looked at her sadly. "And I would give more than that to change the nightmares that I see coming in your future."

Ridley's heart beat faster. "What?"

"You have to remember. Just because I saw it doesn't mean there's no hope." He touched her cheek, suddenly tender.

She pulled away from him. "Nox, what did you see?"

"I saw our future. Mine, and yours."

"And?" She didn't know if she wanted to hear anything more, but she couldn't seem to stop herself from asking.

"And I'm saying there's still got to be hope for both of us. And for this." He leaned forward, as if he meant to kiss her.

She held her breath, but it never happened.

Because the Ripping sound came first.

Then came the inevitable crash that followed when furniture met size thirteen Doc Martens.

Wesley Lincoln, one-quarter Incubus and three-quarters heart, stepped out of the wall between the bedroom and the living room. He straightened a painting and pulled his foot out of a wastebasket, but aside from that, even Ridley had to admit his Traveling skills had seriously improved.

His fighting skills, even more so.

Link didn't waste any time. He barreled right into Nox and pinned him against the wall.

"I didn't see that one coming," Nox said, trying to shove him away.

Link wouldn't budge. "Tell me it's him and not you, Rid," he shouted, without taking his eyes off Nox.

Ridley grabbed Link's arm. "Stop it. What are you doing here?"

"Apparently, trying to kick my ass," Nox said.

Link turned to look at her. "Someone deserves a beatdown, and I'm really hopin' it's him, because I've been waitin' to pound him since the day we got here."

"Don't hold back." Nox closed his eyes. "Go ahead. Take your best shot."

Ridley tried to pull Link away. "Are you out of your mind?" She yanked as hard as she could, but Link still didn't budge. "I'm sorry about what happened. I don't know what I was thinking, but you can't just come barging in here and threaten me—or him—like that."

"Actually, he can. And if he won't, I will." Floyd stepped into the center of the room, and her hands morphed into brass knuckles. "Illusionist-style. No Mortal rules. And none of that complicated conscience crap."

271

She held up her fists.

Nox looked confused. "Take it easy, Fight Club. I'm not going to hurt either one of you."

Link glared. "No, you're not. The hurt is only goin' to go one way around here. Admit what you did, and maybe we can figure this out."

"What exactly am I admitting?" Nox asked.

Link hesitated, looking from Nox to Ridley. "Necro's bad. She may not ever come back."

"What?" Ridley felt her stomach begin to twist. "It's that bad?"

Link's face darkened. "Sampson said it was a Siren who messed her up."

"Link," Ridley began, shaking her head.

"Don't tell me it was you, Rid. Tell me he put you up to it." Link's eyes were wild and red. "Don't tell me he used that house marker on you and had you hurt someone."

Nox and Floyd looked at him. Even Ridley looked surprised by the mention of her Suffer debt.

She shook her head. "Nox? He didn't put me up to anything." She touched Link's arm.

"Really, Rid." Link sounded desperate now. "Because I know you, right? You'd never actually hurt someone. You just wouldn't."

Ridley didn't know exactly what Link was talking about, but she was pretty sure it was about more than Necro being hurt.

"Listen to me, Link. I didn't do anything. Not to Necro or anyone else."

Floyd's expression hardened.

Link looked so relieved that Ridley thought he was going to

hug her. "Good." His voice wavered. "I believed in you. I stuck up for you."

"You did?"

"I knew, deep down, all you were was a whole lotta big talk. You never mean to hurt anyone. You're just one a those sea urchin kind a people. You've got spikes, all right, but that's just because you're scared a sharks. On the inside, you're all soft."

"Or at least, a great home for tiny fish," Floyd added, irritated. "Can we cut the heart-to-heart and get on with the beat-down part already?"

Instead, Link looked from Nox to Ridley again. "If you didn't do it, and he didn't make you do it, then who did? Because Necro's runnin' outta time and if we don't do somethin', we'll need a Necromancer to talk to her next."

"It wasn't us," Nox said. The word echoed between them.

Us.

Link looked from Nox to Ridley. "Is that right?"

Slowly, Ridley nodded. "You know neither one of us would do anything to hurt Necro." *Or you, Link.*

Link shook his head, but he looked like he'd rather be shaking everything in the room. *And maybe throwing it all*, Ridley thought.

"Really? You wouldn't hurt her? 'Cause there's a gash on her neck, and it's bleedin' black blood," Link snapped. "You saw it. If neither one of you did it, why is she headed to the Otherworld?"

"If Necro's sick because of a cut on her neck, then it's my fault." Nox spoke softly, but they all heard him.

Link growled. "What are you talking about?"

"It happened when she was working for me." Nox looked devastated.

"She cut her neck playing the keyboard?" Ridley asked.

Nox shook his head. "That's not the only thing she does for me. She's also my Necromancer. I never should have dragged her into this, but I need her."

"For what?" Link asked.

"She's the best Necromancer I know, and she has the strongest connection to the Ravenwoods I've ever seen." Now it was Nox who couldn't bring himself to look at Rid.

"The Ravenwoods," Ridley repeated, feeling ill. "Of course. Abraham."

This time it was Link's turn to look sick. "Abraham? My Abraham?"

Nox nodded, his head in his hands. "I had to do something for them, and I needed Necro so I could talk to Abraham Ravenwood about it."

"You're his *spy*? Abraham Ravenwood's errand boy? The man who ruined your family and killed your parents? You're working for him?" Ridley was in disbelief. Nox was even more messed up than she'd realized.

Nox didn't answer.

Ridley spat out the words. "And Necro knew?"

"No," Nox said, looking up. "She has no idea. She just wakes up, without a memory of it."

Link crossed his arms tightly. "What exactly did ole Grandpa Abraham want you to do?"

Nox glared at him. "It's not important now," Nox said. "I didn't do it."

Ridley looked incredulous. "How do we know that?"

"Because if I had, you'd both be dead."

The room fell silent.

Link spoke up first. "You're a real hero, and I bet it's an interestin' story, but we don't have time for your crap. Not now. Necro's dyin'. Your boy Sampson is some kind a Darkborn mojo detector, and he said a Siren did this to her, and that person is the only one who can save her."

Nox sounded grim. "I didn't cut her, but it's my knife. It belonged to my mother. I lent it to Necro because I was worried that she couldn't protect herself, given her gifts."

Floyd looked like she wanted to beat Nox to death. "You mean when she's working for you? Here's a thought—what about if *you* protected her?"

Nox ran his hand through his hair. "It's not that easy."

"But talking to the dead is?" Floyd snapped.

Ridley was horrified. "No. You're right. It's better if she looks out for herself. Since according to you, she has *no idea* what's going on."

"Necro entered into a contract with me. The only thing she asked was that I wipe anything from her mind. I used an *Oblivio* Cast."

"Why would she do that?" Floyd asked.

"She was scared. Her powers were getting in the way of everything else in her life. When I met her, she could barely get out of bed or play her music. She didn't want to live like that anymore, but Necromancers are valuable to the wrong kind of people. She knew if she started playing out in the open again, someone would find her eventually. So she came to me for protection." Nox sounded resigned.

"You've done a bang-up job so far," Link said.

Nox ignored him. "The knife is Charmed. It was designed to subdue out-of-control spirits from the Otherworld. I didn't know it could hurt a living Caster, aside from the blade itself."

"Maybe you should've looked into that before you gave it to her," Floyd snarled

"I saw her cut herself," Nox said. "I didn't know she would get sick from it. You have to believe me. I'd never hurt Necro. She's the closest thing I have to a friend."

Had, Ridley thought. *Unless we can help her.* She held up her hand. "Wait, you saw her cut herself? And you didn't do anything?"

Nox sighed. "She didn't do it herself, not strictly speaking."

"Then who did it?"

"Abraham Ravenwood."

"Of course he did." Link punched his fist through the wall, sending a spray of plaster dust into the air around him. "'Cause things weren't bad enough already."

He grabbed Nox by the collar of his shirt, and Floyd by the hand. "It's time to make this right. Grab on to someone, Ridley."

Link didn't have to say the obvious. It wasn't Ridley's hand he was holding now.

CHAPTER 31

Flash of the Blade

It didn't take long for Nox to strip the Charm from Necro's blade. Once he did, all they could do was wait and see if the wound would heal. Even Sampson stopped making his grim predictions about Necro's fate.

Still, nobody knew what would happen now.

The waiting part was the hardest.

Ridley stared at a poster of Sid Vicious. She moved down the wall to Johnny Rotten, then Social Distortion. X. Black Flag. Dead Kennedys. She didn't know much about punk rock, but she was guessing she was looking at the hall of fame.

"The Necros? It's a band?" She lingered over another ancient punk poster. "Is that where she got her name?"

Floyd nodded. "Nec's from Toledo, Ohio. So was the band. I think she felt like it was meant to be." She smiled. "Kind of like Link Floyd."

"You start that again, Supertramp. I dare you." Rid glared.

Link cut them off. "Speakin' a Necro, how much longer you think we gotta wait?" He sounded worried. He'd been like that ever since Nox had undone the Cast.

"The real question is, how many places can a person stick a safety pin?" Rid shook her head, touching the Social D poster. Then next to it, Dead Kennedys. Every single face she could see looked like they should be in Necro's family, or at least her band. Half of them were even more pierced than she was.

Floyd looked at Rid. "Nec loves Dead Kennedys. She says they're her tribe."

Ridley raised an eyebrow. "Necro has a tribe?"

"Sure she does. She has us," Floyd said.

"You guys must be pretty close. I mean, to let her take over the walls like that." Ridley fingered the edge of the X poster.

"Didn't you ever have a best friend?" It was clear from Floyd's tone that she wasn't betting on it. "Or did you always live alone in that cave you call a heart?"

Ridley fixed her eyes on the giant X.

Don't answer.

Don't let her see.

Don't give any of them that satisfaction.

"Cut it out, Floyd," said Link, looking up. "Rid has a lot of friends and a big family, and she has me. She has all of us."

Rid's eyes met Link's from across the room.

"We're her tribe," he said.

And it was true.

She felt like she was going to burst into tears, except she

would've rather stabbed her own eyes out than break down in front of Floyd.

Only a groan coming from the low, rickety bed saved her.

"Holy Toledo," Necro muttered.

Link grinned. "Hey, we were just talkin' about that."

Necro's eyes fluttered open. "I feel like crap."

"You look like crap, too." Ridley smiled at her. She had never been more relieved to see a few more piercings and a blue faux-hawk.

"Hey, buddy." Floyd took Necro's hand. Floyd's other hand bloomed instantly into a bouquet of flowers.

Necro nodded. "Can you make those chocolates?"

"And let you eat my finger?" Floyd's hand fell back into its natural form while Necro turned her head to the rest of the room, smiling weakly.

Link was hovering. "No worries, man. We got this whole thing all figured out. You're gonna be up and jammin' in no time at all." He patted her bed awkwardly.

"Rock on." Necro flashed him the horns, the universal heavy metal hell-yeah. "What's the boss man doing here?"

Nox sat on the floor, leaning against the wall of her room. He was so quiet that they'd almost forgotten he was still there.

Floyd reached up to brush a stray blue wisp away from Necro's face. "He's just worried about you, like the rest of us." Floyd didn't say anything more than that, though Ridley knew she'd have plenty to say on the subject of Nox Gates and his secret relationship with his favorite Necromancer.

They would fight it out later, Ridley suspected. That was what bands did.

Just like tribes.

"I've never done one of these before. I hope it works." Ridley lit the last candle in the Circle of Protection around apartment 2D. A wide ring of flickering light now wound its way from the stage to the beach to Necro's room and back again. Rid wasn't sure Necro was in danger, but they were all too afraid to leave her unprotected in her present state.

Nox looked back after she blew out the last match. He kept his eyes on Ridley. "I'm sorry, Little Siren."

Me, too, she thought. *About this. About everything.* He looked for a second like he didn't quite know what to say, but Ridley didn't, either.

She shrugged it off. "Don't. It was an accident. And anyway, you came back here to help Necro. That's the important thing." *It doesn't matter now*, she thought.

Lines had been crossed. Everything had been said. There was no point in talking about it beyond that.

Nox reached out to touch a pink strand of hair. "I guess this is good-bye." He dropped his hand. "Take care of Necro. And yourself."

"I always do." Her eyes lingered on him.

"I know," Nox said.

He took a tentative step toward her.

"Do you mind?" He gestured awkwardly. "A real good-bye? Seeing as I may never see you again?"

"What?"

Nox extended his arms. One last embrace. A hug between friends. Rid couldn't refuse. But she also couldn't avoid looking over her shoulder before she moved any closer to him. Just to make sure the door was shut.

Ridley and Link might not have been together anymore, but he and Floyd would never let her hear the end of it if they walked in and saw her so much as touching Lennox Gates.

The candles flickered and smoked.

Ridley and Nox stood in the center of the circle—on the shore of the beach that was apartment 2D.

He drew her in for a hug. She could feel his powerful arms beneath his jacket. It seemed like so long ago that they had stood together on the dance floor at Sirene and shared that one exquisite, terrifying kiss.

She hadn't realized it wouldn't be the only one.

He leaned toward her.

His lips touched hers gently. A very different kind of kiss.

It was sweet.

Sweet enough for both of them.

Nox had hurt Ridley, and he knew it. He could feel it, the moment he kissed her.

If only he had told her everything he knew, right from the start.

If only.

He had thought that if he could have one last kiss, maybe it would be like a Cast. Maybe she would forgive him, and everything would revert to the way it had been before he screwed it all up.

But that wasn't possible, because he had been screwing up from the beginning.

When I promised to deliver her to a Ravenwood Blood Incubus. Or when I watched her die in a fire in my own club and I didn't warn her.

If I let it happen that way.

There was a special place in Hell for guys like Lennox.

It was called life.

The only thing he had left was a kiss.

This kiss.

Nox caught a glimpse of candlelight in his peripheral vision, and suddenly he was spinning out of control.

The fire.

The vision hit during the kiss, and there was nothing he could do to stop it.

The vision smoke cleared even as Nox tried to look past it. He was standing somewhere gray and filthy that reeked of garbage and sewage. A thin spray of mold was growing on the stone floor and ceiling.

No light. Underground. A prison cell, probably. It looks more like a dungeon.

Nox found himself standing in the corridor, looking down on the individual lockups. Every steel door was identical— heavy, barred, and bolted.

He walked away from the doors, toward the end of the hallway. At the very end stood two men who looked vaguely familiar. They looked with interest through a square window cut into the cell door immediately in front of them.

The first was a hulking figure, wearing a black suit and cheap leather shoes.

The other man was thinner but imposing, his face hidden behind a black fedora. The sleeves of his expensive dress shirt were pushed up above his elbows carelessly. He was the dangerous one. He stepped back from the door, smoking a cigar.

Nox recognized the gold crown stamped on the side.

Barbadian. He's a Ravenwood.

Nox didn't need to see the family crest stamped into the heavy silver signet ring on the man's finger. There was only one person who fit the description, though Nox himself had never seen him in person.

Silas Ravenwood, the infamous and deadly great-great-grandson of Abraham.

"Keep her chained up until I tell you otherwise," Silas said in a thick accent that Nox couldn't quite place. "To say the Power of Persuasion is valuable to a man in my line of work is an understatement. And my last Siren was useless."

The man in the cheap shoes peered into the shadows of the cell. "Do the chains leave marks?"

"Of course. But I'll make her Charm them away herself. Or maybe I'll let her keep them as a reminder."

"You think this Siren will be better?"

"She comes from a powerful line. And she's made some powerful enemies. How else would she have ended up here?" His voice didn't betray a hint of emotion. "You know Lennox Gates?"

The big guy nodded. "I think I met him once, in one of his clubs."

"His mother was my grandfather's personal Siren, and she was a powerful bitch. The kid sold me this one." Silas Ravenwood laughed.

"Expensive?"

"His life," Silas said.

"You made him pay to keep his own life?" Silas' underling looked shocked.

"Of course not. I made him pay *with* it." He shrugged. "Never bargain with a Blood Incubus."

The pit in Nox's stomach hardened into a lump. It was the closest he'd ever come to seeing his own future, and he suspected it was because it wasn't really about him.

This was Ridley's vision.

She was the Siren they were talking about.

The one chained like an animal.

Then the smoke descended and the terrible faces of the two men vanished...

...and Ridley broke off the kiss.

"Nox? Are you okay?" Ridley stared into his eyes, though they didn't seem to see her. She shook his shoulders, hard. "Nox. You're creeping me out."

He focused his eyes and pulled her into a hug. Now he was holding her so tight that it hurt. "I need to tell you something, Little Siren."

Ridley pulled free from his arms. "What is it?"

"Something I should have told you a long time ago." His eyes held hers. "I don't want to do this. And I've never done it before."

"Done what?" The way Nox was talking, though, Ridley wasn't sure she wanted to know.

"My father warned me not to. Nobody wants to hear it."

"Nox." Ridley was frightened.

"Not even a Caster. We all want to pretend we will live forever."

Ridley's face was pale. "What are you talking about?"

"There's a reason your kiss tastes like fire," Nox began.

⊰ CHAPTER 32 ⊱

Disposable Heroes

Nox told Ridley and Link as much as he could from the relative safety of the Circle of Protection and fifty lit candles. Not that a Circle or a thousand candles could stop a Ravenwood.

Not even apartment 2D was safe, not anymore.

Ridley had to physically restrain Link until Nox finished talking. She would've had to hold off Floyd and Sampson too, except they were both too busy with Necro to care what Nox had to say about anything.

"So let me get this straight," Link said. "You promised Abraham Ravenwood that you'd hand us over to his thugs. You already told us that part."

Nox nodded. "One thug. Silas Ravenwood. His grandson."

"The criminal," Link said.

"Or the Capo. I've heard that's what he calls himself."

"Why me? For what?" Ridley was numb.

"What do you expect? He wants revenge," Nox said. "Your hybrid stabbed his grandfather with a pair of gardening shears."

"And Grandpa had it comin'." Link shrugged. "Guess that makes sense, not that I'm goin' down without a fight. But what does he want with Rid?"

Nox walked over to the window and stared out. It was difficult to look anywhere else. "She lured Abraham there. She delivered him right into your hands."

"So Silas wants to kill her, too?" Link asked. "I'm not enough?" He almost looked insulted.

Ridley was silent, and from the expression on her face, terrified. "Is that it? Is that how I..."

"I'm not sure," Nox said slowly. As if the words themselves were painful. "I've seen your future twice now. Each time it was slightly different."

"But I die? In a fire?"

"Once."

"Once? What about the other time?"

Nox had a strained look on his face now. "Remember when I told you about my mother?"

She nodded.

"Silas is a powerful man. Part of that power comes from the Dark Casters around him. He needs a Siren, and your family is about as powerful as they come, Rid."

"Don't call her that," Link snapped. "Rid's not your friend. Friends don't sell you out to Dark Incubuses."

"But Silas would. And Silas is a businessman. Selling a Siren to the highest bidder, that's good business. Selling the Siren who helped end Abraham Ravenwood, that's even better business."

Ridley stared back at Nox, stunned. "You said your mother

was Abraham's slave. Are you telling me that you were going to hand me over to Silas so he could lock me up in a cage, too? Just like his grandfather?"

Link curled his hands into fists.

"That's one scenario," Nox said carefully. "The fire is the other."

Ridley was incredulous. "And you never said a word?"

Nox stared at the floor. "I tried."

Not hard enough.

Nox looked miserable. "I didn't want to hand you over, period. But before, I didn't really see another way out. It's different now. Now that we're...friends. That's why I'm telling you all this."

Link walked over and stood next to Ridley. "I'm not lettin' you give her to anyone. And I'm not lettin' anyone stick her back in a cage. I'll go instead."

"Link," Ridley began.

Nox turned around to face them. "You don't get it, Mortal."

"Part Mortal," Link said, unflinching.

"Abraham wants both of you, and if I hand you over, you're dead and she's in chains. If I don't hand you over, he'll have Silas find you anyway. So we need to come up with a plan B."

"What if we leave?" Ridley said. "Right now."

Nox nodded. "You should. Get on the road and don't look back. It's the smartest thing to do."

"Tell her the rest." Sampson stood in the doorway, leaning against the frame.

"Shut up," Nox said. "Stay out of this."

Ridley turned to Sampson. "Tell me what?"

"Keep your mouth shut," Nox snapped.

Sampson shoved his huge hands in his pockets and stared back at Nox. "I don't like people telling me what to do. You know that, boss."

Nox's temper flared. "There's only one important word in that sentence: *boss*. We figured this out. Leave it alone."

Sampson nodded, his brown hair hiding his expression. "If those two leave, you won't be my boss anymore. So I guess it doesn't matter if I say anything either way, now, does it?"

Ridley spun around. "Nox, what is he talking about?"

Nox stared back at her, the girl who had changed everything, including him. "If I don't deliver the two of you, Silas won't be happy with me."

"Not happy? He'll kill you." Sampson didn't smile. "Silas, or a handful of Vexes. If he's in a good mood he'll let you choose."

"But hey." Nox forced a smile. "Things haven't been going so well for me anyway."

Ridley's expression crumpled. "Then we stay. We aren't going to let you take on Silas Ravenwood alone."

"She's right," Link said. "I'm not leavin' another guy to take a hit for me, especially not a piece a garbage like you."

Nox shook his head. "You don't get it. He won't stop until the hybrid is dead and you're on a leash for good. You can't escape the Ravenwoods. You should know that by now."

"What if he thinks we're dead?" Ridley asked.

Nox shook his head. "What am I supposed to tell him? That the two of you took a trip to the Bermuda Triangle and your plane disappeared? He's not going to believe the two of you are dead unless he sees it for himself."

"Isn't there a Cast or some Illusionist trick for that? Maybe Floyd can cook somethin' up," Link said. "Some kinda Caster Fakeus Corpsicus?"

But Ridley knew there were some things even a Cast couldn't fix.

Sometimes you just had to go with good old-fashioned planning and manipulation.

Mortal-style.

CHAPTER 33

Oh Yoko!

Hours later, Nox stood at the top of the Empire State Building. The city unfolded beneath him, but he couldn't see it. He was only focused on the moment right in front of him. This was the big game, the last hand, and Nox had nothing in it. There was only one thing he could do now.

What he'd always done.

Bluff.

Nox wasn't sure about any of this. It was Ridley's idea. The hybrid had agreed, but the hybrid would agree to anything—no matter how risky or ridiculous—if he thought it would keep Ridley out of Abraham's clutches.

Nox knew the feeling, which was why he was here now.

He heard the door to the observation platform swing open, then footsteps behind him. "I heard you were looking for me," Nox said.

This is it. Make him think you've got a full house.

Silas Ravenwood circled around him, a wisp of smoke from a Barbadian cigar trailing after him. In a pressed dress shirt, expensive gray slacks, and Italian wing tips, Silas almost could've passed for a CEO instead of a crime lord.

A Blood Incubus CEO.

It was only the smuggled cigars, the way he rolled up the sleeves of his fifteen-hundred-dollar shirt, and the fedora that marked him as a criminal.

And his knuckles.

Businessmen don't have crooked knuckles from beating people to death.

"Where have you been, kid? I left you a message."

Nox shrugged. "Nowhere special."

Silas walked up to him, the cherry of his cigar dangerously close to Nox's cheek. "You think I'm screwing around? When I tell a mutt like you to come in, I expect to see you in my goddamned office with that tail of yours tucked between your legs."

"I've been busy."

"You won't be as busy if you're dead," Silas said. "You have one day to deliver the Siren and the hybrid Incubus."

"Why do you care about the two of them so much, if you don't mind me asking?" Nox knew he was walking a slippery slope. Silas Ravenwood wasn't a fan of questions.

"Why are you suddenly so interested? Feeling sentimental? I know how you feel about half-breeds and wish workers." Silas smiled. "They're almost like *family*."

Nox shrugged, holding in his anger. "Sorry I touched a nerve. I was just curious."

292

"My grandfather wants his name avenged." Silas took a long pull on the cigar. "I have my own reasons for wanting the Siren."

"Is it love?" Nox raised an eyebrow.

Silas grinned. "It is to me."

Nox shuddered.

Ridley in chains. In captivity. Begging for her life. Nox felt ill at the thought, especially knowing how much Silas would enjoy it. "Do what you want. I'm not partial to Sirens myself."

"Too many memories?" Silas leered. "Because if I remember correctly, your mother had no problem granting all my wishes when she worked for my grandfather. At least, when she wasn't busy being Abraham's little whore."

Nox fought back a wave of hot anger.

Steady.

Instead, he imagined taking the Charmed switchblade out of his pocket and holding it to Silas Ravenwood's throat. *How the skin would part, how the blood would rush to the surface. How the body would fall.*

Nox drew a breath, leaving his eyes fixed on Silas. "Fine. Take them off my hands tomorrow night. It'll be easier if I lock them up at the club and you come and get them."

"Tomorrow?" Silas was caught off guard, it seemed.

Nox shrugged. "The hybrid's unpredictable, a real pain in the ass. But he'll be playing at the club, which means the Siren will be there, too. I'll shut them up in the supply room in the basement." He smiled. "À la carte and to go."

Silas thought about it for a minute. Finally, he nodded.

"Be sure to knock the Incubus out first. We're a lot smarter than you Casters, so you have to take precautions. If he's learned anything about Traveling, he'll know he can take the Siren with him."

"Naturally."

Silas stubbed out the cigar on the railing, next to Nox's hand. "Tomorrow night. If they're not there, you'll be the one to pay for it."

Nox tried to keep his expression unreadable. "As if I'd expect anything less."

"Have I ever showed you my tattoo?" Silas rolled up his sleeve another few inches. Two words curved around the front of the Incubus's bicep.

No mercy.

"My grandfather cut it into my arm himself." Silas let his sleeve fall. He snapped his fingers and the door of the observation platform opened behind him.

After Silas was gone, Nox stayed on the roof. There was one more thing he needed to do, and he wanted to do it before he changed his mind.

He pulled a matchbook from his pocket and ran his fingers over the six letters on the cover.

Nox couldn't see his own future, but he wasn't sure it mattered, not anymore. His future wasn't the one he needed to see.

He had to see hers.

Nox had seen the fire and the chains, and he'd started the biggest con of his life. He needed to know if it was going to work—if he could protect her.

No matter how she felt about him, he still had to know.

He struck the match. The smell of sulfur crept into his nostrils.

He lifted his eyes, and there, in the darkness, he saw the last days of Ridley Duchannes' life.

For the third and final time.

And then, as the clouds rolled in, he did something else. He made a plan to change them.

The four of them sat eating hot dogs on a pile of rocks in Central Park, shrouded by trees. The sky was dark, and rain was on the way.

Only rain, if we're lucky.

But when are we ever lucky?

Rid could still hear the traffic from Central Park South. The sound of the chaos was comforting. After what Nox had told her, Ridley didn't feel safe anywhere, but there was only so long the others were willing to stay sandwiched between protective candles.

Hiding in crowded public spaces—Mortal spaces—was the only other idea she'd come up with.

And sticking together.

"That's the big plan? The best you could come up with?" Floyd sounded skeptical. She shoved the rest of her hot dog into her mouth.

"Yeah." Link glared. "Seein' as the marines were already busy."

"You think this could actually work?" Necro tossed her dog back into the paper. "Silas will buy it?" She was bouncing back faster than anyone had thought she could, especially considering it had only been a day since she was lying unconscious on her deathbed.

Even so, the hot dog was ambitious.

"He might." Link sighed. "Maybe."

Ridley couldn't eat, either. "It's a long shot. If you guys don't want to do it, I understand." She jammed her hands into the pockets of her leather jacket and shivered.

"What does that mean?" Necro picked at the awkward bandage on her neck.

"It means that I wasn't straight with Link, and I wasn't straight with you. And I'm sorry about that." Ridley sounded miserable. "About a lot of things."

Necro looked at her. Floyd didn't.

Link stayed silent.

In the distance, two taxi drivers cussed each other out. Horns blared, and cars roared past.

"You want to know what I think?" Necro asked.

Rid wasn't sure.

"You, Ridley Duchannes, are a giant bitch. A full-blown Yoko Ono." Necro said the words slowly. Then she looked at Floyd, who shrugged.

Ridley stiffened. "And?"

"And I think John Ono Lennon was one of the greatest musicians in the history of the known universe." Necro smiled.

Ridley was caught off guard. "What's that supposed to mean?"

"Every band needs a Yoko. And Silas Ravenwood can suck it. Nobody messes with my band. Right, Floyd?"

Floyd wadded up her hot dog wrapper. "The girl has a point."

Necro held up her fist. "Pound it, sister. Silas Ravenwood is going down."

Floyd held up hers.

Then Link. "Don't leave a guy hangin'."

Ridley didn't.

"Now," said Necro, rubbing her blue faux-hawk. "Think you can do anything with this hair? I'm feeling like tonight calls for a Brooklyn Blowout."

"No time. We have to meet Nox back at the apartment." Ridley slid down from the rock, her short kilt snagging on the way.

"Tell me he's bringing us a pizza," Necro said, sliding down after her. "Anything but hot dogs."

"Even better," Ridley said as Link and Floyd climbed down from the rock. "He's bringing us the blueprints to Sirene."

CHAPTER 34

Symphony of Destruction

"This is a hellhole," Ridley muttered from her seat on the dank basement floor.

"You think?" Link sat next to her, staring up at the ceiling, where some kind of plumbing leaked through the planks and plaster.

Not just a hellhole. A prison, she thought. You could almost hear the rats scurrying behind the kegs.

How did I end up in a dirty basement in the bottom of a nightclub in Brooklyn? Afraid for my future? Hiding from Silas Ravenwood?

They waited in silence. There wasn't much left to talk about at a time like this.

Twenty-four hours of planning didn't make tonight any better. The band had still ridden to the club in tense silence. The moldy basement beneath Sirene was still dank and deserted. Nox was still pacing in his office as if it was opening night.

It wasn't.

There were no Casters crowding in. No DayGlo Sirenes selling Nectar of the Gods. No bartenders, no band.

Not on this level of the club, which had been locked off from the rest of the world, just as Nox had promised Silas it would be.

This storage room made the Underground look like the Happiest Place on Earth.

Ridley could feel the bass beat begin pounding through the walls. Nox had his house DJ covering for them. Every sound made her jump.

"Music's come up," Link said, listening.

"Yep." *Won't be long now,* she thought.

"We should be out there." He sounded wistful.

"Not tonight, we shouldn't."

"Guess not."

Rid smiled at him. "You had a good run, Shrinky Dink."

"Yeah. Sirensong." He said the name like he was filing it away in his graveyard of failed bands.

Who Shot Lincoln. The Holy Rollers. Meatstik. Sirensong.

Rid picked at a pink glitter nail. "It wasn't all Nox, you know. Not all of it."

Link didn't take the bait. "Sure. It was also his mom's Siren lyre."

"Link."

"Guess there's no way to find out now." Link sighed and looked at her. "It doesn't matter, Rid. We gotta get outta here and get safe." *Get you out of here and get you safe.* That was what he was thinking. Ridley knew Link well enough to know that, no matter how mad he might be at her.

She had always been his first priority. Taking care of her. Doing the right thing by her. Caring about her. She didn't know why it had taken her so long to believe it.

Guess there's no way to find out now.

She resisted the urge to reach out to him, if only to lay her hand on his arm. It was strange, having to remember not to touch him.

I did this.

I did this to myself.

"Ow—" A yelp from Link broke the silence, and he shook his hand like he wanted to shake it right off. "Is your ring burnin' up?"

She held hers up, wincing. The glowing red light cast shadows on the wall around them. "Like crazy."

It was quiet for a moment.

Ridley stole a sideways look at Link. "I would have, too, you know."

He raised an eyebrow. "Woulda what?"

"Taken your place. With Abraham, I mean. Back there, what you said. How you would have let him take you instead of me."

Link stared at the wall in front of him intently. "Yeah?"

Ridley shrugged. "I just wanted you to know."

He turned to her. "Rid—"

But the banging at the door startled them, and Ridley pulled herself to her feet, Link scrambling up after her. "Nox?"

"It's me," the familiar voice said from the other side.

Link unlocked the door. "Took you long enough."

"Sorry," Nox said. "I had to organize a few things. A few thousand things. Floyd and Necro are ready to go. I have them at each end of the stage, waiting for my signal."

Ridley looked at Nox. "Necro. Is she—"

"Fine. Stronger than you think. Believe me." In some ways, Nox knew her better than any of them, Ridley realized.

Link looked relieved.

Nox took in the dismal room. "How do you kids like it down here? Pretty luxurious, right?"

"We couldn't have waited in your office?" Ridley asked.

"I said I was holding you down here," Nox said. "That was the plan. This has to seem legit. Silas has eyes on the club. He's not exactly a trusting guy."

"So what's next?" Ridley asked, shivering. She knew the plan, but knowing it didn't make her feel any better about it.

Nox pulled a little crimson matchbook from his pocket and held it in the air between his fingers. Ridley recognized it immediately. The word SIRENE was printed across the cover.

Nox took her hand with his free one, and Rid could almost feel Link watching them. "You're sure you want to go through with this, Little Siren?"

"If you're sure it's the only way," she answered.

He nodded. "It's the only way I can think of."

Link's eyes were fixed on the matches. "Is that for what I think it is? Or are you plannin' to take up smokin'?"

"It's time," Nox said.

"So just a small fire, right? A diversion?" Rid started to get nervous.

"Not that small," Nox said. "Maybe a little bigger than I let on."

"Nox." Ridley pulled her hand away.

"Okay, maybe not small at all." Nox shrugged. "Don't worry. I've shown everything to Necro and Floyd. The Illusionist can handle it. They'll get everyone out of the club before they even know what's going on. And, hopefully, before it blows."

"Hold on, dude." Suddenly, Link was paying attention. "You're gonna burn your own club down?"

"The only way Silas Ravenwood will leave you both alone is if he thinks you're dead, and it has to be convincing. Something he can see—or at least his men can see—with their own eyes. They'll see Sirene when she burns." Nox waved the matches. "Get it?"

"Wait. Seriously." Ridley put a hand on his arm. "You'd burn down Sirene for me?"

"Why not?" Nox shrugged, looking at her. "I built it for you."

For a second, no one said a word.

Then Link gave Nox a hard look. "How about you keep that crap to yourself, pretty boy? Otherwise, the wrong Supernatural might go up in flames."

Nox ignored him.

Ridley looked away. "No."

"Ridley. Please. Let me do the right thing, for once in my life."

"I said no." She shook her head. "Call it off. There has to be a better way."

Link looked at her. "The guy has a point. As much as I don't like it, we don't have a whole lotta choices right now, Rid."

"Exactly." Nox sighed. "They come for you. The place goes up in flames. We carry out the bodies."

"Our bodies." Ridley was still having trouble wrapping her mind around it.

He nodded. "Eventually, Abraham will figure it out when you don't show up on the other side. But by then, you'll have a head start on him. You'll just have to lay low."

"Like, witness protection low." Link nodded. "We'll figure something out."

Nox lowered his voice. "You saw the blueprints. You can't go out the front door, or Silas' men will see you. There's only one way out from down here." Nox pointed down the hallway. "The service door is at the end of that hall. Go out that way."

"Won't Silas have men at that door, too?" Rid asked.

"Yeah," Nox said, "but they won't be standing very close, if that's where the fire starts."

"You're not saying—" Ridley couldn't bring herself to finish.

"The fire starts here." Nox nodded. "You're going to have to get out through the fire. It's the only way."

"Hello." Link waved. "Hybrid Incubus in the room. We're not goin' out the door. I'll Rip us both out. I've gotten a lot better lately."

"You can't," Nox said. "Silas isn't stupid. He's already got that one covered. The club is Bound—on top of my own Binding, he's done his own. Can't you feel it? No one can Travel in or out. No Rip letter could get through that now. You have to use the doors, like a Mortal."

Ridley panicked. "But you said I die in a fire." She stared back at him, her heart pounding in her chest. "This is what you warned me about. Tonight."

Nox nodded. "You die in a fire. That's one possibility. But

not this one. I never saw anything like this. I never saw a future where we were the ones starting the fire."

"How do you know?" Ridley felt desperate.

"I saw wooden stairs. I saw a fire. I saw the sky. Not a basement below the club itself."

She shook her head. "What if it's the same thing?"

"It's not. Not if we're in control of the whole thing."

"Are you sure?" She could tell from the look on his face that he wasn't.

"Ninety-nine percent. This isn't one of the futures I saw for you. This isn't one of your paths."

Ridley was silent for a moment.

What other choice do I have?

"I'd rather die in a fire than end up as part of Silas Ravenwood's harem," she said finally.

Link grabbed her hand. "Yeah, well, you aren't gonna do either. Not on my watch."

"Our watch," said Nox.

"Back up." Link frowned. "If I can't Rip, how are we gonna get outta this place? I'm pretty badass, but I'm not fireproof."

"I am," Sampson said from where he stood just outside the door. Ridley had no idea how long he'd been there watching them.

Link raised an eyebrow. "Seriously?"

The Darkborn gave Link a hard stare. "Of course not, you idiot. But I can control it." Sampson ducked his head under the doorframe and came inside. "Ever heard of the butterfly effect? They say if a butterfly flaps its wings in China, it can cause a hurricane on the other side of the world."

"I sorta failed bio in summer school, so you might wanna hit the high points."

Sampson continued. "When your cousin screwed up the Order of Things, that's what she did. She changed the nature of the supernatural world, right down to the source."

"The Dark Fire," Ridley said in a low voice.

Sampson's gray eyes met hers, and he smiled. "Why do you think they call us Darkborns?"

"It's true. Sampson's kind draw their strength from the Dark Fire," Nox said. "So Mortal fire? Not such a big deal."

"Yeah? What about Mortal smoke inhalation?" Link was suspicious.

"There's fire, and then there's fire. Let's just say it bends to my will," the Darkborn said, looking at Ridley. "The way guys bend to yours."

"I thought you didn't care what happens to Mortals?" Ridley looked at Sampson suspiciously. "I thought you didn't get involved with Caster business?"

He shrugged. "There's an exception to every rule. I'd hate to break up the band."

Link stared at Sirensong's lead guitarist with his mouth hanging open. "You're the Magneto of Supernaturals. Holy crap." Magneto was the one comic book character Link revered above all others. It was the highest compliment he could've paid Sampson.

"I'd go with Metallica," Sampson said. "But I'll take it."

Link whistled to himself. "You bet your Dark balls a fire it's a compliment."

"So that's it." Nox held up the matchbook. "It's time to take the future into our own hands. We light the fire. We set the Wheel of Fate in motion."

Link grinned. "I'm startin' to get what you're sayin'. The Wheel can't roll over us if we're the ones pushin' it."

Nox handed Link the matches. "You're not as stupid as you look. For a messed-up Incubus with Mortal limitations."

"I get that a lot."

Nox turned to Ridley. "You ready?"

She tossed her head. "I was born ready." It was the second time she had tried to bluff him.

She hoped this time he believed her.

Link held the matchbook. Ridley and Sampson stood next to him, somber. They might as well have been at a funeral—which, in a way, they were.

"*Incendio*," Nox said. He drew a poker chip from the inside pocket of his jacket. "Time to get this party started."

Ridley stared at the chip as if it was haunted. She was transfixed.

"What's that?" Link asked.

"A little something I won in a game of Liar's Trade. A marker. I won a very powerful Cast from a very powerful Cataclyst." Nox looked at Ridley. "Not, you know, Duchannes powerful." He smiled. "But a hottie all the same."

Ridley looked at him. "I guess you never know who you'll meet at the table."

He smiled at her, flipping the chip in his hand. "We light this on fire, and the *Incendio* Cast goes up in smoke. Literally. The Cast, and the club."

"Really?" Link scratched his head. "Just like that?"

"I have no idea. I've never tried it before."

Nox raised the chip.

He looked around the basement, and then up to the ceiling above them, where the main dance floor was. Rid almost couldn't bear to watch.

"Good night, Sirene."

Nox kissed the chip and handed it to Sampson.

"Now. Before I change my mind."

Sampson twisted the chip in his hand and slowly held it out, palm up. "Light me up, Link."

Rid stepped back. "Be careful."

Link turned his head as he held the match, ready to strike. "Always, Babe." He looked at Sampson. "It's been real, bro. See you on the other side."

Link flicked the match and it flared to life. The moment felt like an eternity as he waited for the flame to grow.

Nox looked away. Sampson's jaw was set. Link took one last look at Ridley. He held the match above the chip and dropped it in Sampson's hand.

Then everything went white.

The blinding burst of flame and heat blew everyone back. Link hit the wall behind him hard. Ridley fell next to him. Nox was on his knees.

Only Sampson was left standing. He held out his arm, with an intense ball of flame in his hand, glowing like a sun. He tossed it down the hallway toward the exit doors.

Just like Nox had wanted him to.

Within seconds, flames licked up the wooden beamed ceiling and the wood-paneled walls.

Sirene was going up in smoke and taking Nox's dreams right along with it.

———

"Time to go," Sampson said, smoking and soot-covered but otherwise unharmed.

Link stood, pulling Rid up with him. "Remind me to buy you a new shirt when we get out of here."

"Not from where you shop." Sampson didn't even smile. He stared hard at the rest of them. "You need to stay right behind me, unless you want a serious sunburn."

"Duck and cover," Link said. "Got it."

Sampson caught his eye. "I'm not talking about your kind of Third Degree Burns."

"I figured."

The fire grew before their eyes, swelling and roaring with every passing second. Wood crackled and snapped as if the whole place was somehow coming alive, if only to die again. Smoke was already filling the basement hallway, and fire rolled across the ceiling in waves. Sampson stepped out into the flames, and even though Nox had told them what to expect, it was hard to believe. The burning waves curled away from Sampson, spreading up the walls and around him, like the Darkborn was enclosed in a bubble.

When it came to Mortal fire, he was.

Nox watched in horror as the whole room ignited, surrounding them on all sides, filling the space behind them each time Sampson took a step forward.

Link reached out his hand toward the edge of the bubble.

"Don't do it," Sampson said. "It only works for me, hybrid."

Link let his hand drop, patting the Darkborn's shoulder. "You really are Magneto."

"Just stay close."

Ridley was behind Link, and Nox kept his hand on the small of her back.

This is going to work. It has to.

Even though the flames bent away from Sampson, the heat was intense, and the walls, floor, and ceiling began to fall apart around them, disintegrating into ash and flame and charred bits of wood.

The floor shuddered, wooden planks giving way beneath their feet as they walked. It was a life-and-death game of leap-frog as Sampson carefully led them down the hall.

Then the exodus began.

They could hear it, all around them, the feet pounding and the people screaming, even through the roaring of the flames.

One by one, the fire alarms began shrilling through the air.

The screaming only grew louder—and then quieter.

Floyd and Necro must be doing their jobs, just like they said they would.

It was all Ridley could think.

At least, it was all she could hope. That they would get the whole upstairs crowd out of the building. Because they had to.

Those girls are as tough as Sampson, maybe tougher.

Even Necro, even now.

As the four Supernaturals moved down the hall, the flames arched over the invisible barrier protecting them.

They made good progress until one of the support beams in the ceiling began to splinter.

Ridley felt it before she heard it. *My hand is burning. Why is my hand burning?* She looked down to see her ring glowing red.

Something was wrong.

"Link—" she began.

But Nox saw it first. "Rid! Watch out—"

A hunk of burning wood ripped free just as Ridley looked up. She screamed and jumped back.

No!

Nox tried to push her forward, but there was already too much distance between the two of them and Sampson and Link.

The fire streaked across the floor between them, and the ceiling beam crashed to the ground, taking Ridley with it. The burning beam now separated Ridley and Nox from Sampson and Link, and the flames were closing in quickly.

I've seen this, Nox thought. *This is how it ends.*

That thought was followed by another, only a fraction of a second later.

No. It can't be. I won't let it.

"Rid!" Link shouted from the other side of the wall of smoke.

Nox scooped Ridley up off the floor. Her expression was a mixture of confusion and panic. "I've got you, Little Siren."

He coughed as the smoke seared his lungs. The fire was so intense, he could barely see. The world was collapsing around them. Without the Darkborn, they wouldn't last long.

He searched the smoke for a sign of Sampson, but he could

barely see a few feet in front of him. If the Darkborn wasn't coming back, there was a reason. Nox knew he wouldn't leave them behind.

Nox stumbled away from the hottest part of the narrow hallway, holding Ridley against his chest with one arm and running his hand along the stone wall with the other. Flames crept closer, and the smoke blew ash and embers in their faces.

Not now. Not like this.

Nox fell back into a recessed doorway, finding a temporary reprieve from the heat and flames.

But they were running out of options.

The door behind them was locked, and they were cornered by the fire. There was no sign of Link and the Darkborn.

Ridley was stunned and coughing. "We're trapped, aren't we?" Nox looked around but shook his head. "I'll figure this out, Rid. We're going to make it, I promise."

We aren't going to make it.

Nox positioned himself between the fire and Ridley in a vain effort to shield her from the heat, but now he was coughing as hard as she was. His back burned as the pain grew too much to bear.

His stinging eyes closed.

"Nox, stay with me." He could hear Ridley's voice, though it sounded like she was far away.

I'm here, he thought, though his mouth wasn't making any sounds.

Because it was hopeless—that was his next thought. And the fact that they were never getting out.

I'm so sorry, Ridley. I'm sorry that the shadows follow me wherever I go. That they followed me to you.

"Stop it, Nox. Open your eyes. I'm right here."

His head fell onto her shoulder.

"Lennox!" Sampson called out through the flames.

The cloud of smoke cleared and Sampson burst through it, untouched. He grabbed Ridley and Nox with each arm—and the heat suddenly and mercifully dissipated. "The crazy hybrid lost it. He wanted to come back in here and get her himself. Took everything I had in me to knock his dumb ass out before Silas' men got a look at him."

"We need to get her out of here," Nox said, struggling to hold his head up.

"I'm okay. I can walk." Ridley sounded like herself again, and Nox was feeling better. He didn't take his eyes off her, now that they were open. He knew it might be his last chance to have her this close.

Sampson led the way, and when they reached the last stairwell, Link was slumped against the side of the stairs.

Nox and Ridley could feel a draft of fresh air blasting toward them.

The outside world is so close now.

Nox pulled Ridley close, gasping for air.

"Thank god," he said.

Ridley didn't speak. She was just trying to breathe. Still, she reached for his hand.

Nox bent his face toward hers as he caught his own breath, letting his lips graze her cheek one last time.

Then Nox let go of Ridley, pushing her toward Sampson. "You have to go, Little Siren."

"You mean *we* have to go." She was still holding his hand.

Sampson turned away, trying to give Nox a moment alone with her while still keeping the fire at bay.

There wasn't much time.

"That's not part of the plan. Someone has to stick around and face Silas, or he won't believe the two of you are dead," Nox said.

"No, I already told you. We *talked* about this. I'm not leaving you in here. Not with them."

"I'll be right behind you, or close enough. But I need to make a dramatic exit for Silas' benefit. I can't do that with you on my arm. I have to go out the main doors. I'll see you in the outside world, when it's safe again."

"You're lying," she said.

It was true.

Nox looked up to the blackened ceiling beams. *How long before these rafters fall?* He had to make her understand. "When Silas finds out you're alive, he'll never stop looking for you. I can help you, but only if I stay. You have to get out of New York. Go anywhere you want, as long as it's far away from here."

Light fixtures began to pop, one at a time.

Old wine bottles began to explode and ignite.

Another support beam crashed against the floor behind them.

The club was coming down.

Ridley bit her lip. "What about my marker? What about what I owe you? Or have you forgotten?"

Nox reached into his pocket and pulled something out, pressing it into her palm. "Take it. It's yours."

Her fingers curled around what looked like a harmless poker chip. "Nox," she said.

"I didn't forget. I remember every single thing about you," Nox said gently. "And you don't owe me anything. You never will."

"You know that's not true."

"You got me my drummer, remember?"

"I'm not talking about that marker, and you know it."

Nox put his arms around her, pulling her close. "What you owe me, Little Siren—what you owed me all along—wasn't something that should be won in a game. Not even when you're playing for TFPs."

Her voice was trembling. "It was a house marker. It was your call, Nox. You could have taken anything you wanted. Anything I had to give."

"I know," Nox said. *I know better than anyone. I've thought about it a thousand times, every day.* "I wish I'd never won it. I wish I hadn't made you come here. I wish I hadn't even asked you for the drummer. It was wrong, all of it. I'm sorry." The truth of his words was undeniable, as well as the emotion behind them.

Ridley leaned and tossed the chip as hard as she could, flinging it into the hot red heart of the fire.

A tear rolled down her cheek. She wiped it with the back of her soot-streaked hand. "I forgive you."

A Siren's tear.

He'd only seen a Siren cry once. His mother, on the day Abraham Ravenwood took her from him. He'd never forgotten that moment.

And I'll never forget this one.

Nox didn't watch as Sampson carried her out the back door. The deception was a good one; Ridley was limp as a rag and covered in soot. Silas and his men would never know a heart was still beating in the little Siren's chest.

It was an unsettling sight.

I might never see her again. I don't want to remember her like that. He touched his fingers together, still wet from her tears, wonderingly.

I want to remember this.

Nox walked back toward the doors of the club, probably for the very last time.

By the time he had finally made it out, there was nothing left of Sirene. He watched the firefighters saturate the framework and the remaining roof, if only to keep the fire from spreading to nearby buildings.

Mortal fires, Mortal firefighters. They were remarkably good at their job. Too bad they wouldn't remember any of it tomorrow.

A black SUV pulled up to the curb behind him.

The tinted window rolled down, and Silas Ravenwood stared back at him from underneath his fedora. He glanced at what was left of the club. "Hope you've got insurance, kid."

You just have to bluff one more hand.

For her.

Nox thought about his mother, and the night he found out his father was dead. He thought about every terrible thing that had ever happened in his miserable life. Then he remembered the one thing that was even more painful—the way he'd felt when he thought of Ridley in chains, just like his mother in a cage.

And the way he felt now.

Totally and completely empty.

Nox raised his bloodshot eyes to meet Silas' empty ones. "What do you want, Silas?" He gestured at the club. "I'm out. I've got nothing left for you to take."

Silas lit a cigar and climbed out of the car. He walked over to Nox and brushed the ash off the shoulder of Nox's burnt shirt. "I hate hearing you talk like that, kid. There's always something left to take."

Fear shot through Nox's veins.

Don't react.

The Incubus slung his arm around Nox's neck, then tightened it.

Nox struggled against him, fighting for breath.

"Did you think I'd fall for this piss-poor act of yours? I know you let that little bitch go." Silas tightened his grip, cutting off the air Nox had left. "You're a sucker, Gates, just like your old man. Threw your life away on a Siren who won't live long enough to benefit from all that misguided devotion."

Silas' driver opened the back door, and Silas tossed Nox into the car. For an older Incubus, he had an iron grip. *Dealing in other people's powers your whole life will do that for you,* Nox thought as the door slammed on him. *I should know.*

Nox laughed at the irony. He had more in common with Silas Ravenwood than he'd ever imagined.

Air tore through his lungs, and he choked on every breath. Nox knew Silas Ravenwood was going to kill him—and enjoy doing it. But his future didn't matter to him anymore.

Because Nox had seen hers, in the third and final vision. The last time he'd looked at the last days of Ridley Duchannes' life.

Let her have today. Leave tomorrow to the angels.

There was always more Darkness.

Lennox Gates knew that better than anyone. Whether you were pushing the Wheel or it was headed straight for you, Darkness always found you in the end.

He just hoped he was the only one who knew it.

Nox closed his eyes as the car started to move.

He was going to pass out.

I should have told her how I felt about her, the first time I had the chance. That's my only regret. All those years ago, when we were kids.

On that beach in Barbados.

The first day I met the only person in the world who would ever be able to understand me. The girl who knew what it felt like to do the things I could do.

I should have told her.

Nox blacked out before he could remember why he hadn't.

⊰ AFTER ⊱

Fade to Black

The road out of New York unrolled quickly, the same way they'd come. Except this time, Lucille Ball sat in the front seat, between the Caster and the quarter Incubus, purring.

"What is wrong with that cat? It's like she has no idea we're on the lam." Ridley was annoyed.

"She doesn't. She's a cat."

"Lucille Ball is as big a gossip as the Sisters," Ridley said. "She knows everything. We're on the run from a bunch of Caster Underground lowlifes. The apartment isn't safe. The city is worse. Probably most of the country is full of Silas Raven-wood's thugs. That cat should not be purring."

Ridley was twitching enough for them both. She didn't care if she ever saw a city again. All she knew was they had each other, and they were alive.

But for how long?

"Stop lookin' over your shoulder," said Link.

"I can't help it if I don't want to die," said Rid. "And it feels like I'm—like we're being watched."

"You're not gonna die. Well, I mean, you are. We all are. But not yet." Link accelerated, all the same. "If Nox did his part, Silas Ravenwood has no idea where we are or where we're headed—and the rest of the band is long gone."

Ridley glanced out the window. She didn't want to think about Nox and what he was or wasn't doing. She didn't want to think about what he'd given up by staying behind. "We can't hide from Silas forever."

"Speak for yourself. I'm great at hidin'. Last year, Principal Harper couldn't find me for the better part of a semester. It's just one a my many gifts." Link winked. Ridley knew it was true. Plus, Link had been hiding most of his life from his own mother, long before that. By now, she figured, he was as good with invisibility as Savannah Snow was with visibility.

"Principal Harper isn't Silas." Ridley was doubtful. But Link was starting to calm her down, smoothing out her rough spots, like he always did.

"Maybe. But Silas also isn't the most powerful Blood Incubus of all time. Maybe we can ditch him. Maybe we can buy ourselves some time."

Until Abraham gets involved again, Ridley thought. *Which I hope is never.*

"So what now?" She looked at him. Back in the Beater once again, where everything that had to do with Link began and ended. Where Lena had met Ethan, now that she thought about it. The Beater had seen it all. It was a wonder the thing could still move.

Link looked sideways at her. "What do you mean, what now?"

"We can't go back to New York."

"No, ma'am. Not unless you're fine with a permanent stop at His Garden of Perpetual Peace," said Link. "Then we could haunt just about anywhere we felt like it. Seein' as we'd be dead."

"Stop joking around. I'm serious. You have no idea what you're dealing with here. It might as well be a Caster death sentence. We're done. And nobody will ever hire you again. Forget Sirensong. You can kiss your whole music career good-bye." *Please*, she thought desperately. *Please, please, kiss it good-bye.*

Link tapped the wheel. "Aw, Chicken Wing."

Ridley practically screamed. "Don't. Call. Me. That."

He grinned, ignoring her. "We're only done in New York, darlin'. Weren't you listenin' to me all those other times? When I told you how all those bands made it big without ever settin' foot in New York?"

She just looked at him. "You're crazy. You know that?"

"Hey, I may not have a band, but I have you, don't I?"

"Don't you always?"

"You didn't answer the question."

Link pulled her hair back until he could see the tiny sparkling S studs in her ears. "What are those?"

"The earrings? I guess I forgot to take them off." S for Siren. S for Sirene. *From a certain Caster closet.* They reminded her of dinner under the stars, on the roof of the Met.

Cinderella at the ball of the damned, she thought.

"Those real diamonds?" Link looked at her. "Don't tell me." He shook his head. "I can't compete with that."

"With what?" Ridley smoothed her hair back over her ears, self-conscious now.

"With Mr. New York City. With all the flash and the cash."

"Mr. New York City saved our lives," she said.

"Sure, from himself. From what he was plannin' to do to us in the first place. If you want to get technical."

"I don't."

"I'm not him. I'll never be him." Link fixed his eyes on the road. "I'm a Southern boy. When I get you earrings, they're gonna come from the mall. You should know that by now."

Something inside Ridley broke. She was overwhelmed by feelings, more than she'd ever wanted. More than she knew what to do with.

For what I have, and what I've lost. Who I have, and who I've lost.

But Ridley and Link had survived. They were together. They had now, and they had each other. That was the most important thing.

She only wished she knew how to tell him that.

Ridley looked at Link. "I don't want you to be anyone except Wesley Lincoln, from Gatlin, South Carolina."

"That's sweet as sugar, Sugar. I wish I believed you, but that doesn't make it any less sweet."

"Link."

"Come on. We both know Lennox Gates owns guys like me."

Rid touched his shoulder. "I don't care about any of that. I just want you to kiss me, you idiot."

She realized it was true the moment she said it.

Link bit his lip, thinking. "No way. If you're going to be with me, it's not going to be because we made out in the alley one time and then you felt sorry for me."

"We're not in an alley. Now kiss me."

"I said no. If we're going to be in this together, it's going to be because we both want to be. Because we respect each other, and we need each other. And we love—"

"Kiss me," she said.

Slowly, he pulled the car over to the side of the highway.

Link walked around to the passenger side of the Beater and pulled open the door. He was down on one knee, mostly because that was the only way he could fold his supersized body compactly enough to bring his head to her level.

Ridley looked down at him from her seat. "Can I help you, Wesley Lincoln?"

"Ridley Duchannes. Is there even one stupid tiny little part of you that loves one stupid tiny little part of me?"

She looked at him, blinking back tears. She could've prevented all this if she had just flung her arms around him the first time he'd told her he loved her, and kissed his sweet face, and confessed that she'd always loved him, too.

They wouldn't have fought. She wouldn't have fled the country and, ultimately, the whole Mortal world. She wouldn't have tried to lose herself in a stupid card game.

Suffer was the perfect name for the club where she'd almost lost it all. And it described what both of them had been doing since the moment she'd set foot in that place. But if Ridley was honest with herself, she had already been suffering for three months by the time she found her way there.

Why?

Because she couldn't tell one stupid boy who she loved with every muscle in her stupidly broken heart that she loved him more passionately and more deeply than she'd ever loved anyone in the world?

Ridley couldn't go back to that afternoon in the Dar-ee Keen. It hurt too much. She couldn't walk back through any of the wrong paths she'd taken.

Instead, she closed her eyes and started to cry, really cry.

She melted into Link's arms, burying her face in his shoulder, pressing her runny nose into his spiky hair, like he'd been waiting for her to do since that first time he said it.

Wesley Lincoln finally got his answer, even if it was wet snot on his neck. Even if Ridley Duchannes was speechless and all she could manage was a nod.

Even if it was a long time coming, longer than back-to-back Shark Weeks, longer than a whole summer vacation of E-rated video games, and even longer than Summerville's marathon Battle of the Bad Bands.

Link would take it. He could wait for the rest, even if it took the rest of his long life.

In that moment, the longest standoff in recorded history— at least, all the history recorded between this particular Caster and this particular quarter Incubus—came to a short, sweet end.

Together they were ready to take on the world.

Or hide from it, indefinitely.

They were still working out the plan.

"Next question, darlin'."

"You're full of questions today, Shrinky Dink." Ridley sat with her pink toes in his lap while he drove, and Link held on to them with his hand.

She wiggled them and he smiled.

"Only one more question, and I promise this one'll be easier than the last."

"All right, then," she said.

"Should we go back to Gatlin?"

He was wrong. This wasn't easy, either.

This one kept them talking for a hundred miles.

As much as Ridley wanted the answer to be yes—more than she'd ever thought she'd want to go back to Gatlin, to everything that meant—she knew in her heart there was no way she could risk everyone she cared about. She wouldn't even risk telling them where she and Link were headed.

Not when Silas Ravenwood was involved. *Or worse, Abraham.*

"Then where do we go? If we can't stay in New York, and we can't go home?" Ridley hadn't quite figured that out yet.

"Did you actually call Gatlin *home*?"

"Don't avoid the question," Ridley said, avoiding the question.

Link grinned, tapping on the steering wheel. "Where are we goin'? You and me? That's music and magic, Babe. I got just the place. There's only one."

"Yeah?"

"Sure. It was supposed to be chapter ten in my autobiography. You know, *Carolina Icon*. Did I ever tell you that one?"

Rid had to think about it. "Viva Link Vegas?"

"Nah, that's all fake magic. Plus, that's chapter twelve, the one with the white tigers. For when my vocal cords are shot and I'm fat from eatin' fried peanut butter." He winked at her.

Ridley smiled. She hadn't known they weren't shot now. "Where, Hot Rod? Don't die on a toilet before you tell me."

"Aw, come on. It's not the worst way to go."

Ridley didn't know about that, but at least it wasn't a fire or chains. She wondered what Nox's third vision was, the last one he'd seen.

The one he wouldn't tell her about.

Rid looked back at Link. "Cough it up. Where are we headed?"

Link was going to tell her, but then "Stairway to Heaven" came on the radio, and they had to stop talking.

It was the only rule of the Beater.

Ridley would have to wait a few minutes to find out.

She wrapped a strand of pink hair around her finger and thought about where she was going and what she was leaving behind.

Link was singing, the radio was playing, and the wind was blowing. Rid's window was down and her hand was hanging out to feel the warmth of the sun. There were cows on one side of the highway and horses on the other. Everywhere she looked, round bales of hay sat tied up with string, like birthday presents.

Ridley felt pretty good, for someone with a banged-up heart and a bounty on her head. Her ring tapped against the side of the car, but she couldn't see if it was glowing, and right now she didn't care.

Which was also the reason she didn't see the truck coming right at them.

Sugarplum—

People said the gas tank alone burned more than two stories high.

Hot Rod, don't you leave me—

The back of the Beater? Smashed like a dropped accordion.

Stairs. Flames. The sky.

"Stairway to Heaven" kept playing right up until the radio caught fire.

To be continued...

Acknowledgments

SO MANY PEOPLE HAVE WORKED together to bring our readers the continuing adventures of Link and Ridley and the Caster world in the Dangerous Creatures novels. The last six months have been nothing short of miraculous.

Our agents, Sarah Burnes (and everyone at the Gernert Company, on behalf of Margie) and Jodi Reamer (and everyone at Writers House, on behalf of Kami), have collaborated, as always, with grace and general awesomeness.

Our editors, Kate Sullivan (for Margie) and Erin Stein (for Kami), as well as our former editor, Julie Scheina, have been not just patient and brilliant but passionately #TeamLinkAndRidley from the start.

The publishing, sales, editorial, marketing, publicity, school and library services, art direction, and copyediting groups at Little, Brown Books for Young Readers have continued to work tirelessly on behalf of Casters everywhere.

The teachers, librarians, booksellers, bloggers, journalists, tumblr-ers, tweethearts, Facebook followers, cousins, aunts, uncles, friends, writer friends, YALLFestians, and most of all DEAR READERS (NOTE: THIS IS YOU) who make up the larger Caster world have become the GREATEST FANDOM OF ALL HUMAN HISTORY.

We offer up a giant, Wesley Lincoln–sized thank-you to all of you.

But most especially, we want to thank our families. You, darlings, are the collective loves of our respective lives. You Charm us every day.

Lewis, Emma, May & Kate, and Alex, Nick & Stella, we'll save you the biggest cherry lollipops of them all.

XO,
Margie & Kami

GUARD YOUR HEART....

TURN THE PAGE FOR A PEEK AT MARGARET STOHL'S ROMANTIC THRILLER *ICONS*!

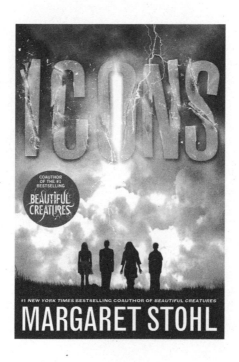

AVAILABLE NOW
HOWEVER BOOKS ARE SOLD

The Pietà of La Purísima

Feelings are memories.

That's what I'm thinking as I stand there in the Mission chapel, the morning of my birthday. It's what the Padre says. He also says that chapels turn regular people into philosophers.

I'm not a regular person, but I'm still no philosopher. And either way, what I remember and how I feel are the only two things I can't escape, no matter how much I want to.

No matter how hard I try.

For the moment, I tell myself not to think. I focus on trying to see. The chapel is dark but the doorway to outside is blindingly bright. That's what morning always looks like in the chapel. The little light there prickles and stings my eyes.

Like in the Mission itself, in the chapel you can pretend that nothing has changed for hundreds of years, that nothing has happened. Not like in the Hole, where they say the buildings have fallen into ruins, and Sympa soldiers control the streets with fear, and you think about nothing but The Day, every day.

Los Angeles, that's what the Hole used to be called. First Los Angeles, then the City of Angels, then the Holy City, then the Hole. When I was little, that's how I used to think of the House of Lords, as angels. Nobody calls them *alien* anymore, because they aren't. They're familiar. We never see them, but we've never known a world without them, not Ro and me. I grew up thinking they were angels because back on The Day they sent my parents to heaven. At least, that's what the Grass missionaries told me, when I was old enough to ask.

Heaven, not their graves.

Angels, not aliens.

But just because something comes from the sky doesn't make it an angel. The Lords didn't come here from the heavens to save us. They came from some faraway solar system to colonize our planet, on The Day. We don't know what they look like inside their ships, but they're not angels. They destroyed my family the year I was born. What kind of angel would do that?

Now we call them the House of Lords—and Ambassador Amare, she tells us not to fear them—but we do.

Just as we fear her.

On The Day, the dead dropped silently in their homes, never seeing what hit them. Never knowing anything about our new Lords, about the way they could use their Icons to control the energy that flowed through our own bodies, our machines, our cities.

About how they could stop it.

Either way, my family is gone. There was no reason for me to have survived. Nobody understood why I did.

The Padre suspected, of course. That's why he took me.

First me, and then Ro.

I hear a sound from the far end of the chapel.

I squint, turning my back to the door.

The Padre has sent for me, but he's late. I catch the eye of the Lady from the painting on the wall. Her face is so sad, I think she knows what has happened. I think she knows everything. She's part of what General Ambassador to the Planet Hiro Miyazawa, the head of the United Embassies, calls the old ways of humanity. How we believed in ourselves—how we survived ourselves. What we looked up to, back when we thought there was someone up above.

Not something.

I look back to the Lady a moment longer, until the sadness surges and the pain radiates through me. It pulses from my temples and I feel my mind stumble, folding at the edge of unconsciousness. Something is wrong. It must be, for the familiar ache to come on so suddenly. I press my hand to my temple, willing it to stop. I breathe deep, until I can see clearly.

"Padre?"

My voice echoes against the wood and stone. It sounds as small as I am. An animal has lurched into my leg, one of many more entering the chapel, and my nostrils fill with smells—hair and hides and hooves, paint and mold and manure. My birthday falls on the Blessing of the Animals, which will begin just hours from now. Local Grass farmers and ranchers will come to have the Padre bless their livestock, as they have for three hundred years. It is Grass tradition, and we are a Grass Mission.

Appearing in the door, the Padre smiles at me, moving to

light the ceremonial candles. Then his smile fades. "Where's Furo? Bigger and Biggest haven't seen him at all this morning."

I shrug. I can't account for every second of Ro's day. Ro could be lifting all the dried cereal cakes out of Bigger's emergency supplies. Chasing Biggest's donkeys. Sneaking down the Tracks toward the Hole, to buy more parts for the Padre's busted-up old *pistola*, shot only on New Year's Eve. Meeting people he doesn't want me to meet, learning things he doesn't want me to know. Preparing for a war he'll never fight with an enemy that can't be defeated.

He's on his own.

The Padre, preoccupied as always, is no longer paying attention to himself or to me. "Careful..." I catch his elbow, pulling him out of the way of a pile of pig waste. A near miss.

He clicks his tongue and leans down to chuck Ramona Jamona on the chin. "Ramona. Not in the chapel." It's an act— really, he doesn't mind. The big pink pig sleeps in his chamber on cold nights, we all know she does. He loves Ro and me just as he does Ramona—in spite of everything we do and beyond anything he says. He's the only father we have ever known, and though I call him the Padre, I think of him as my Padre.

"She's a pig, Padre. She's going to go wherever she wants. She can't understand you."

"Ah, well. It's only once a year, the Blessing of the Animals. We can clean the floors tomorrow. All Earth's creatures need our prayers."

"I know. I don't mind." I look to the animals, wondering. The Padre sinks onto a low pew, patting the wood next to him. "We can take a few minutes to ourselves, however. Come. Sit."

I oblige.

He smiles, touching my chin. "Happy birthday, Dolly." He holds out a parcel wrapped in brown paper and tied with string. It materializes from his robes, a priestly sleight of hand.

Birthday secrets. My book, finally.

I recognize it from his thoughts, from yesterday. He holds it out to me, but his face is not full of joy.

Only sadness.

"Be careful with it. Don't let it out of your sight. It's very rare. And it's about you."

I drop my hand.

"Doloria." He says my real name and I stiffen, bracing myself for the words I fear are coming. "I know you don't like to talk about it, but it's time we speak of such things. There are people who would harm you, Doloria. I haven't really told you how I found you, not all of it. Why you survived the attack and your family didn't. I think you're ready to hear it now." He leans closer. "Why I've hidden you. Why you're special. Who you are."

I've been dreading this talk since my tenth birthday. The day he first told me what little I know about who I am and how I am different. That day, over sugar cakes and thick, homemade butter and sun tea, he talked to me slowly about the creeping sadness that came over me, so heavy that my chest fluttered like a startled animal's and I couldn't breathe. About the pain that pulsed in my head or came between my shoulder blades. About the nightmares that were so real I was afraid Ro would walk in and find me cold and still in my bed one morning.

As if you really could die from a broken heart.

But the Padre never told me where the feelings came from. That's one thing even he didn't know.

I wish someone did.

"Doloria."

He says my name again to remind me that he knows my secret. He's the only one, Ro and him. When we're alone, I let Ro call me Doloria—but even he mostly calls me Dol, or even Dodo. I'm just plain Dolly to everyone else.

Not Doloria Maria de la Cruz. Not a Weeper. Not marked by the lone gray dot on my wrist.

One small circle the color of the sea in the rain.

The one thing that is really me.

My destiny.

Dolor means "sorrow," in Latin or Greek or some other language from way, way before The Day. BTD. Before everything changed.

"Open it."

I look at him, uncertain. The candles flicker, and a breeze shudders slowly through the room. Ramona noses closer to the altar, her snout looking for traces of honey on my hand.

I slip my finger through the paper, pulling it loose from the string. Beneath the wrapping is hardly a book, almost more of a journal: the cover is thick, rough burlap, homemade. This is a Grass book, unauthorized, illegal. Most likely preserved by the Rebellion, in spite of and because of the Embassy regulations. Such books are usually on subjects the Ambassadors won't acknowledge within the world of the Occupation. They are very hard to come by, and extremely valuable.

My eyes well with tears as I read the cover. *The Humanity Project: The Icon Children*. It looks like it was written by hand.

"No," I whisper.

"Read it." He nods. "I was supposed to keep it safe for you and make sure you read it when you were old enough."

"Who said that? Why?"

"I'm not sure. I discovered the book with a note on the altar, not long after I brought you here. Just read it. It's time. And nobody knows as much about the subject as this particular author. It's written by a doctor, it seems, in his own hand."

"I know enough not to read more." I look around for Ro. I wish, desperately, he would walk through the chapel door. But the Padre is the Padre, so I open the book to a page he's marked, and begin to read about myself.

Icon doloris.

Dolorus. Doloria. Me.

My purpose is pain and my name is sorrow.

One gray dot says so.

No.

"Not yet." I look up at the Padre and shake my head, shoving the book into my belt. The conversation is over. The story of me can wait until I'm ready. My heart hurts again, stronger this time.

I hear strange noises, feel a change in the air. I look to Ramona Jamona, hoping for some moral support, but she is lying at my feet, fast asleep.

No, not asleep.

Dark liquid pools beneath her.

The cold animal in my chest startles awake, fluttering once again.

An old feeling returns. Something really is wrong. Soft pops fill the air.

"Padre," I say.

Only I look at him and he is not my Padre at all. Not anymore.

"Padre!" I scream. He's not moving. He's nothing. Still sitting next to me, still smiling, but not breathing.

He's gone.

My mind moves slowly. I can't make sense of it. His eyes are empty and his mouth has fallen open. Gone.

It's all gone. His jokes. His secret recipes—the butter he made from shaking cream together with smooth, round rocks—the rows of sun tea in jars—gone. Other secrets, too. My secrets.

But I can't think about it now, because behind the Padre—what was the Padre—stands a line of masked soldiers. Sympas.

Occupation Sympathizers, traitors to humanity. Embassy soldiers, taking orders from the Lords, hiding behind plexi-masks and black armor, standing in pig mess and casting long shadows over the deathly peace of the chapel. One wears golden wings on his jacket. It's the only detail I see, aside from the weapons. The guns make no noise, but the animals panic all the same. They are screaming—which is something I did not know, that animals could scream.

I open my mouth, but I do not scream. I vomit.

I spit green juices and gray dust and memories of Ramona and the Padre.

All I can see are the guns. All I can feel is hate and fear. The black-gloved hands close around my wrist, overwhelming me, and I know that soon I will no longer have to worry about my nightmares.

I will be dead.

As my knees buckle, all I can think about is Ro and how angry he will be at me for leaving him.

Tracks

I am alive.

When I open my eyes I'm on a train—alone in a prison transport car, gunmetal gray, pushed by an old coal-fueled steam engine. Nothing but four walls lined with metal benches, bolted to the floor. A door to my left, a window to my right. A pile of old rags in the corner. That's it. I must be on the Tracks, hurtling toward the Hole. The dim blue waters of Porthole Bay flip in and out of sight, rhythmically punctuated by shuffling old comlink poles. They stick up from the land like so many useless skeleton fingers.

I watch my reflection in the window. My brown hair is dark and loose and matted with dirt and bile. My skin is pale and barely covers the handful of small bones that are me. Then I see my reflection twist, and in the plexi-window I look as sad as the Lady in her painting. *Because the Padre is dead.*

I try to hold on to his face in my mind, the grooves by his eyes, the mole on his cheek. The cocky spike of his thinning hair. I'm afraid I'll lose it, him—even the memory. Tomorrow, if not today.

Like everything else, there's no holding on to the Padre.

Not anymore.

I look back out at the bay, and I can feel the bile churn inside me, strong as the tides. Usually the water calms me. Not today. Today, as I clutch the blue glass bead at my throat, the ocean is almost unrecognizable. I wonder where the Tracks are taking me. *To my death? Or worse?*

I see a glimpse of the rusting, abandoned cars on the highway along the rails, junked as if all life stopped and the planet froze in place, which is pretty much what happened on The Day. After the House of Lords came, with their Carrier ships, and the thirteen Icons fell from the sky, one landing in each of the largest cities in the world.

The Padre says—said—that people used to live all over Earth, spread out. There were small towns, small cities, big cities. Not anymore. Almost the entire population of the planet lives within a hundred miles of a mega-city. The Padre said this happened because so much of the world has been ruined by people, by the rising waters, rising temperatures, drought, flooding. Some parts of Earth are toxic with radiation from massive wars. People stay in the cities because we are running out of places to live.

Now everything people need to live is produced in or near the cities. Energy, food, technology—it's all centralized in the cities. Which makes the Lords' work that much easier.

The Icons regulate everything with an electronic pulse. The

Padre said the Icons can control electricity, the power that flows between generators and machines, even the electrical impulses that connect brains and bodies. They can halt all electrical and chemical activity at any time. Which is what happened to Gold-engate, on The Day. And São Paulo, Köln-Bonn, Greater Beijing, Cairo, Mumbai. The Silent Cities. Which is why we gave in to the Lords and let them take our planet.

But out in the Grasslands, like at the Mission, we have more freedom. The Icons lose their strength the farther away you go. But the Lords and the Ambassadors are in control, even then, because they have the resources. They have weapons that work. And there's no power in the Grass, no source of energy. Even so, I have hope. The Padre always tried to reassure me—everything has a limit. Everything has an end. Beyond the borders of the cities and the frequencies of the Icons, life goes on. They can't turn everything off. They don't control our whole planet. Not yet.

Nothing in the Grass works that isn't pulled by a horse or cranked by a person. But at least we know our hearts will be beating in the morning, our lungs pumping air, our bodies shivering from the cold. Which is more than I know about myself tomorrow.

The pile of rags groans from the floor. I was wrong. I'm not alone. A man, lying facedown, is splayed across from me. He smells like a Remnant, which is what the Embassy calls us, another piece of worthless garbage like me. He even smells like he lives with the pigs—drunk pigs.

My heart begins to pound. I sense adrenaline. Heat. Anger. Not just the soldiers. Something more.

Ro's here.

I close my eyes and feel him. I can't see him, but I know he's near. *Don't*, I think, though he can't hear me. *Let me go, Ro. Get yourself somewhere safe.*

Ro hates Sympas. I know if he comes after me the rage will come after him, and he will probably be killed. Like the Padre. Like my parents, and Ro's. Like everyone else.

I also know he will come for me.

The man sits up, groaning. He looks like he is going to be sick, leaning against the swaying side of the car. I steady myself, waiting by the window.

The comlink poles go slapping by. The Tracks turn, and the watery curve of the Porthole shoreline comes into view, the Hole beyond it. A few crude skiffs float on the water nearest the shore. Beyond them, rising above the water, is the Hole, the biggest city on the west coast. The only one, since Goldengate was silenced. I don't look at the Icon, though I know it's there. It's always there looming, from the hill above the city, a knife in the otherwise flat skyline. What once was an observatory has been gutted and transformed by the black irregularity that juts out from the structure. It's also a reminder, this disturbingly nonhuman landmark, sent by our new Lords to pierce the earth and show us all that we are not in control.

That our hearts beat only with their permission.

If I'm not careful, I can feel all of them, the people in the Hole. They well up in me, unannounced. Everyone in the Hole, everyone in the Embassy. Sympas and Remnants and even Ambassador Amare. I fight them off. I try to clear my mind. I will myself not to feel—I've felt too much already. I try to press back against the welling. If I let them in, I'm afraid I will lose myself. I'll lose everything.

Chumash Rancheros Spaniards Californians Americans Grass. I recite the words, over and over, but this time they don't seem to help.

"Dol!"

It's Ro. He's here now, right outside the door. I hear a rattle and see the skull of the Sympa slam into the plexi-door and sink out of sight. There is a dent where he hit. No one else could destroy a Sympa like that, not with only his hands. Ro must already be out of control, to throw him so hard. Which means I don't have much time. I push myself up to my feet and move across the car to the door. It doesn't open, but I know Ro is right outside. I can see a glimpse of the narrow hall through the small plexi in the door.

"Ro! Ro, don't!" Then I hear shouting. Too late.

Please. Go home, Ro.

The shouting grows louder, and the train lurches. I stand up and stumble, almost stepping on the other prisoner, the Remnant. He rolls over and looks up at me, a pile of filth and rags, his face so covered with muck I can't tell what he is or where he's from. His skin is the color of bark. "Your *Ro* is going to get you both killed, you know." The voice is mocking. He has an accent, but I can't place it—only that it's not from the Californias. Maybe not even the Americas.

He moves again, and I see the welt that runs down the length of his face. He's been beaten, and I can imagine why. I want to kick him myself for mocking Ro, but I don't. Instead, I feel for the binding beneath my sleeve, wrapping it more tightly around my wrist and my secret.

One gray dot the color of the ocean.

The Padre's gone. Only Ro knows now.

Unless that's why the Sympas came.

I can't worry about it much longer, though, because the man answers himself in a strange falsetto, which I imagine he means to be me. "I know. I'm sorry about that, mate."

Sleepwalker

As my bare feet sank into the wet earth, I tried not to think about the dead bodies buried beneath me. I had passed this tiny graveyard a handful of times but never at night, and always outside the boundaries of its peeling iron gates.

I would've given anything to be standing outside them now.

In the moonlight, rows of weathered headstones exposed the neat stretch of lawn for what it truly was—the grassy lid of an enormous coffin.

A branch snapped, and I spun around.

"Elvis?" I searched for a trace of my cat's gray and white ringed tail.

Elvis never ran away, usually content to thread his way between my ankles whenever I opened the door—until tonight. He had taken off so fast that I didn't even have time to grab my shoes, and I had chased him eight blocks until I ended up here.

Muffled voices drifted through the trees, and I froze.

On the other side of the gates, a girl wearing blue and gray Georgetown University sweats passed underneath the pale glow of the lamppost. Her friends caught up with her, laughing and stumbling down the sidewalk. They reached one of the academic buildings and disappeared inside.

It was easy to forget that the cemetery was in the middle of a college campus. As I walked deeper into the uneven rows, the lampposts vanished behind the trees, and the clouds plunged the graveyard in and out of shadow. I ignored the whispers in the back of my mind urging me to go home.

Something moved in my peripheral vision—a flash of white.

I scanned the stones, now completely bathed in black.

Come on, Elvis. Where are you?

Nothing scared me more than the dark. I liked to see what was coming, and darkness was a place where things could hide.

Think about something else.

The memory closed in before I could stop it....

My mother's face hovering above mine as I blinked myself awake. The panic in her eyes as she pressed a finger over her lips, signaling me to be quiet. The cold floor against my feet as we made our way to her closet, where she pushed aside the dresses.

"Someone's in the house," she whispered, pulling a board away from the wall to reveal a small opening. "Stay here until I come back. Don't make a sound."

I squeezed inside as she worked the board back into place. I had never experienced absolute darkness before. I stared at a spot inches in front of me, where my palm rested on the board. But I couldn't see it.

I closed my eyes against the blackness. There were sounds—the stairs creaking, furniture scraping against the floor, muffled voices—and one thought replaying over and over in my mind.

What if she didn't come back?

Too terrified to see if I could get out from the inside, I kept my hand on the wood. I listened to my ragged breathing, convinced that whoever was in the house could hear it, too.

Eventually, the wood gave beneath my palm and a thin stream of light flooded the space. My mom reached for me, promising the intruders had fled. As she carried me out of her closet, I couldn't hear anything beyond the pounding of my heart, and I couldn't think about anything except the crushing weight of the dark.

I was only five when it happened, but I still remembered every minute in the crawl space. It made the air around me now feel suffocating. Part of me wanted to go home, with or without my cat.

"Elvis, get out here!"

Something shifted between the chipped headstones in front of me.

"Elvis?"

A silhouette emerged from behind a stone cross.

I jumped, a tiny gasp escaping my lips. "Sorry." My voice wavered. "I'm looking for my cat."

The stranger didn't say a word.

Sounds intensified at a dizzying rate—branches breaking, leaves rustling, my pulse throbbing. I thought about the hundreds of unsolved crime shows I'd watched with my mom that began exactly like this—a girl standing alone somewhere she shouldn't be, staring at the guy who was about to attack her.

I stepped back, thick mud pushing up around my ankles like a hand rooting me to the spot.

Please don't hurt me.

The wind cut through the graveyard, lifting tangles of long hair off the stranger's shoulders and the thin fabric of a white dress from her legs.

Her legs.

Relief washed over me. "Have you seen a gray and white Siamese cat? I'm going to kill him when I find him."

Silence.

Her dress caught the moonlight, and I realized it wasn't a dress at all. She was wearing a nightgown. Who wandered around a cemetery in their nightgown?

Someone crazy.

Or someone sleepwalking.

You aren't supposed to wake a sleepwalker, but I couldn't leave her out here alone at night either.

"Hey? Can you hear me?"

The girl didn't move, gazing at me as if she could see my features in the darkness. An empty feeling unfolded in the pit of my stomach. I wanted to look at something else—anything but her unnerving stare.

My eyes drifted down to the base of the cross.

The girl's feet were as bare as mine, and it looked like they weren't touching the ground.

I blinked hard, unwilling to consider the other possibility. It had to be an effect of the moonlight and the shadows. I glanced at my own feet, caked in mud, and back to hers.

They were pale and spotless.

A flash of white fur darted in front of her and rushed toward me.

Elvis.

I grabbed him before he could get away. He hissed at me, clawing and twisting violently until I dropped him. My heart hammered in my chest as he darted across the grass and squeezed under the gate.

I looked back at the stone cross.

The girl was gone, the ground nothing but a smooth, untouched layer of mud.

Blood from the scratches trailed down my arm as I crossed the graveyard, trying to reason away the girl in the white nightgown.

Silently reminding myself that I didn't believe in ghosts.

Scratching the Surface

When I stumbled back onto the well-lit sidewalk, there was no sign of Elvis. A guy with a backpack slung over his shoulder walked by and gave me a strange look when he noticed I was barefoot, and covered in mud up to my ankles. He probably thought I was a pledge.

My hands didn't stop shaking until I hit O Street, where the shadows of the campus ended and the lights of the DC traffic began. Tonight, even the tourists posing for pictures at the top of *The Exorcist* stairs were somehow reassuring.

The cemetery suddenly felt miles away, and I started second-guessing myself.

The girl in the graveyard hadn't been hazy or transparent like the ghosts in movies. She had looked like a regular girl.

Except she was floating.

Wasn't she?

Maybe the moonlight had only made it appear that way. And maybe the girl's feet weren't muddy because the ground where she'd been standing was dry. By the time I reached my block, lined with row houses crushed together like sardines, I convinced myself there were dozens of explanations.

Elvis lounged on our front steps, looking docile and bored. I considered leaving him outside to teach him a lesson, but I loved that stupid cat.

I still remembered the day my mom bought him for me. I came home from school crying because we'd made Father's Day gifts in class, and I was the only kid without a father. Mine had walked away when I was five and never looked back. My mom had wiped my tears and said, "I bet you're also the only kid in your class getting a kitten today."

Elvis had turned one of my worst days into one of my best.

I opened the door, and he darted inside. "You're lucky I let you in."

The house smelled like tomatoes and garlic, and my mom's voice drifted into the hallway. "I've got plans this weekend. Next weekend, too. I'm sorry, but I have to run. I think my daughter just came home. Kennedy?"

"Yeah, Mom."

"Were you at Elle's? I was about to call you."

I stepped into the doorway as she hung up the phone. "Not exactly."

She threw me a quick glance, and the wooden spoon slipped out of her hand and hit the floor, sending a spray of red sauce across the white tile. "What happened?"

"I'm fine. Elvis ran off, and it took forever to catch him."

Mom rushed over and examined the angry claw marks. "Elvis did this? He's never scratched anyone before."

"I guess he freaked out when I grabbed him."

Her gaze dropped to my mud-caked feet. "Where were you?"

I prepared for the standard lecture Mom issued whenever I went out at night: always carry your cell phone, don't walk alone, stay in well-lit areas, and her personal favorite—scream first and ask questions later. Tonight, I had violated them all.

"The old Jesuit cemetery?" My answer sounded more like a question—as in, exactly how upset was she going to be?

Mom stiffened and she drew in a sharp breath. "I'd never go into a graveyard at night," she responded automatically, as though it was something she'd said a thousand times before. Except it wasn't.

"Suddenly you're superstitious?"

She shook her head and looked away. "Of course not. You don't have to be superstitious to know that secluded places are dangerous at night."

I waited for the lecture.

Instead, she handed me a wet towel. "Wipe off your feet and throw that away. I don't want dirt from a cemetery in my washing machine."

Mom rummaged through the junk drawer until she found a giant Band-Aid that looked like a leftover from my Big Wheel days.

"Who were you talking to on the phone?" I asked, hoping to change the subject.

"Just someone from work."

"Did that *someone* ask you out?"

She frowned, concentrating on my arm. "I'm not interested

in dating. One broken heart is enough for me." She bit her lip. "I didn't mean—"

"I know what you meant." My mom had cried herself to sleep for what felt like months after my dad left. I still heard her sometimes.

After she bandaged my arm, I sat on the counter while she finished the marinara sauce. Watching her cook was comforting. It made the cemetery feel even farther away.

She dipped her finger in the pot and tasted the sauce before taking the pan off the stove.

"Mom, you forgot the red pepper flakes."

"Right." She shook her head and forced a laugh.

My mom could've held her own with Julia Child, and marinara was her signature dish. She was more likely to forget her own name than the secret ingredient. I almost called her on it, but I felt guilty. Maybe she was imagining me in one of those unsolved crime shows.

I hopped down from the counter. "I'm going upstairs to draw."

She stared out the kitchen window, preoccupied. "Mmm... that's a good idea. It will probably make you feel better."

Actually, it wouldn't make me feel anything.

That was the point.

As long as my hand kept moving over the page, my problems disappeared, and I was somewhere or *someone* else for a little while. My drawings were fueled by a world only I could see—a boy carrying his nightmares in a sack as bits and pieces spilled out behind him, or a mouthless man banging away at the keys of a broken typewriter in the dark.

Like the piece I was working on now.

I stood in front of my easel and studied the girl perched on a rooftop, with one foot hanging tentatively over the edge. She stared at the ground below, her face twisted in fear. Delicate blue-black swallow wings stretched out from her dress. The fabric was torn where the wings had ripped through it, growing from her back like the branches of a tree.

I read somewhere that if a swallow builds a nest on your roof, it will bring you good luck. But if it abandons the nest, you'll have nothing but misfortune. Like so many things, the bird could be a blessing or a curse, a fact the girl bearing its wings knew too well.

I fell asleep thinking about her. Wondering what it would be like to have wings if you were too scared to fly.

I woke up the next morning exhausted. My dreams had been plagued with sleepwalking girls floating in graveyards. Elvis was curled up on the pillow next to me. I scratched his ears, and he jumped to the floor.

I didn't drag myself out of bed until Elle showed up in the afternoon. She never bothered to call before she came over. The idea that someone might not want to see her would never occur to Elle, a quality I'd envied from the moment we met in seventh grade.

Now she was sprawled on my bed in a sea of candy wrappers, flipping through a magazine while I stood in front of my easel.

"A bunch of people are going to the movies tonight," Elle said. "What are you wearing?"

"I told you I'm staying home."

"Because of that pathetic excuse for a guy who's going to be the starting receiver at community college when we graduate?" Elle asked, in the dangerous tone she reserved for people who made the mistake of hurting someone she cared about.

My stomach dropped. Even after a few weeks, the wound was still fresh.

"Because I didn't get any sleep." I left out the part about the girl in the graveyard. If I started thinking about her, I'd have another night of bad dreams ahead of me.

"You can sleep when you're dead." Elle tossed the magazine on the floor. "And you can't hide in your room every weekend. You're not the one who should be embarrassed."

I dropped a piece of charcoal in the tackle box on the floor and wiped my hands on my overalls. "I think getting dumped because you won't let your boyfriend use you as a cheat sheet rates pretty high on the humiliation scale."

I should've been suspicious when one of the cutest guys in school asked me to help him bring up his history grade so he wouldn't get kicked off the football team. Especially when it was Chris, the quiet guy who had moved from one foster home to another—and someone I'd had a crush on for years. Still, with the highest GPA in History and all my other classes, I was the logical choice.

I just didn't realize that Chris knew why.

The first few years of elementary school, my eidetic memory was a novelty. Back then, I referred to it as photographic, and kids thought it was cool that I could memorize pages of text in only a few seconds. Until we got older, and they realized I didn't have to study to earn higher grades than them. By the time I hit junior high, I had learned how to hide my "unfair advantage," as the other students and their parents called it when they complained to my teachers.

These days, only a handful of my friends knew. At least, that's what I'd thought.

Chris was smarter than everyone assumed. He put in the time when it came to History—and me. Three weeks. That's how long it took before he kissed me. Two more weeks before he called me his girlfriend.

One more week before he asked if I'd let him copy off me during our midterm.

Seeing him at school and pretending I was fine when he cornered me with his half-assed apologies was hard enough. "I didn't mean to hurt you, Kennedy. But school isn't as easy for me as it is for you. A scholarship is my only chance to get out of here. I thought you understood that."

I understood perfectly, which was the reason I didn't want to run into him tonight.

"I'm not going."

Elle sighed. "He won't be there. The team has an away game."

"Fine. But if any of his loser friends are there, I'm leaving."

She headed for the bathroom with her bag and a smug smile. "I'll start getting ready."

I picked at the half inch of black charcoal under my nails. They would require serious scrubbing unless I wanted to look like a mechanic. The giant Band-Aid on my arm already made me look like a burn victim. At least the theater would be dark.

The front door slammed downstairs, and Mom appeared in the hallway a moment later. "Staying home tonight?"

"I wish." I tilted my head toward the bathroom. "Elle's making me go to the movies with her."

"And you're okay with that?" Mom tried to sound casual, but I knew what she was worried about. She had baked brownies and listened to me cry about Chris for weeks.

"He's not going to be there."

She smiled. "Sounds dangerous. You run the risk of having a good time." Then her expression changed, and she was all business. "Do you have cash?"

"Thirty bucks."

"Is your cell charged?"

I pointed to my nightstand, where my phone was plugged in. "Yep."

"Will anyone be drinking?"

"Mom, we're going to a movie, not a party."

"If for some reason there is drinking—"

I cut her off, reciting the rest by heart. "I'll call you and you'll pick me up, no questions asked, no consequences."

She tugged on the strap of my overalls. "Is this what you're wearing? It's a good look."

"Grunge is coming back. I'm ahead of the curve."

Mom walked over to the easel. She put her arm around me, leaning her head against mine. "You're so talented, and I can barely draw a straight line. You certainly didn't get it from me."

We ignored the other possible source.

She looked at the black dust coating my hands. "Earth-shattering talent aside, maybe you should take a shower."

"I agree." Elle emerged from the bathroom, ready enough for both of us in tight jeans and a tank top strategically falling off one shoulder. Whoever she planned to flirt with tonight would definitely notice her, along with all the other guys in the theater. Even in a tangled ponytail and barely any makeup, Elle was hard to miss.

Another difference between us.

I wandered into the bathroom, my expectations for myself considerably lower. Getting rid of the charcoal under my nails would be a win.

Mom and Elle were whispering when I came back out.

"What's the big secret?"

"Nothing." Mom raised a shopping bag in the air, dangling it by the handle. "I just picked up something for you. I thought you might need them. Evidence of my psychic powers."

I recognized the logo printed on the side. "Are those what I think they are?"

She shrugged. "I don't know...."

I pulled out the box and tossed the lid on the floor. Resting in the folds of tissue paper was a pair of black boots with leather straps that buckled up the sides. I'd seen them a few weeks ago when we were shopping. They were perfect—different, but not too different.

"I thought they'd look great with your uniform," she said, referring to the black jeans and faded T-shirts I wore every day.

"They'll look amazing with anything." I pulled on the boots and checked myself out in the mirror.

Elle nodded her approval. "Definitely cool."

"They'll probably look better without the bathrobe." Mom waved a black tube in the air. "And maybe with a little mascara?"

I hated mascara. It was like fingerprints at the scene of a crime. If you cried, it was impossible to get rid of the black smudges under your eyes, which was almost as embarrassing as crying in front of everyone in the first place.

"It's only a movie, and that stuff gets all over my face whenever I put it on." Or hours later, something I learned the hard way.

"There's a trick." Mom stood in front of me, brandishing the wand. "Look up."

I gave in, hoping it might make me look more like Elle and less like the girl-next-door.

Elle leaned over my mom's shoulder, checking out her technique as she applied a sticky coat. "I would kill for those eyelashes, and you don't even appreciate them."

Mom stepped back and admired her work, then glanced at Elle. "What do you think?"

"Gorgeous." Elle flopped down on the bed dramatically. "Mrs. Waters, you are the coolest."

"Be home by midnight or I'll seem a lot less cool," she said on her way out.

Elvis peeked around the corner.

I walked over to pick him up. He froze for a moment, his eyes fixed on me. Then he tore back down the hall.

"What's the deal with the King?" Elle asked, using her favorite nickname for Elvis.

"He's been acting weird." I didn't want to elaborate.

I wanted to forget about the graveyard and the girl in the white nightgown. But I couldn't shake the image of her feet hovering above the ground—or the feeling that there was a reason I couldn't stop thinking about her.

Blackout

The house was dark when Elle dropped me off five minutes before curfew, which was strange because Mom always waited up. She liked to hang out in the kitchen while I raided the fridge and gave her a slightly edited play-by-play of the night. After my self-imposed exile, she'd be amused when I reported that nothing had changed.

Elle had dragged me around the lobby with her while she flirted with guys she would never go out with, and I got stuck making awkward small talk with their friends. At least it was over and no one had asked about Chris.

I unlocked the door.

She hadn't even left a light on for me.

"Mom?"

Maybe she fell asleep.

I flipped the switch at the base of the stairs. Nothing. The power was probably out.

Great.

The house was pitch-black. A rush of dizziness swept over me as the fear started to build.

My hand curled around the banister, and I focused on the top of the stairs, trying to convince myself it wasn't that dark.

I crept up the steps. "Mom?"

When I reached the second-floor landing, a rush of cold air knocked the breath out of my lungs. The temperature inside must have dropped at least twenty degrees since I left for the movies. Did we leave a window open?

"Mom!"

The lights flickered, casting long shadows down the narrow hallway. I stumbled toward her room, my panic increasing with every step. The memory of the tiny crawl space in the back of her closet fought to break free.

Don't think about it.

I edged closer.

This end of the hall was even colder, and my breath came out in white puffs. Her door was open, a pale yellow light blinking inside.

The stench of stale cigarette smoke hit me, and a rising sense of dread clawed at my insides.

Someone's in the house.

I stepped through the doorway, and the wrongness of the scene closed in on me.

My mom lay on the bed, motionless.

Elvis crouched on her chest.

The lamp in the corner flashed on and off like a child was toying with the switch.

The cat made a low guttural sound that cut through the silence, and I shuddered. If an animal could scream, that was what it would sound like.

"Mom?"

Elvis' head whipped around in my direction.

I ran to the bed and he leapt to the floor.

My mother's head was tilted to the side, dark hair spilling across her face, as the room pitched in and out of darkness. I realized how still she was—the fact that her chest wasn't rising and falling. I pressed my fingers against her throat.

Nothing.

I shook her roughly. "Mom, wake up!"

Tears streamed down my face, and I slid my hand under her cheek. The light stopped flashing, bathing the room in a faint glow.

"Mom!" I grabbed her shoulders and yanked her upright. Her head swung forward and fell against her chest. I scrambled backward, and her body dropped down onto the mattress, bouncing against it unnaturally.

I slid to the floor, choking on my tears.

My mother's head lay against the bed at an awkward angle, her face turned toward me.

Her eyes were as empty as a doll's.